EVOLUTION WITH A TWIST

A Novel By

Ian T. Hill

iUniverse, Inc.

New York Lincoln Shanghai

Evolution With a Twist

iUniverse books may be ordered through booksellers or by contacting:

iUniverse
2021 Pine Lake Road, Suite 100
Lincoln, NE 68512
www.iuniverse.com
1-800-Authors (1-800-288-4677)

Because of the dynamic nature of the Internet, any Web addresses or links contained in this book may have changed since publication and may no longer be valid.

This is a work of fiction. All of the characters, names, incidents, organizations, and dialogue in this novel are either the products of the author's imagination or are used fictitiously.

ISBN: 978-0-595-45057-2 (pbk)
ISBN: 978-0-595-69161-6 (cloth)
ISBN: 978-0-595-89368-3 (ebk)

Printed in the United States of America

CONTENTS

PROLOGUE

▼

Through out human history the search for new knowledge has led mankind down many paths. The resulting journey inevitably provided both opportunities and consequences which were almost always unpredictable and irreversible. They often changed the course of human progress. This is a story of one such journey.

---▼---

CHAPTER 1

THE PROFESSOR

In the year 2028, very few people would have thought that Johnsonville, Pennsylvania would be the location for a development that would rock the world of science and eventually, change the meaning of life itself. Just as surprising, would have been the source of this development; John Cupar, who was about to wake up and change the world.

It was quite cold on this special day in February as Professor John Cupar began to wake up. John's normal way of waking up was to drift from a dreaming state into a kind of semi-conscious thinking mode, and that would gradually bring him into the reality of his surroundings. His thoughts would usually be about some problem that had been bothering him from the day before but this morning was different. As his thinking process started, his heart began to beat faster and suddenly, he was wide awake. A rapid succession of thoughts raced through his mind. Today was the start of the technical conference at his university; a conference for which he was the host. It was the first time that John had been chosen to be the host and also the first time it was being held at his university. Being the host for the first time was not why John's heart was beating faster. Tomorrow, during the first full day of the conference he was going to make a presentation that he had been hoping to present for eight years. Being the conference host was a distraction from that event. He knew he had to do it, and he had devoted a fair amount of time in preparing to do it, but to John, it was just a duty and a distraction.

John looked at the clock and quickly came back to reality. He jumped out of bed and initiated the morning ritual that he and Helen had come to practice during their seventeen years of marriage. They had an unspoken agreement that he would get up first and prepare a cup of tea for both of them down in the kitchen. When she came down that would be his signal to go upstairs to dress while she prepared a second cup of tea and watched over the family breakfast.

As usual, he was the first one to enter the kitchen and as he prepared the tea his mind was torn between reviewing all the things he had to do during the day and the presentation. It was going to be one hell of a day. He had to make sure that all the preparations had been made to greet the conference attendees and that all the exhibits had been finished over the weekend. He had to give a lecture to a class of freshmen starting the new semester, greet some of his colleagues and friends who would be arriving during the day and, finally, host the dinner that would be the first event of the conference. Of course, he knew it was absurd for him to be giving a lecture to the class of freshmen today but that was one of John's idiosyncrasies; he felt that he had to give that lecture to every freshman class regardless of what else was going on. Thank God he had good friends to help him with the conference.

His thoughts on his presentation kept interrupting his thoughts on everything else. The presentation would describe the results of eight years of research conducted by him and a small team of specialists he had recruited during those eight years. The feeling of being able to tell the world about what they had accomplished was the kind of feeling John was not used to handling. He was a man who prided himself on always being organized and in control, but now, in the middle of all his other thoughts, the "presentation" kept taking over his mind. He couldn't control it. It wasn't just excitement. His feelings went from excitement to pride and periodically, even fear.

Helen had now come downstairs. Glancing at her preoccupied husband she wondered why John was still sitting drinking his tea instead of going upstairs to get dressed.

"Is everything all right?"

"Yeah, I was just doing a little planning in my head for today." John's voice betrayed his emotions.

"Okay." Helen could tell this was not the time to press him about what he was thinking. He was not the only one trying to appear calm and in control. She was fully aware of what he was about to present at the conference because, in more than a few ways, she had helped him with his project. No one on his team had Helen's perspective as a doctor, which, it turned out, had been very useful. John and Helen had been married in 2011 when both of them were twenty-eight and he had supported her, without complaint, during the tumultuous years that followed as she had started her career as a doctor, while also having two children in quick succession. They were very close and she knew that when he was ready he would come to her for one of their long talks to check his reasoning with her. That mutual confidence and respect was what made their marriage so strong and so important to both of them.

Helen's emotions about John's presentation were quite different than John's. She was both amazed and enthusiastic about what had been accomplished, but she was also very concerned about what affect the presentation might have, not just on John, but on their family and the life they enjoyed in their quiet little community. As a doctor and a mother she was also very concerned about the wider implications of what had been accomplished.

Finally, John roused himself and started up the stairs to get dressed and prepare for the day. Climbing the stairs his hand glided appreciatively up the curving mahogany banister burnished by generations of hands and downward-sliding boys and girls. He loved this old house with its winding staircase and big rooms with their high ceilings. It was located on Brookwood Road in a part of town that had not changed much during their lifetimes. All the homes on the street were of the same era and they liked the idea that they could stand in their front yard and almost imagine that they were living in the nineteen thirties. Both of them had grown up in the town and liked to reminisce about their childhood in this pleasant part of the world. They'd had to scrape together the down payment thirteen years ago but life in this gracious old home had been worth every penny. He savored it now with the heightened awareness of what tomorrow might bring to his comfortable, quiet life at the university. Once in the shower, his reveries and preoccupation with the conference gave way to planning for the day; breakfast, a quick call to his parents, then to the university to meet with his conference helpers and then, give the freshmen lecture.

When he joined the others for breakfast, Helen was watching Suzie unload the dishwasher, Amanda was counting out grapes to keep within her calorie count and Jack was late. Everything was normal except—where was his tea? Helen always prepared his second cup of tea and had it waiting at his place.

"Where is it?" He looked around as he spoke.

"Where's what?" Now Helen's voice mirrored his tension.

"My tea!"

Amanda, their sixteen-year-old daughter, looked up and with a hint of a smile on her face whispered, "It's over here behind me, Dad." Amanda loved her parents and was fully aware of how lucky she was to be in a family with two really interesting and sometimes funny parents. The fact that her mother was a doctor was also a tremendous inspiration for her.

"Thanks, Am, could you hand it to me"? John's voice softened as he spoke to his daughter. Whenever he looked at Amanda he could see Helen at that age with her beautiful blond hair and graceful body.

Helen looked over her shoulder at John, her expression saying, "Well, at least I made it." John knew better than to say another word.

Of course, she could have let Suzie do it. Suzie did almost everything else around the house, but making the tea was a caring ritual that had begun in their first years together and they wanted to continue it always.

"Good morning, Suzie. Is everything okay?" This was another ritual that John went through every morning.

"Good morning, John, all systems are working properly." Suzie had a very pleasant voice and for whatever reason, John liked hearing her morning report.

Getting Suzie had been a tremendous break for Helen. The fact that she was only a humanoid or as some people preferred to call her 'a robotic housekeeper', was something the family now took for granted. In many ways she had become part of this family. In the year of 2028 these devices were very common and appreciated. Suzie was a very up-to-date model and had been a nice benefit from some of John's work. She was about the same size as Helen and, sometimes, Helen dressed her in some of her own clothing. In fact, she was quite human-looking and John had more than a few times talked to her as if she were Helen, especially if he was in one of those 'absent minded' modes for which he was so famous. It always shocked him when she would turn and inform him of where Helen really was after he had called her "honey". Her usual response was "John, honey is upstairs". She knew all the names the family used for each other. Amanda and her brother, Jack, never stopped laughing at her when she did this.

Of all the crazy things that John had brought into their house from his lab, Suzie was the one that Helen appreciated the most. Having Suzie allowed Helen to pursue her career and still have time to take an active part in her children's lives.

John knew why Helen was on edge. Intuitively, the entire household was reflecting his tension. John and Helen referred to the morning bustle in their kitchen as a "family breakfast", but if anyone ate with anyone else it was purely coincidental. Household members executed their independent agendas, working around each other in the same space. Amanda was the oldest child and her thoughts this morning were with her peers, and definitely not on anything going on in the family kitchen. She was sixteen and a cheerleader for her school's basketball team. Tonight, after practice, she wanted to study with Willie who was on the team and who was her current love.

The youngest member of the family, Jack, finally ran into the room and as usual Copper, the family dog, was tagging along at his heels. Copper was the family terrier and like Suzie, was a benefit from John's work at the University. He was robotic, but in a way that would have amazed everyone in town if they knew what he really was, but John was not ready for that disclosure yet. Copper was very attached to the member of the family who paid him the most attention and in this case, that was Jack. Copper ran to every member of the family for a 'good morning' greeting which he received even from Suzie.

Both Amanda and Jack knew about the conference at the university and the importance of what their father was going to present but they were not able to make a connection between their own lives and the disclosure of what their Dad had accomplished. Their lives were very busy and for the most part, very enjoyable and although they had heard their parents discussing possible ramifications of the presentation they were in a state of denial about the possible effect on their own lives.

Ignoring the increased noise level and confusion caused by her brother's arrival, Amanda looked up at Helen and raised her voice. "Mom, is it okay if Willie and I use the dining room for homework tonight?"

Helen was not at all happy to consider that arrangement but she also knew not to fight a losing battle. "You do remember that your father and I are going to be out this evening, don't you?"

Amanda answered with her innocent child intonation, "Sure, but Brenda and Jack will be here won't they?"

Jack stopped in his tracks with that statement. His voice was a mixture of a plea for a "no" decision and an expression of anger at his sister's request. "I know what that means! It means I won't be able to come downstairs or if I do, she is going to yell at me." Amanda and Jack usually got along pretty well but when it came to who could do what in their own home, that wasn't always the case. The increased tension of the morning was having its effect.

"Jack, you know that just isn't true! You can go anywhere you want to tonight. Don't give Mom the wrong idea just because you don't like the idea of me having a friend over to help me." Amanda's voice was quiet and self-assured. She knew she was going to win this one.

Helen acknowledged her defeat. "Okay, but only until ten at the latest."

"Thanks, Mom, I knew you wouldn't mind so I told him it would be okay." This forethought on Amanda's part surprised no one and with that she was the first to finish breakfast and the first to rush out. As she did, Brenda, John's assistant, walked into the room. Brenda lived with John and his family in one of their spare rooms upstairs which was not all that unusual in this college town with all its old, large homes. After her normal cheerful 'good morning everybody' Brenda sat down across from Jack.

Jack, like his sister, knew he was lucky to have parents like John and Helen. He more than anybody in the family, was always excited when his Dad brought home a new gadget for the family to see. These days his attention was usually focused on the church league basketball team or his new girl friend, Patricia. This morning it was focused on the fact that his math homework, due tomorrow, was not done. "Brenda, could you help me with my homework after school today?"

John glanced at Brenda. "Jack, you know this is a busy week for Brenda and me and tonight your mother and I have that special dinner over at the university. Brenda has some things she's got to do, but if she's back in time maybe she can help you."

Brenda smiled across the table at Jack. "You know I'll be glad to help you and I'll try to get home early."

The relief on Jack's face told John he had gotten the answer he'd been hoping for. "Thanks Brenda, I knew I could count on you.

With Brenda's promise of help, Jack grabbed his last piece of toast and was gone. In the time that Brenda had been with the family she had become like a sister to Jack and Amanda. She enjoyed helping them with their homework almost as much as she enjoyed playing games with them. She had been with them only four years but it seemed much longer to the family.

With the children on their way, John and Helen had a chance to talk for a few moments before she left for the hospital. John didn't want Brenda to hear what he had to say to Helen. "Brenda, why don't you get our stuff and wait for me in the car. I want to talk to Helen for a few minutes."

After Brenda left the room Helen took John's hand. "I know you're nervous about the conference but I know you can handle what you've got to do. After all, many of the people who are coming are old friends."

John tried to keep his feelings under control as he spoke. "This responsibility of being the conference host is driving me a little crazy. I hope Brenda is going to be okay with her part of our presentation. She's never had to face a large audience before and it's critical that she stays calm and does her part of the presentation. I'm getting a lot of help from Sonny and Dede so I think everything will be okay.

Of all the people on the faculty those two can organize anything. Besides, we don't make our presentation until tomorrow afternoon. If I think there's going to be any problems as I listen to tomorrow morning's presentations, I'll have some time to figure out how to deal with them. Could you call Mom and Dad and talk to them about tomorrow night. I'll be home by five so I'll see you when you get here. Remember, we have to get to Ross Hall by six thirty for the Conference dinner and opening ceremonies so make sure you leave the hospital on time."

She knew that wasn't the whole story. "Aren't you worried about what the reaction will be tomorrow?"

"You know I am but who knows, maybe someone will have something even bigger and better and our presentation will get lost in the excitement."

"You don't believe that for a minute! Don't try to con me with your no-big-deal speech. I know what this means to you. It's important to all of us. Would it help if I were there when you and Brenda make your presentation?"

John moved close to Helen and put his arms around her. "You're right, it is a big deal and this whole thing is driving me crazy. I'll try to take your advice and keep things in perspective. You don't have to come to the presentation. I'll be fine. My team will be there to help and I know you're busy at the hospital. If anything weird develops during the day I'll give you a call."

Helen felt relieved. John did seem to be okay, much to her relief. Now she could go to her patients and give them the attention they deserved. Later, when John and Helen remembered this day, it would be difficult for them to understand how they failed to see what was about to happen.

After she was gone John went out to his car. "Brenda, you drive. My mind is so wrapped up with this damned conference I would probably forget to go to the University." John wasn't sure what he would do without Brenda as his assistant. He really was a little worried about how the presentation would affect her. Actually, Brenda was looking forward to the presentation. As a key member of the team it was an event that she had been anticipating for months.

As they drove, John took in the scenery; something he rarely got to enjoy since he almost always did the driving. It was not that Brenda was a bad driver, John just liked to drive. A feeling of contentment came over him as he gazed at this neighborhood in which he had grown up, when his dad was a professor at the university. The town was located in the upper part of Pennsylvania and even at this time of year, with the snow on the ground and the barren trees, it was an inviting scene. Growing up in a small college town had its advantages. Though the students came and went, the long-time residents formed the heart of the town and they were for the most part, long time friends.

They parked in front of Ross Hall where the exhibits were being assembled and where most of the conference activities were to be held. As they got out of the car, John stopped to think for a moment.

"Brenda, you don't need to come with me for this meeting. In fact, it's probably better that you don't. Go on over to the lab and check on the work we gave the team on Friday. I'll come over after my lecture; and after I check on how the reception group is doing, I'll pick you up there."

She started to walk away and then stopped and slowly turned toward John. "I think you're right. I'd better get over there." With that she turned and began to quickly walk toward the lab.

John stared at her retreating figure. What was that about? He didn't have time to worry about it and he knew he would find out what was going on after his lecture.

Ross Hall served as a center for many of the town's events and resulted in business coming into the town that would not have been possible without it. For the conference it was ideal because it could not only hold the exhibits and the multiple simultaneous presentations, but it also had a large auditorium and dining area.

When John entered the meeting room he found that he was the last one to arrive. "Am I late? This is the nine o'clock meeting, I hope." John was laughing, as was everyone else around the table.

Sonny McMahon was at the other end of the table with stacks of papers in front of him. "Yes, John, this is the right meeting and we're all relieved that you remembered to come." Nobody around the table was surprised at the comment because they knew the relationship between these two good friends, the absent minded professor and the always organized administrator. "Sit down, John, and let's get on with it."

John felt very lucky to have so many faculty members and student volunteers ready to help him with all the things that had to be done to host the conference. They reviewed the arrangements for greeting the attendees coming in that afternoon and for ensuring that everyone had transportation and places to stay "When I walked in today I didn't see any signs outside that will show our guests where they should enter the building." John looked around the table.

Dede was Sonny's wife and not known for keeping her opinions to herself. "Let's see if I heard you correctly, John. When you walked under the sign over the front entrance with the big red letters—ADVANCED HUMANOID DEVELOPMENT CONFERENCE—you thought that was just the name of the building?"

This time the group tried to muffle their amusement but not very successfully. John was embarrassed and his face turned red. "I—I must have been looking down. I apologize for my—mistake. Dede, am I forgiven?"

For all her honesty and outspokenness, Dede was a very kind and fun person to be around and John knew that. Like John and Helen, Sonny and Dede were a matched set, one complementing the other. Sonny was always deliberate and organized and Dede was spontaneous and eager to try anything new. They had been friends with John and Helen for many years and Helen always enjoyed the time that she could spend with Dede. Her personality was contagious and always made Helen feel positive about some of their mutual problems, including husbands absorbed in their work and teenage children absorbed in everything.

"John, you know I always forgive you and besides I know you have too much on your mind right now. Just leave all the details to us and get ready to enjoy your conference. It's going to be great."

John was thinking that it had better be. This was the fifteenth anniversary for the conference and everyone was expecting it to be very special. This was quite a change from the humble beginnings in 2014. At that time, very few people thought it was a good idea. By then, the technical developments for automated and robotic devices had made significant changes in a number of industrial areas. Conferences for those developments were being held every year in a number of countries around the world. The use of human looking robotic devices was expanding rapidly for commercial applications and in Japan, they were already being used in many private homes. John had been lucky enough to get involved at the beginning of their development.

After the meeting, John and Sonny took a quick tour of the exhibits. This gave them a chance to review their arrangements for dividing the various responsibilities that had to be taken care of as the week progressed.

"You know, John, I have to confess that when you asked me to help with this conference I didn't fully appreciate what an important event it would be. When I read the names of the companies that will be here and the media representation I was amazed. How'd you ever arrange for a conference like this to be held at the university?" John smiled. Until now he wasn't sure that his helpers, especially Sonny, fully realized the importance of what he had done or what this conference was all about. "Sonny, I have been working with some of the people who will be attending today, for over ten years. Bob Schultz, our group president, is known all over the world for his work with robotic control systems and his wife, Diane, is almost as famous for her work with visual interpretation systems. To be honest with you, I never thought I would be able to convince them that the work we do here is just as important as the work being done at MIT, Berkley or Carn-egie-Mellon.

Sonny interrupted. "How about your reputation, John? Aren't you just as well known for your interpretation and duplication of human brain functions for applications in robotic operations? I think you guys call that neuromorphic engineering don't you?"

John was surprised that Sonny knew about his work and the name neuromorphic, but he shook his head and waved his hand in front of Sonny. "No, that wasn't it. The real deciding factor was the recommendations of the companies that have been using our consulting services. The University finally woke up to the money that was coming in from that work and started to lend a hand to my efforts to host the conference. While we're on the subject, let me thank you and Dede again for all your help. I think you know how badly I needed it. My skills at organizing something like this are pretty bad and yours are second to none."

He glanced at his watch. "You won't believe this but I've got to go. I have to lecture a bunch of freshmen over at the Bernard Building." John held up his hand when he saw the expression on Sonny's face. "Yes, I know, I should have arranged for someone else to do that today but I like to open the second semester of this course just to watch the reactions I get from the students."

Sonny was always impressed with John's devotion to teaching. Unlike many of the other professors at the university who were more concerned with publishing papers than teaching, John had always had a sincere interest in actually teaching his students. Sonny waved his hand at John. "I understand, John, don't worry about things over here. We've got them under control but please remember to come back to greet some of your friends as they arrive."

John left the building feeling very relieved that the conference arrangements seemed to be going so well. Just as he enjoyed the town's scenery, he enjoyed walking on campus, cold breeze or not. The graceful, imposing buildings imparted a sense of security and permanence. It was during these walks that he had developed some of his best ideas and it was on these grounds that he had enjoyed many creative discussions with both friends and students. His thoughts today were not just on the presentation but also on some of the conference attendees. He liked most of his fellow researchers at the various universities but he felt uncomfortable with some of the company representatives. Their focus was always on the money to be made with each new development. The media personnel were the most unpredictable group who would be present. Sometimes they would oversimplify a topic and completely miss its importance. Other times they would blow something out of context and get everyone excited or concerned about a development that was not important.

The university was built on the western edge of the town toward the mountains. When driving into town on the main highway the university could be seen in the distance with the mountains looming up behind it. It was a beautiful scene, especially in autumn. The main buildings of the university were laid out in a large U shape and the buildings along the arms of the U were designated for each of the different disciplines being taught at the University. The Quadrangle formed by the center of the U was a gathering place for the students during good weather, but today it was snow covered and the only students visible were those hurrying between classes. The walk between Ross Hall and his building on the Quadrangle where his class was located was not far. He looked forward to today's class. It was always kind of an exhilarating experience to watch the student's reactions to his first lecture. When he was about half way there, Michelle came running toward him. "You only have five minutes before your lecture!"

"Michelle, I appreciate your concern but I've been doing this before you entered kindergarten. I know what time it is and we'll be there in plenty of time." His smile belied his curtness. Her attention pleased him. She was an important and favorite member of his project team with more energy and enthusiasm than everyone else combined. She was a little bit like Dede with an energetic and positive approach to everything. She had been a member of his special team for five years. "Relax and walk over with me. Is everything ready for the lecture? Are there many students there?"

"I think you're going to be surprised at how many there are. Everything is ready to go except that Alex hadn't arrived when I left to find you."

John wasn't concerned about his Lab manager. "I wouldn't worry about it. He's probably still over at the lab. Brenda just went over there and they're probably absorbed in some discussion about tomorrow. He'll probably be there by the time we arrive."

Entering the lecture hall, John actually was surprised to see how many students were there. He still was not used to the effect of the university's decision to make the course an undergraduate requirement. Michelle was right, dependable Alex was nowhere to be seen. Michelle shrugged at him as she took her chair off to his right. John walked on stage and took possession of the podium. The murmur of voices rose momentarily. Then the class fell silent in anticipation.

"Good morning!"

John's greeting was followed by a murmured "good morning" from about a dozen members of the class.

"I want to welcome everyone to this opening lecture for the second semester of a course most of you probably never expected to take or, for that matter, ever wanted to take. Welcome to 'The Effects of Humanoid Development on Modern Society'. Before this semester is over I think you will realize just how useful the information you are learning will be to you."

At this, there was the usual rolling of eyes and muffled groans.

"During the first semester I hope you learned why the course on The Affect of Automation Developments on Modern Society is now a requirement for all students. You are about to learn why this course is in the same category.

Near the end of the last century, technological changes began to take place that changed the lives of millions of people all over the world. Your studies in the first semester explored these changes and the technologies that caused them. At one point, it was said to be the beginning of the Information Age but it was actually much more than that. Certainly, the changes connected to information processing, transmission, and storage brought about significant economic, cultural and political changes but as I know you're all aware, advances in other areas have also had a great impact on humanity. The advances made in biological and medical knowledge have changed people's expectation about life itself. The food we eat, the medicines we take and in some cases, even the processes within some people's bodies have been modified by DNA manipulation.

The technologies, which brought about these changes are still advancing and still causing change. The University recently decided that it was important for all of you to understand what these changes might be and how they will affect your lives and your work and, believe me, they will affect you no matter what you choose to do."

He paused and looked up at his audience. As with any university class, most of the students were looking at him. The usual ten percent were already half asleep or staring into space. That was okay. If he could reach half this class with his message he would consider the course a success. He continued with his lecture.

"In this semester, as a continuation of the first semester's work, we will go into a more detailed study of a product development that has resulted in some surprising and unexpected applications. Of course, I'm talking about our now ubiquitous humanoids. These human looking, robotic devices have come a long way since the awkward, lumbering lab experiments of the late nineteen hundreds. The course will cover the history of their development and the technologies behind these developments. It will also cover the impact they have had on our economy, our culture and our daily lives. You will have the opportunity to see some of the earlier designs and experiment with some of the features now being introduced in the new humanoids."

As John glanced up from his notes he saw a hand go up. "Professor, isn't there a conference on humanoids being held here starting tomorrow?"

John was surprised to hear the question from one of the freshmen. They were usually unaware of things outside their own, highly focused world.

He smiled and said "yes, and that is the reason why Michelle, up here on my right, will be giving these lectures for this week."

Michelle gave a little wave at the group. The happy faces on at least the male half of the class showed him that he would not be missed. He couldn't blame them; he would rather have a lecture from her than someone like himself any day of the week. She was a pretty woman in both face and figure and her personality made her very popular with all the students.

"We're going to try to give you some understanding of where humanoid developments are headed. We'll also try to speculate how their new capabilities will affect us. I'm sure that many of you already have a humanoid in your home and will appreciate these new features. I've been lucky enough to have a humanoid for my own use for about ten years and I must say it has become almost like a member of my family. To complete today's lecture I'm going to give you a quick overview of humanoid development and the controversies that swirled about them as they were introduced. Most of the technologies that made modern humanoids possible were developed for applications which had very little to do with humanoids. It was not a single technology but a convergence of many technologies, which provided the tools for their creation.

First, there were the incredible advances in data processing and the coincident shrinkage in both the size and the power requirements of the processing devices. The emergence of quantum computing and the techniques of complexity-adaptive processing gave the humanoid development groups the computing capacity of the human brain at incredibly low power levels."

John glanced up and saw several hands raised and pointed to one of them. "Do you have a question?"

"Professor Cupar, are we expected to know what you mean by quantum computing or complexity whatever?"

"No, we are not going to teach you the technology involved in humanoid operations and in this case, let's just say that electronic processing got very fast and the software started to get smart enough to fix itself. Please, if any of you have any questions regarding what I'm talking about during this or any future lectures, feel free to ask."

With that answer the other hands went down and John continued. "We have now reached a point where for many functions, it is possible to not just match but exceed the complexity and the capability of the human brain. Of course, I am not saying that the control mechanisms in these "machines" operate like the brain, but for certain applications, including even some forms of deductive reasoning, they are now superior to the brain. As they evolved, they provided humanoid developers with the ability to give their creations greater and more complex capabilities up to the point where now, unless you can see whom you are dealing with, it is usually difficult to tell whether you are dealing with a human or a humanoid.

Just as humans must 'sense' the world around them, humanoids must do the same if they are to have any practical applications. Fortunately, this problem was also solved by developments in other areas. First, there was the need to 'understand' human speech and other sounds. This problem was one of the first to be solved because it had so many important uses in business. I'm sure all of you talk to a number of devices that were developed with this technology, almost every day. In a similar way, the ability to interpret images was also driven by potential business and military applications. Advances in this technology probably resulted in more job losses than all of the others put together as machines started to 'see and interpret' what they saw."

Again, John glanced up and saw a student with a raised hand. "Professor, can these humanoids be made to feel pain with their skin?"

John had to laugh at this question. "No, their programming can be designed to react to temperature or types of pressure but these machines don't 'feel' anything. They follow their internal programming and that's all.

As all of these technological developments I have mentioned became available, they were quickly adapted to the task of designing a useable humanoid by the universities and companies involved in this work. At first, their work was not taken seriously and their efforts were poorly funded. This situation changed when the results of some of their early experiments showed the advantages of having a mobile, reliable worker whose duties could easily be changed and who could work without a break, twenty four hours a day. At this point in humanoid development there were several problems which limited their use. They were expensive, their reliability and safety were unproven and people were nervous about working near or with a humanoid.

One of the most important turning points, which seemed to surprise everybody, was the ability to make the humanoids 'more human' in their behavior and appearance. It was found that when they were made to the size of a normal human, dressed in human clothing, and made less 'machine like' in appearance and movement they were more quickly accepted by human workers. Encouraged by this development, changes were made to give their faces more expression, even to the point of simulating lip and jaw movements related to the words they spoke. These changes also gave them the ability to simulate a variety of different emotions including laughter. Remember, I said simulate, not *feel*, different emotions. The results were astounding. The fear that people initially felt quickly diminished and the number of uses involving direct human interaction increased substantially.

It was at this point when humanoids hit the magic crossover, which many devices had reached in their development history. As people lost their fear of working with humanoids, more companies started to use them. The increased demand lowered the cost to produce them and mass production techniques lowered them even more.

The places and types of applications they were used for started to expand exponentially. The new uses weren't just in the offices and factories, they started to be use in hospitals and nursing homes and individual homes.

A more recent application, introduced by the Japanese, is the use of a humanoid as a sex partner. I'm not sure if any of you have utilized one, but I understand that both the male and female versions perform quite well and have an interesting number of optional techniques. Maybe they will help control our 'population growth' problem."

That woke the class up. It was interesting to see how every student, boys and girls changed their seating posture as they reacted to the introduction of the topic of sex. All the boys laughed and looked around at the other members of the class. Most of the girls did not look around, but they did laugh.

As he went on John finally looked at his watch and realized that he needed to bring the class to a close. "I see we are running out of time so let me wrap this session up. Are we now at the end of all these changes in humanoid and other technologies? Of course not! That is what we will be studying for the next few months. We have time to answer just a few more questions."

John pointed to a raised hand in the front row. The question was from a girl who spoke very softly "Do you think that any of these advanced humanoids are actually alive or will ever be alive?"

CHAPTER 2

▼

REMEMBERING A BIRTHDAY

That was the question that was always asked and, normally, one that John had no trouble answering. He took a deep breath and hoped that his standard answer would be sufficient and that he could avoid a long discussion on the subject.

John turned to look at the young girl who had asked the question. When he replied it was with a smile.

"The simple answer to your question is 'no', they're not alive and the advanced models are not intended to be alive; but it's an interesting question and one which has been asked by every class that has been given this lecture. When you start getting into that area the first thing you run into is the question of definitions, but let me ask you a question. Why would you want them to be alive?"

She was obviously not expecting a return question and started to blush as she stuttered her reply.

Would ... wouldn't they be more fun to have around if they were alive? Wouldn't they be more useful?"

John's response was quick "what do you mean by 'alive'?"

She pondered the question and said "You know, not so perfect, more emotional and more.... more human."

John couldn't resist "You mean like us; able to be distracted from what they're doing, able to make mistakes because they aren't paying attention or refuse to function because they are in a bad mood? Would you like one of your 'alive' humanoids watching over your medication in the hospital or taking care of your grandmother when she's alone? Why do you think we made these things in the first place?"

He stopped the class laughing with a wave of his hand.

"Let's go back to what you meant by the word 'alive'. If you look it up in the dictionary you will find most definitions describe a living thing as something that exists by using biochemical actions to store and use energy derived from nutrients and excreting waste products from this process and also, of course, able to reproduce itself. When you asked your question, based upon what you wanted the humanoid to do, you probably should have used the word conscious.

When that word is used it opens up a completely new set of questions. The concept of consciousness has intrigued mankind for as long as the words for it have existed. Most dictionaries define "conscious" as having a feeling or knowledge of one's own feelings or of external things. Sometimes the words 'aware' or 'cognizant' are used as in 'being aware of oneself as a thinking being'. Unfortunately, these definitions use words, which are also poorly defined. What does being aware or having feelings mean? If someone were going to try to make a humanoid 'conscious' they would first have to define, very precisely, what consciousness is and how it could be made to exist in a humanoid. As I said before, I would be willing to bet that many of you have had a phone conversation with a computer-controlled device that made you wonder if the thing you were talking to was "alive", as most of you like to put it. Of course, what you were dealing with was some very clever programming. It is not terribly difficult to duplicate the normal human responses in a wide range of conversational topics."

John knew he was on the edge of getting into a discussion that he definitely did not want to have today.

"If some of you are interested perhaps we can explore this topic during the course of this semester. Are there any other questions?" Fortunately, there were only a few and these were the usual ones that were easily answered.

"Okay, then, that's it for today. I think most of you will find this course both interesting and useful. I'll see you in class next week."

As the students filed out of the hall he turned to Michelle. "What do you think happened to Alex?"

She had that worried look on her face that he had become so familiar with over the past three years. "I don't know. I saw him at the lab just before I came over and he didn't say anything about not coming."

He knew that Michelle and Alex were in love with each other and that she almost always knew where he was and what he was doing. "Why don't you go over to the lab and find out what's going on? After I check with the reception group over at Ross Hall I'll come over to the lab to pick up Brenda and she can tell me if there're any problems that I should worry about." John was puzzled but he didn't have time to worry about Alex now.

When Michelle left, he was left alone in the hall. The question about humanoids being 'alive' always caused him to remember his early thoughts on the subject and remembering them took John back to a time when he started to dream of the impossible. As he gathered his notes together and started the walk from the Quadrangle building back to Ross Hall he continued to reminisce about the past. It was not a long walk but with the snow on the ground it gave him enough time to remember what had brought him to this point in his life.

In 2000 when he was only seventeen, he began to wonder how mobile robots operated and how he could build one for himself. At that point in their development they were being used for some very specialized tasks where the risks of injury to humans was high, or where their high cost could be justified because of the importance of continuous and reliable performance. Some were used where their mobility was very limited for jobs like distributing and collecting mail or other items along a defined path. They were certainly not human looking and the idea of a human looking robot or 'humanoid' was more of a topic for science fiction than for science.

Like any curious teenager absorbed by his own interests, John pestered his parents to allow him to own his own robot. Kits for robotic devices were available for kids of various ages and he was allowed to build a few, but he quickly became bored with their limited capabilities. He modified them and even won a prize in one of his science classes for one of his creations but what he really wanted them to do could not be done.

As his education progressed so did humanoid development. The technical problems that he had described to the class were gradually solved and applications for industrial and military tasks increased rapidly. When John received his Master's Degree in 2007 and began his association with the university's School of Engineering and Applied Science, the potential for the large scale production of humanoids was just beginning to be seriously explored especially in Japan. When the opportunity was presented for him to work with a section within the engineering school, specializing in robotic development, he jumped at it as if it were a dream come true, as in fact, it was. As it turned out, the progress in humanoid technology was quite rapid and in the year 2011 when John and Helen were married, commercial humanoids were being produced in fairly large numbers.

John had stumbled into the right business at the right time, but in his mind the business opportunities didn't matter. What mattered was the opportunity to work in an area that fascinated him. He knew he could make more money working on the "outside", but he chose instead to work part time as an industry consultant. During his twenty-two years of research he had done a fair amount of consulting and it was because of this work that he had been able in 2017, to obtain some advanced prototype humanoids for his personal use. He was eventually able to use them not just in the lab, but also in his own home. His kids had named their humanoid, Suzie, and Helen had helped him test and improve her capabilities in a home environment.

As improvements were developed in his lab he incorporated them into Suzie and some of these improvements were really amazing. To John's family these events were not just useful but exciting as Suzie became more and more "human". John, of course, was happy to see their interest but he also felt these things were a distraction from his main goal. He wanted to make a humanoid that was actually conscious.

Like many other people with his technical interests, John often thought about how he would go about doing that. It was the excitement and the challenge of doing so that occupied his mind with very little thought about what would happen if he actually reached his goal. That lack of forethought was not surprising, but when he looked back on his work, he often wondered why he never gave it a thought. Unlike most of the others, John had the advantage of working in a laboratory equipped to study this problem and which actually encouraged new areas of research.

Fortunately, he found that there were others in his field who also had thought about the question of a conscious humanoid and in the various conferences they would talk for hours on end about the various ways that this might be done. The difference was that John was actually determined to do it.

He was under no illusions about the difficulty of the task. He had spent a fair amount of time studying the human brain, with help from Helen and his biologically inclined friends at the university. When Helen first met John, she thought his humanoid work was very interesting but when she found out about what his real interest was and what he wanted to do she was flabbergasted. She couldn't believe he was serious about it but as time passed and her understanding of his work increased, she became almost as deeply interested in the challenge as he was.

In effect, she became the first member of the team; the team he knew he would require in order to reach his goal.

During the years that he had been learning and studying humanoid development, there had been many advances in the understanding of how the brain operates to enable the function of consciousness to exist. It was apparent, even from the beginning of these studies that the conscious function of the brain is only one of its many functions and that most of the brain's operations are performed without any involvement of the conscious function. A critical discovery, which gave scientists an understanding of how the brain functioned, was the determination of precisely how the brain stores and retrieves information. It was discovered that this information was 'self related' or in effect, 'tagged with self'. It was not only 'self related' but also 'tagged' with its body part of origin. With the realization that this 'self related' memory information starts to be stored even before the brain's owner is born and continues to be stored in ever increasing complexity as life goes on, the understanding of the nature of consciousness was becoming more clearly understood.

As John studied these brain functions, his mind was always trying to connect what he was learning with how he could perform the same functions with an electronic data processor operating as part of a humanoid. People had thought throughout the ages that the brain was a mysterious, magical thing. To John it was a physical thing, operating within the laws of science. True, it was enormously complicated in its operation and was a product of evolution over a period of billions of years, but it looked to him that at least some of its operations could be performed with other approaches and other technologies. As far as he was concerned that could include the conscious function. At each level of research John would think, "I can do that" and would develop an approach to do it and then would move on to the next challenge. John decided that it might be possible to duplicate the conscious function in a robotic device but not at the complexity level of the human brain. John decided to work with the concept of consciousness at a more basic level and try to find ways of achieving this level with something he could actually create.

His first decision was to decide what sort of 'thing' he could actually create. He realized that he would have to make something that was big enough to use the equipment that was at his disposal and something that he could instrument to determine how it was operating. He wanted his creation to have mobility and because of the uncertainty of what his experiment might do, he needed something that could easily be constrained if the need arose. He decided to create a conscious dog.

This was actually an easy choice because robotic dogs had become very popular. The advantages of these "pets" were obvious. They didn't excrete anything but carbon dioxide and water vapor; they didn't shed, their personality could be changed as desired and they could be turned off. For John, the advantage was that all the work of mobility and structural design had been done. With the easy part out of the way John's real work now began.

He gradually assembled a small team of associates and swore them to secrecy and began the task of creating the dog. The first member, after Helen, was Alex. He was John's assistant responsible for running his laboratory. The only concern that John had about Alex was his lack of concern for following the rules and protocols expected of university employees but, on the other hand, he was brilliant. It was Alex who was responsible for Michelle joining the team because of their personal relationship. Because of the unique requirements of his project, John needed to recruit personnel in fields not normally related to humanoid research. That turned out to be a relatively easy task once they understood what he was trying to do. Helen was actually better than John was at convincing some of these prospects to join the team.

As he had suspected from his earlier work, he quickly realized that their dog would have to start out like a newborn puppy. In order to attain a level of consciousness it had to obtain and store information from its own body parts and with the appropriate programming, the information would be tagged as self obtained.

When the team tried to let the dog become conscious or in other words, turned it on, the results were a disaster. It was fortunate that the dog was tied down and small or the special lab they had set up would have been destroyed. It became obvious that the programs adapted from robotic dogs were totally worthless for this application. Even with all of their advanced equipment and testing devices it took the team two years of trial and error to achieve their goal. It was only after the team mastered the process which let the internal programs be modified automatically with real time 'self learning' experiences, just as a real dog's developing brain functions, that they were rewarded with success. They raised their 'puppy' in the lab and in spite of themselves; each member of the team gradually became attached to it. Each team member received a duplicate copy of the puppy. That was easy since they could make a physical copy of the dog and then simply download the 'brain' contents into the new copy. When John brought the dog home he did not tell his family what he had done; he just told them it was an advanced robotic dog but, as time went by, they realized that this was not a normal robotic dog. Amanda named it "Copper" for reasons known only to her. In

John's absence, Helen, Amanda and Jack agreed that they would never question what Copper was until John was ready to tell them and in the meantime, they loved their puppy.

After the completion of Copper, John held a meeting with the team to decide what they would do with their project. Should they publish their achievement and legally protect their work? The problem was proving their claim. To prove that they had developed a conscious being was filled with potential challenges from their competitors in the academic world. They also feared that publishing the details at this early stage would provide too much information for potential competitors. So with a strong belief in their own expertise and ability they decided to keep going and reach a level of development that would be difficult to dispute and much harder to duplicate. Now they would create a conscious humanoid or more precisely, an android.

Using the hard lessons that they had learned by creating Copper, they planned to use the physical structure of an existing humanoid but to throw out the existing processor and programming. This time they paid close attention to the lessons learned by the scientists studying the genetically determined processing found in the brain for handling sensory inputs from the eyes, ears, nose and other body parts and organs. They realized that the visual and sound processing mechanisms were the most important functions that it would need to survive as a conscious being and they concentrated on these functions. Using the lessons learned with Copper's programs they gave the brain the function of continuous operation which included an 'eight hour' sleep function. As they had done with Copper a survival instinct was included and thus a desire to live and function. They named their creation "Brenda".

They chose a female name because in the discussions leading up to the project they decided to pattern the brain structure to be more like the processing found in a human female brain. The brain research that had been done over the past forty or more years clearly indicated that there was a distinct difference between the male and female brain. The team decided that the female brain pattern would more quickly adapt to the challenges the conscious humanoid would encounter. When the team was ready to activate 'Brenda' a strange thing happened. They knew that Brenda would be like a baby. To achieve true consciousness she would have to learn everything using her own body parts in order to 'self tag' the memory information. Experimenting with a robotic dog was one thing, but experimenting with a human-looking being that would be conscious was quite another. Every member of the team worried about how Brenda would 'feel' and how she would react to her consciousness. She was their baby. They decided to disable the sleep function and operate on a 'round the clock' basis with at least two members of the team present at all times and with the ability to initiate the sleep function instantly, if needed. In this way they felt that she could learn more quickly.

On Brenda's birthday, the day she was first activated, all the team members were there. They all knew what should happen based upon their program knowledge, but after the experience with Copper they knew better than to be too confident. To their amazement, everything went almost perfectly. The lessons learned with Copper had paid off. Brenda was, in fact, like a baby. She had to learn about herself through trial and error and to learn about her environment the same way. The difference was that she was already 'fully grown'. With the 'sleep cycle' turned off and the team working on a 24-hour schedule they found that she learned quickly. Instead of confining her to the lab as they had done with Copper, they took her outside and because of her appearance, people who saw them who were not on the team just thought that the Humanoid Group was just working on a new model. All the work they had done on the language processing paid off nicely as Brenda quickly learned to talk. One of the interesting features of Brenda's communication skills was the ability to talk to her electronically. Her internal communication equipment both received and transmitted. It was continuously connected to the team's laboratory processing system. She quickly learned the difference between vocal speech which she heard with her ears and 'radio' speech which seemed to come from inside her brain. She was not aware that her thoughts could be 'downloaded' and her processing could be changed. The team tried many different processing modifications to give Brenda a variety of 'feelings' which they felt would help her communicate with humans, not just by words, but also by facial expressions and body language. They realized that these 'feelings' were not an exact duplication of human feelings in the true sense but were, nevertheless, real feelings for Brenda's consciousness. With a great deal of trial and error they did achieve an apparent level of humanness that amazed even them.

After about six months and about the time when the team was becoming exhausted with their twenty-four hour work schedule, it was decided to try having Brenda live in a normal home. It was then that John told his family what was going on, including the truth about Copper. To his surprise and pleasure everybody in the family agreed to give Brenda a try in their home. The year was 2024 and John's family was about to make history but, not necessarily, the history they might have expected.

No one was quite sure what to expect from this arrangement, and it was to everyone's surprise that Brenda had a distinct personality and a cheerful one at that. It became clear that this was the result of all the care and attention she had received from the team. Although she was programmed to survive and protect herself from harm, there had never been any threats to her survival. She had only known care and consideration. That is what she received from John's family as well. They thought she was wonderful! Although she was only six months old, to the family she seemed to be like a very bright, ten-year old girl. She was very naïve but she wanted to know and try everything. Her ability to learn and remember was astounding, and because she did not feel pain in the same way that a human feels pain, she had to be carefully taught the things that could seriously damage her. She knew she was different but she seemed to accept that fact without any concern. While the family ate, she refueled but when they slept, she slept and when they watched television she watched television. She continued to be taught by members of the team and she learned to help them just as they and the family members helped her. They took her out in public as part of her 'growing up' process and even taught her how to drive a car. Since humanoid drivers were fairly common, obtaining the necessary legal permission for Brenda to drive was not difficult. It seemed to the team and the family that Brenda aged a year for every month that went by and within a very short time she began to help John and became his live-in assistant. One of the interesting features that Brenda possessed was her capability to electronically 'communicate' with normal humanoids like Suzie and even other processors not related to humanoids. This feature was the team's idea and was created to speed Brenda's ability to learn, but since no human could ever have this capability it was uncertain what effect it might have on Brenda. It was difficult to imagine 'self tagging' that kind of information in the same way that 'seeing something' with one's eyes is 'self tagged'. Brenda could not describe the 'feeling' of learning that way, but for John it was a real help since Brenda could, in effect, 'translate' for John in his efforts to utilize various digital devices.

As Brenda continued to develop, John was surprised by Brenda's descriptions of what she was feeling. It was clear that Brenda had not just the feelings that the team had given her but as a result of 'just living' she had developed new ones. She 'liked' certain activities and 'disliked' others. She had been given the ability to laugh in certain situations but as she 'matured' and learned, she laughed in situations totally different from what was expected. It was clear that the process of 'program' oneself, so vital to the development of a human child's brain was in operation within Brenda as a result of what had been learned with Copper's creation. The extent of this process was never fully understood by the team because of the incredible complexity that had been achieved with Brenda's brain. Its ability to change its own programs on a continuous basis made the task of monitoring and analyzing the brain's operations very difficult. They had created a new life form and had created it in such a way that the consequences of what they had done were not totally understood.

John was so lost in his remembrances that he almost forgot where he was going but as he approached Ross Hall he caught sight of a couple that quickly brought him back to reality. It also brought him a feeling of relief as he recognized Bob and ran toward him. "Hey Bob! Over here!" It was Bob and Diane Schultz from the University of Rochester. Bob was the president of the Conference group and had been the host of last year's Conference. Diane was also a university faculty member and had been active in supporting past conference activities. "Hi, John, we were wondering when you would show up. Aren't you supposed to be in charge of this affair? They had been friends for many years and both John and Helen enjoyed being with this wonderful couple. Diane gave him a hug. They were both about ten years older than John and had been almost like an older brother and sister to him.

She looked around at the people moving about them. "Where's Helen? Isn't she helping you with all this?

"No, as usual, she's busy at the hospital. She'll be with me tonight at the dinner and then you two can share all the latest gossip. Bob, you should be grateful that I remembered to come at all. How about giving me a few clues as to how to pull this thing off? John wasn't kidding about needing some help. "How do I handle all the media people and their requests for special treatment?"

"It's not that hard. Just have a special meeting for them tomorrow morning and let them ask anything they want. That will make them feel that you understand how important they are and how important it is for them to know everything, before anyone else does. We both know you haven't a clue what most of the presenters will present but if they have their brains engaged they should know that anyway."

John felt a sense of relief having Bob to talk to. "I learned from what you did last year and I've already arranged for that meeting tomorrow morning. As group president, how about joining me at the meeting and then you can help me run around in circles when they ask their questions?"

"Sure, no problem. I noticed when Diane and I were registering that Noreen Stern is covering the conference for CBS. I'm surprised that we have attracted that kind of coverage."

Diane jumped into the conversation with that special look she would get when she was excited. "Have you seen her on TV when she is interviewing someone who she thinks needs to be taken down a few steps? She chews them up and spits them out all the time with that cute smile on her face. She must know something special about this conference or she wouldn't be here."

Bob looked at John with that 'is there something you want to tell me' look and John shrugged his shoulders. "You've seen the schedule. It is just like the one you used last year. Maybe she has heard that something special will come out of the Legal Issues meeting that will be presented on Thursday." With that sentence John hoped he had put that subject to rest and he looked around as if he had other people to greet.

"Yeah, you might be right. We know you've got other things to do right now and we've got to get over to our motel so we'll get going. See you at seven and don't forget to bring your beautiful bride." With that Bob and Diane walked toward the street.

John went into the Hall and found that most of the attendees had registered and everything seemed under control. Thank God for Sonny and his crew. Dede told him that Walt, the university president, was looking for him but John decided to wait and call him after he got home. He walked out to his car and started to drive over to his lab to pick up Brenda. As he drove he called the lab to tell Brenda he was on his way. Michelle answered the phone. "As I'm sure you may have guessed, the big problem over here was an argument between Alex and Steve about what the team should be doing after tomorrow. I'll let Brenda give you the details when you pick her up and I'll make sure she's waiting outside."

Michelle was right. John had suspected that the problem that had caused Alex to miss the student lecture was a disagreement with his assistant Steve. When he pulled up to the lab he could see by the way Brenda was moving, that she was upset. Brenda got in the car before John said anything. "Michelle told me about the argument so you don't have to worry about giving me the details. I'm not surprised because, let's face it, those two are always arguing about something."

"Yeah, but this time it was a real shouting match. I've never seen them argue like that. I think I should talk to Steve tonight after he cools down."

John drove for a minute before answering. "Brenda, why don't we worry about them after tomorrow's presentation? We've got enough on our plate without trying to solve Steve's problems tonight. I hope you remember you promised Jack that you would help him with his math homework tonight."

With that reminder John could see Brenda start to relax. "Yes sir, I think I would rather be doing that than doing what you and Helen will be doing tonight. Besides talking to Steve when he is angry is a pain in the butt."

John laughed. "What do you mean, don't you think I like taking Helen out?"

Brenda became serious again. "I didn't mean that. I was talking about having to listen to all those speeches and talk to all those people who will try to find out what you are going to say tomorrow."

John was amused at Brenda's intuitiveness but not surprised. Brenda had become very protective when it came to John and the rest of the family. John looked over at Brenda as they drove. "I've done this before and, believe me, there won't be any problems. Most of those guys would rather hear themselves talk than listen to someone else."

As they drove up to the house John turned to Brenda with a request. "Don't mention the Lab argument to Helen. I think she's got enough on her mind for tonight, having to guard her conversation with everyone while also trying to have a good time." As soon as he got out of the car John's mind was quickly absorbed by the details of preparing for the evening ahead. Brenda went up to her room on the top floor of the house, and John went up to the bedroom where Helen was still getting ready. He started to change his clothes for the evening ahead but his mind was not on getting dressed. It was on who would be at the dinner and what rumors they might have heard about his and the other presentations. The academic and business people who would attend the opening ceremonies and the conference presentations were a 'tight knit', if not always friendly group of people. Many of them had made a fortune when the idea of 'mass produced' humanoids became a reality. With very few exceptions, they were not a group of people concerned about the social ramifications of replacing people with humanoids. Their main concern was how to make them better and/or cheaper. The last thing on their minds would be how to make them conscious.

In addition to Bob and Diane, he knew most of these entrepreneurs quite well and was actually looking forward to hearing the latest ideas, especially after everyone had had a few martinis. Unfortunately, he liked martinis, too, and he hoped that Helen would help him keep his mouth shut. She only drank wine and was an unusually gifted observer of people. She instinctively knew who was trying to 'con' the rest of them and who was keeping a secret that they desperately wanted to share with someone. On more than one occasion she had steered him to the right guy at the right time to find out the latest new development.

Much to John's surprise Helen was ready to go at six thirty and also to his surprise, she already knew that they did not have to be at Ross Hall until seven.

"Okay, what's going on? You're ready and I'm not. "John was both pleased and puzzled. He looked at Helen and felt a sense of pleasure and pride. She was beautiful and smart and she was his.

She laughed at his surprise. "Don't you think I've got you figured out by now? I knew you wouldn't tell me the right time but I decided to get ready early anyhow. I've been watching you get ready and your mind must be in a dozen different places at one time. Are you going to be okay tonight? I haven't seen you act like this since the time I was having Amanda and you didn't know whether to jump out the window or faint."

John didn't quite know where to begin. "I'm excited about tomorrow, worried about tonight and beginning to be full of doubt about what we're about to do. When my 'fellow researchers' find out what is going on I am not sure if they will just yawn or blow my head off."

"Come on, John, is this my professor who always knows what he is doing and why he is doing it? You are about to tell the world that you've created a new life form. It's a dream you've had all your life. Are you going to let a few last minute jitters spoil this for you?"

John glanced at her with a look that could not be put into words. "You're right, as usual. Let me finish getting ready and let's get this show on the road."

By the time John came downstairs; Brenda had come down and was talking to Jack in their library about getting started with his homework. He left Helen in the hall putting on her coat and went to make sure Brenda understood his thoughts about Jack's homework. "Brenda, make sure it's Jack who does the homework and understands what he did. I think we'll be home about eleven this evening so you'll probably still be up when we arrive and you can tell me how it went."

"Dad, give us a break. Brenda knows what she's doing. Just go to your dinner and have a good time. We'll be fine."

John took a deep breath and sighed before going on. "Brenda, are you still planning to talk to Steve tonight?

"Yes, as soon as I finish helping Jack I'll start talking to him—again. I contacted him when you went to get dressed for your dinner. He's still mad, so I said I would talk to him later after Jack and I are finished. I have a feeling that it's going to be a long talk. Why don't you just take Helen to the dinner and have a good time."

"You're right but tell Steve to keep his temper and give us a chance to resolve his problems after we get through tomorrow." With that John left the room and headed out the door with Helen.

As Brenda turned to start working with Jack her thoughts were not on math homework, they were on what she was going to say to her brother, Steve.

As John and Helen drove over to Ross Hall for the conference dinner and opening ceremonies John tried to focus on the evening ahead. He felt confident that Sonny and his group had taken care of the dinner arrangements and had made sure that all the guests were properly informed about everything. All he had to do was to concentrate on introducing Bob and covering the conference schedule. Unfortunately, his mind kept returning to the argument that had occurred in the Lab between Alex and Steve. John always knew that the time would arrive when he would have to deal with Steve's problems but he had hoped that it would be after the conference. He remembered when Steve had been added to the project. The team had completed Brenda's development, to the point where they felt she was ready to try living in a normal home and there had been a discussion about making clones of her. The idea was to allow other team members to try living with their own 'Brenda' just as they had done with their own Copper. It was an intriguing idea because they all felt that information needed for the continuing improvements of Brenda's capabilities could be developed faster if there were more than one prototype. They finally decided that only one duplicate could be created because of their concerns for the security of their work and the extra load that the duplicate would place on them. Alex was eager to try living with a duplicate and, after some heated discussion; it was decided to let him try it. They named the duplicate, Steve.

The actual creation of Steve from a physical standpoint was not difficult because of the team's experience with Brenda but when it came time to transfer Brenda's brain contents to Steve the team created a problem for themselves that they would later regret. After several long discussions they decided to use a male brain structure so they could test and observe the differences that would occur with a conscious male humanoid as compared to the experience with Brenda. That decision of course, made the transfer of information from Brenda's brain much more difficult. At that point in Brenda's development, she was still very much a child. They tried to explain to her that when she woke up she would be in two places at the same time. They told her that in one place, she would be just as she was when she went to sleep but would see someone on the other side of the room, who would say that he was Brenda. The team had decided that the two should look like brother and sister. They told her she would also be that other person and would see herself on the other side of the room but when she looked in the mirror she would see that she now had a new face and looked like a boy. They explained that she would not only have a new face and body but would also have a new name. She would be called Steve.

Of course, it was impossible to make Brenda understand, even when they showed her Steve's body before he was activated. They decided to just 'do it' and see what would happen.

Brenda was just fine. She hadn't changed and she felt the same as always. Steve was a different story. If he had been given the capability to cry he would have done so but his distress was obvious. Somebody had his body and he had a new face and everybody called him Steve when he knew his name was Brenda. They kept Brenda and Steve together and allowed them to get used to the idea of being brother and sister. During the week that followed, Steve slowly adapted to the idea that he was okay but now he had a friend that was strangely, both himself and someone else. When the team looked back at what they had done and how Steve's personality developed, they realized that Steve was actually seriously disturbed by the experience, just as any human child would have been by such a traumatizing event. Unfortunately, the team was composed of technical specialists not psychologists, and their understanding of this type of event was rudimentary at best. Of course, Steve still had the same people caring for him and teaching him and now he had someone who knew what he was feeling. The two new friends had something that nobody else had; they could talk electronically and share information and as far as they could understand, nobody knew they were doing it. They even had the ability to exchange visual information so that one could literally see what the other one was seeing. The one doing the original seeing controlled whether the information was transmitted or not. Of course, the team knew they were communicating electronically and monitored most of the exchanges. They decided to tell Brenda and Steve that they could monitor their location and physical condition but did not tell them about monitoring their communications.

The experiment had confirmed something that the team hoped would happen with the duplication. Everything that Brenda had learned up to the point of transfer was transferred to Steve so that he did not have to learn how to walk, talk and control his body. Now, as one of them learned something new, it could be transferred to the other and thus, for certain types of information, the two of them could learn twice as fast. They lived in two different homes and although they could communicate continuously, they didn't always do so and thus did not always share their experiences. Most humanoids being made in the early twenties were made with different facial features and skin coloring to meet the desires of their owners and allow them to be distinguished from each other. Brenda and Steve looked very much like normal humanoids. That appearance made it very easy to take them out in public. Once they learned the importance of acting like ordinary humanoids, when they were in the presence of humans who were not on the team, they were taken out frequently as part of their development.

As time went by, the team continued to make them 'more human' in their behavior. They experimented with trying to duplicate some of the functions that a living brain is genetically programmed to perform, especially in the areas of expressed emotion and desires. Since they were essentially gender neutral, even though their names were masculine and female, the area of sexual desire was not addressed. As each change was made, it was made to only one of them so that the team would have a basis for comparison. When it was determined that a change was not successful it was removed. Unfortunately, because of the complexity of their continuously changing internal 'programs', the removal process was not always complete. The result was an ever-increasing difference between Brenda and Steve. When presented with the same information each one processed this information in a distinctive way. This difference was obvious when they expressed their thoughts about the information. Steve became noticeably more aggressive than Brenda. John had just recently realized that in addition to the gender differences in their brain structures, one of major reasons for their different personalities was the home in which they lived. Brenda lived with a loving family that was eager to share their experiences with her. Steve lived with Alex, a somewhat eccentric scientist who was also madly in love with his girlfriend, Michelle. Alex cared about Steve and his development but he cared much more about Michelle. Steve was left alone more frequently than Brenda and had to figure out how to use that time as best he could. When Steve 'connected' with Brenda he could see their different situations and was envious of the life that Brenda was leading. His only passion became learning all that he could about the world he lived in and his place in that world.

CHAPTER 3

▼

DINNER
CONVERSATIONS

As John drove to the conference dinner his memories of all that had happened since Steve's creation dominated his thoughts and he knew that the argument which had occurred between Alex and Steve had to be resolved as soon as possible. It might be dangerous to try to put it off until after the conference. Helen looked over at her husband and recognized his expression and his behavior. She had seen that intense concentration many times. "What's bothering you John? Are you worried about what's going to happen tonight or about what's going to happen tomorrow?"

The expression on Helen's face and her soft voice made John realize her concern and the fact that he had been ignoring her. "To tell you the truth I feel a little numb. I'm trying to concentrate on everything I am supposed to be doing tonight but I can't stop thinking about tomorrow, and today we had some problems with Steve that are on my mind. I'll be glad when tonight's over. I just want to make my presentation and get back to my work."

Helen could feel the tension in his voice and she knew that nothing she could say would make any difference. They arrived at Ross Hall exactly at seven. As they drove into the parking lot it was clear that only about half the people expected had arrived.

They left the car to walk to the Hall and could feel the cold evening breeze and as they walked John put his arm around Helen. It was something that John did without thinking and that made Helen feel very warm inside. As they entered the Hall through the big doors at the entrance they were eagerly greeted by the students who had volunteered to check names and take tickets.

"Hi, professor Cupar! Mrs. Cupar, you really look great." It wasn't hard to tell that they were excited about the evening and all the important guests. John and Helen were well liked by the students and they both enjoyed the attention. That was one of the advantages of being in a small university, getting to know your students as individuals rather than just as a crowd.

"Professor Cupar, Mister McMahon asked me to tell you that the extra tables and dinners you requested have all been arranged. He also said that he had personally tested the sound system and that you should just relax and have a drink." The smile on the student's face made John laugh and he could feel himself 'unwinding' a few notches.

"That sounds like Sonny, he probably also wrote everyone's speech and told them where to sit. By the way, did he say that he had informed some of the guests that they are supposed to sit at the head table?" John was sure he probably had done that but it never hurt to ask.

"I'm not sure but I'll go find him and I'll let you know."

"Don't worry about it, I'm sure I'll see him in the crowd and I'll find out myself." With that, John and Helen entered the main dining area. It was a large area that could easily handle up to five hundred people but tonight there would only be about half that number. For presentations there was an elevated platform in the middle of one wall opposite the main entrance. Two bars had been set up, one at each end of the room.

One of the advantages of being early or at least, on time was the speed with which one could get a drink and John was quick to take advantage of that fact, ordering a martini for himself and a glass of wine for Helen. As he took his first sip he felt a tap on his shoulder. "Good evening John. Did Dede give you my message?"

John turned and quickly recognized the university president. Walt and John had known each other for many years and were good friends. John lightly hit his forehead and shook his head. "I'm sorry Walt. I totally forgot to call you. I hope I haven't screwed up anything?"

"No John, I know how busy you are and I just wanted to know if everything was okay. It looks like you've got a damn good turnout. How did you get so many media types to come to this thing?"

John was beginning to wonder the same thing because he hadn't done anything but follow the ideas that Bob Schultz had given him and those were the same things that Bob had done last year. "I don't know what the hell I did, Walt. Maybe it's just because our humanoids are becoming so popular with everyone. Whatever it is I'm glad they're here because that will make our corporate sponsors happy and what makes them happy, is usually good for us."

"I can't argue with that. Don't hesitate to let me know if you need anything or if anything goes wrong."

"Thanks Walt. I appreciate your offer. Now let me get this glass of wine over to Helen before she comes after me. We'll get a chance to talk some more later."

That was fine with Walt and John started over to where Helen was waiting. As he walked through the crowd he was happy to see more people coming in. He remembered how the conference used to be back in the 'old days'. Then the Conference wasn't even an annual event. It was held at a different location every other year and usually the same people attended. The original intent of the conference was to allow the researchers from the academic world to exchange ideas and present the latest advances in the world of humanoid development. Beginning about seven years ago, the companies that were trying to commercialize humanoids, started to attend because of their close association with many of the academic researchers. With the greater involvement of the companies came a significant increase in funding for the exhibits and activities of the conference. Coverage by the media also increased and it became an annual affair. Most of the companies were now sending at least half a dozen representatives while the Universities usually sent only about two or three people.

John had been his University's representative for about ten years. Normally, when the conference was held he would take one or two members of his faculty with him. Since the conference was being held at his University this year, all the members of his faculty were invited to attend. Alex, as a member of the faculty was coming and naturally, had asked Michelle to come with him.

They were late in coming and as they walked up to John and Helen, John was already on his second drink and Helen was already on his case warning him to go easy with the gin.

"Michelle, you look beautiful but who is your shy looking date?" John knew he shouldn't make them uncomfortable but he couldn't resist. Helen looked at him with a disapproving squint and turned toward Michelle and Alex.

"Hi, Alex. Michelle, you look marvelous in that dress. I know that you've both been looking forward to this conference and are probably relieved that it's finally getting started."

Michelle was obviously very excited. "Yes, but we don't know whether to be afraid or as you said, relieved. Whatever happens, life will never be the same after tomorrow."

"John, have you had a chance to talk to anyone yet?" Alex was clearly focused on why they were there and noticed that his boss didn't look totally sober. He was not going to get into any small talk if he could avoid it. "Michelle, why don't we circulate and see what chatter we can pick up?"

John's slightly slurred response showed the effect of the martini. "Wait up Alex. Let's have a little talk before you go anywhere. Helen, you talk to Michelle for a minute while I talk to Alex."

John grabbed Alex by the arm and led him to the side of the room. Alex wasn't sure what was going on. What's your problem John? Did something happen today?"

"You tell me Alex. What the hell happened in the lab today? The last thing we need is for Steve to run around yelling at you. He could really screw things up tomorrow. Is this the result of your letting him access that information I warned you about?"

Alex's response was close to anger. "No it's not. He's angry because we won't let him access that information." He took a quick look around before continuing. "Look, this is a hell of a time to have this discussion. I see people starting to stare at us already. Why can't we meet tomorrow morning with him and reach some kind of agreement?"

John's common sense finally kicked in and he paused before answering. "You're right, this isn't the time and I shouldn't talk about it while I'm not totally sober. Let's get together after I have my meeting with the media group in the morning."

They walked back to where Helen and Michelle were talking. From the expression on their faces it was obvious that the girls were worried about what John and Alex had been talking about and equally obvious that they were relieved when they saw the two men calmly returning. As Alex and Michelle excused themselves John couldn't resist giving them one last bit of advice. "You two go ahead and see what you can find out but watch what you say. Some of these guys are pretty good at reading between the lines."

As they walked away Helen put herself squarely in front of John. "If you have another one of those you won't be able to talk to anyone." She knew how nervous he was and if a drink helped him relax that was fine, but she also knew that he would never forgive himself if he said the wrong things tonight.

"Hey, Helen! Where have you been hiding yourself?" It was Bob and Diane Schultz and Helen felt a sense of relief when she saw them. Helen knew just seeing Bob and Diane that afternoon had given John a feeling that he was among friends. Bob was not just a good friend but like John, he was a department head and a top researcher in this field. He was very modest about his accomplishments and very down to earth. He was a man you could trust and tonight Helen knew that is what John needed.

"Diane, you are looking lovely tonight, as usual. How are you enjoying your Rochester winter this year?" Helen's words were normal but her expression was not. Her sense of relief as she saw Diane was certainly real. Diane and Helen had been commiserating with each other for years as both tried to cope with the trials and tribulations of being married to husbands totally absorbed in their work. Diane was a smart woman and very practical. She was one of Helen's favorite people.

"Helen, you look like a cat in a room full of rocking chairs. What's John been doing to you? Diane's expression was a mixture of happiness to see Helen and concern for her obvious discomfort.

"Does it show? I was hoping that no one would notice. You know how John can be, all wrapped up in some technical thing and ignoring everything else but this time he can't do that. He's got to be the conference host and also one of its presenters but tonight he has decided to be the conference martini drinker."

Before Diane could reply, Bob grabbed John by the arm. "While the girls talk about everything that is wrong with us why don't we go over there and have a quick talk about what's going on?"

"Here we go again."

Helen's expression told Diane that she had better step in before Helen continued. "Let them go, we can talk better without them anyway." With that, John and Bob walked over to the side of the room.

"Well?" Bob stared at John expecting him to talk.

"Well what? What do you want me to say?"

John was surprised at the intensity in Bob's voice. "Did you honestly think that you could keep what you are doing secret? Have you looked at the E-mail traffic coming out from some of your people down here? You know these young people are in contact with their friends all over the country and they are usually playing games with each other and I don't mean Monopoly. They also don't stay sober twenty-four hours a day. My crew is telling me that you have this special team of yours ready to drop a bombshell tomorrow. Do you deny it?"

John was still not sure what to say. He paused. "Okay, sure, we have a paper to present that might raise a few eyebrows, but bombshell, I don't think so." He looked at Bob to see if he bought it.

Bob was not 'buying it'. "John, how many years have we known each other, twelve, thirteen years? Who the hell do you think you are talking to; your crew is acting like they just discovered aliens from another planet? Don't you think you can trust me?"

John was torn with what to do. Bob was a trusted friend but he had promised his team that nobody would know until the presentation. "Okay, look, it *is* a big deal. We are going to present something very special and, I think, very important, but I promised my team that there would be no leaks before the presentation. I swore them to secrecy with a threat of instant death if they talked to anyone about it before then. With all the E-mails I bet that not one of them gave it away. We're old and good friends but I can't break a promise. Can you understand that and give me a break?"

Bob stared at John for what seemed to John to be a long time but was actually only about five seconds. "Okay, I respect your promise to your team but you've got to realize that probably half the people in this room know that something is going on and they aren't going to let up until they find out what it is. You better stop drinking right now and get ready for them." They started to walk toward 'the girls' when Pat stopped suddenly and turned to John. "For Christ's sake, it isn't that 'conscious' thing that you have been mumbling about for the last ten years is it?"

John stopped cold. Again, he didn't know what to say. His face turned even redder than it already was from the martinis and his speech had a noticeable slur. "I told you that I am not talking about what we're doing until tomorrow. Why don't you just come to the presentation and see for yourself."

"Oh, my God!" The expression on Bob's face was hard to describe but it was not a happy one.

At this point, Les Zuchert walked up to them. Les was not one of John or Bob's favorite people. He was the lead representative of The Companions Inc, one of the biggest companies producing humanoids in the country. Both Bob and John knew that this company had a reputation for 'borrowing' other people's ideas and pushing the legal limits of patent infringement. In other words, they were thieves and Les was their chief crook.

"Just the two guys I've been looking for." He walked up between them and put his arms around both their shoulders. "I hear that John has some big news for us. How about a little preview of your presentation tomorrow?"

Bob looked at John and took Les's arm off his shoulder. He was afraid of what John and his martinis might say so he answered quickly. "Why does a guy like you need a preview, Les? Your guys have probably paid off one of John's people and are half way through your first production run on his ideas."

Les laughed. "Come on, give me a break. This is a cutthroat business and if I let someone get in front of me, my company will dump me like a sack of potatoes. Have I ever hurt either one of you? All I need is a little help and I could make both of you richer than you will ever be teaching at any university in the country."

John finally spoke but his slur caught Les's attention immediately. "You mean *you* would be richer, don't you Les?"

"John, you old fox, I heard that you've got something that will knock our socks off! Come on over here and let me buy you a drink so we can get reacquainted."

Before John could say a word he heard "Professor Cupar, I wonder if I could introduce myself?" Both John and Bob quickly turned around to see who had asked the question and who owned that sexy voice. "My name is Noreen Stern and I wanted to introduce myself before we sat down for dinner." Her voice was well matched by her long dark hair and beautiful face and figure.

Bob looked like he had just swallowed a bug but John was all smiles. "Noreen, I heard that you were attending our conference and I was looking forward to meeting you. This is Bob Schultz from the University of Rochester and this is Les Zuchert from The Companions Company.

"It's a pleasure to meet you gentlemen." Her greeting was polite but it was clear that her attention was focused on John. "Professor, did you know that Debbie Hull is my sister? She is part of your team isn't she? "Now her expression was like a cat that had cornered a mouse.

Now it was John's turn to swallow a bug. "Debbie is your sister! No, I didn't know that. Is Stern your married name?"

"Why yes, I'm surprised she hasn't mentioned me to you. Wasn't she the one who told you that I was coming to your conference? Well, that doesn't matter. I understand that you've got something really interesting to present tomorrow."

"Yes John, why don't you tell us all about it." Les was smiling from ear to ear as he moved over next to Noreen.

She looked at Les like he was a fly in her soup. "Professor, would you like to go somewhere where we can talk after the dinner. I'd really like to give your work the attention that I'm sure it deserves and I can do that if you could give me a private interview."

Before John could speak, Bob finally found his tongue and stepped closer to John. "Noreen, I'm sure you realize that John is the host for this conference and has a lot on his mind, especially tonight. Perhaps after tomorrow's activities he might be able to consider your request." He looked at John, hoping that it wouldn't be the martinis that would give his reply.

Apparently, the danger of the situation helped John override the alcohol because he paused and seemed to take a deep breath. "Thank you for your kind offer, Noreen, but Bob is right. Let me think about it and perhaps we can discuss your request tomorrow."

Noreen also paused and sized up the situation as she looked at both John's and Bob's expressions. She smiled and said "that will be great and I'll look forward to listening to your presentation and talking to you afterwards." Both John and Bob thought the same thing. How can a woman, with a smile like that, have such a dangerous reputation?

It was with great relief for both men when they heard the announcement by Sonny. "Will everyone now take your seats; dinner will be served in five minutes."

"Come on John, let's find the girls and sit down. It was a pleasure meeting you Noreen. We'll see you later, Les." Bob grabbed John by the arm and led him toward the head table where their wives had already seated themselves. When Bob felt that they were far enough away he stopped John. "Who is Debbie Hull?"

John's expression was very serious. "She is the senior software engineer on my team developing our advanced humanoid. I've got to contact her to find out what she told Noreen. I'm going to blow her away if she has given her any information about our project. Right now, though, I have got to get through this evening. Let's get going over to the table."

Bob had no response. As they approached, Helen looked up at Bob. "Did John behave himself?"

Their eyes met and with that look Bob told Helen that he had. He saw the relief in her eyes and felt relieved himself.

Before John could relax for dinner he had to introduce another friend to his audience. When he stood up and started to speak both the distractions and martinis seem to have eased their hold on him as he spoke into the microphone. "Ladies and gentlemen, can I please have your attention?" There was a gradually diminishing noise level from the audience as they turned their attention to John.

"Let us begin this evening with a prayer by Father Kevin Brooks."

John sat down and Father Brooks looked out over the audience. "In the name of the Father, Son and Holy Spirit let us bow our heads. Almighty God, please give your blessing and your guidance to these talented men and women as they bring their efforts to this conference. Give them the resourcefulness and courage to do your work in a spirit of cooperation and unity. They need your light and guidance to see there way clearly and your strength to go ahead resolutely. Let them be aware of both the benefits and the consequences of their work. Give them the wisdom to understand the effects of what they do and the courage to apply their knowledge for the betterment of all of mankind and not the enrichment of a privileged few. We ask these things with the hope and certainty that you will support their efforts to do your will through your Son, our Lord, Jesus Christ, Amen."

John looked up at the audience and could immediately see that the prayer was not one they expected to hear and not one that they necessarily had wanted to hear. He was surprised himself. It was not what he expected from Father Kevin but he didn't have time to worry about it as he stepped up to the microphone once again. "Thank you Father Brooks. Ladies and gentlemen, please enjoy your dinner."

Dinner went as expected and everyone seemed to be enjoying themselves. Their companions at the head table were all old friends and the conversations were more about family members and family activities than about the conference. By the time dessert was served John's martinis had totally released their hold on his brain and he began to concentrate on his opening speech.

He stood up and addressed the audience again. "Ladies and gentlemen, if I can have your attention we will begin our program. Tonight is the start of the twentieth conference on Humanoid Research and Development. As I am sure all of you know, our conference concerns developments which still boggle the minds of many of our fellow citizens, especially those over the age of forty. These developments have changed the lives of many people all over the world. Not all of those changes have been welcome and that is an issue that will be addressed during this week. When the conference first began it attracted very little attention from the media. Now, as I'm sure you are all aware, at least twenty percent of the people who are attending this event are from the media. Before the evening is over we will hear from the president of our association about some of the events that have occurred during the year and he will make several presentations in recognition of the accomplishments of some of our members. I will close the evening by giving you a quick review of the presentation topics for each of our sessions. Before I forget to mention it, there are copies of the final version of the conference agenda at both entrances to the Hall. The version that was sent to you during the year in preparation for the conference is generally correct, but there have been a few changes in the names of those who will be giving the presentations. It is now my privilege and honor to introduce our association president, Robert Schultz, a man that we all know and respect and a man that I consider to be one of my best friends."

Bob came to the microphone and thanked John for being this year's host and then proceeded to give a short speech outlining most of the significant events that had occurred during the year in the world of humanoid developments and applications. He then presented an award to a scientist from the MIT development laboratory near Boston for her work in improving the precision and sensitivity of humanoid hands. This work had made possible a number of new applications where a humanoid needs to manipulate its hands in ways that could not be pre-programmed, just as a human must sometimes do for unexpected and difficult tasks. The next award was presented to the leader of a Carnegie-Mellon team in Pittsburgh that had developed an advanced program that allowed a humanoid to more accurately forecast the consequences of its actions. This work had also made possible a number of new applications where a humanoid could be safely used in interfaces with humans that had previously been prohibited.

When Bob finally turned over the microphone to John he could see that the audience, which like John, had 'had a few', and was ready to call it a night.

He whispered to John as they passed each other. "Make it short or you'll lose them."

"Thanks Bob." John then turned to the microphone. "I would personally like to congratulate this year's award winners. I think we all realize that with each passing year the work that we do has an ever increasing and profound impact on our society. As you reviewed the agenda that was sent to you earlier, I think most of you were reminded of that fact by the number of concerns being presented which are the direct result of actions by our friends in the legal profession. As I mentioned earlier, the agenda that was mailed to you needs a few corrections and corrected copies are on the table at both entrances to the hall. I want to point out that we have tried to arrange the presentations for each day in a logical sequence. We hope the result is one which causes each general area to lead logically into the next general area. This sequence is as follows. The New Technical Developments will be presented tomorrow. Commercial Applications will be presented on Wednesday morning. On Wednesday afternoon Personal Applications will be presented. Legal Considerations and Concerns will be presented on Thursday morning and Humanoid Economic and Social Issues will be presented on Thursday afternoon. That will be the final topic covered by this conference.

If any of you need assistance with your living or working arrangements or for that matter, anything else, please feel free to contact me, Mister McMahon or our assistants using the telephone numbers listed in the agenda. I want to thank you all for coming tonight and for your support of the conference."

As the audience filed out of the room Bob approached John and put his hand on John's shoulder. "John, I don't know exactly what you are presenting tomorrow but I hope you know what you're doing. I hope you have thought about what effect it might have on the conference and for that matter, on our work."

The seriousness on Bob's face made John uneasy. "Really Bob, I don't think it's that big a deal. I don't expect any reactions other than the usual ones that you hear after one of us has done something a little different from the rest. There may be a little excitement at first and then everybody will go on to the next presentation and probably, forget about most of what I said."

"I don't believe that but okay, I'll have Diane give Helen a call tomorrow so we can get together. I want to hear about what you and your family have been up to for the last six months. See you in the morning." With that Bob and Diane left the hall.

After a quick check with Sonny and Dede and their helpers, John and Helen left for home. As they drove, Helen looked at John. "Well, what happened? What was Bob talking to you about?"

"I think he has guessed what I'm going to present tomorrow and is concerned about its effect on everybody." John's voice was very matter of fact in its tone.

Helen was not as calm. "What do you mean? What does he think will happen?"

John was irritated by her tone. "Look, he is just guessing and he has no idea of what will happen. He is probably worried that I will steal the headlines from the conference but I don't think that will happen. I'll tell you one thing that happened that has me worried. Do you know that Noreen Stern is Debbie Hull's sister? I don't know what Debbie has told her but I am going to give her a call when we get home and find out."

"Noreen Stern? Was she there tonight? Have you ever seen her on TV when she was doing one of her famous interviews? If you start talking to her she is going to have you for breakfast. What did she say?"

John was annoyed at Helen's implications. "She was very nice to Bob and me. She just introduced herself and asked if she could talk to me after my presentation and I told her that I would think about it. I'm only worried that Debbie told her things that she might not understand and might release them before I have a chance to explain to everybody what we have done. You just relax and let me get a good night's sleep after I talk to Debbie. That's what I need right now."

Helen was clearly still concerned. "Please don't agree to do anything with her until you've had a chance to get some advice from someone like Bob. Will you promise me that?"

"Sure, I promise. You know I would always talk to Bob about something like that." They drove the rest of the way in silence. When they arrived home everyone was in his or her bedroom except Brenda who was waiting in the living room.

"How did it go tonight? Did you enjoy yourselves?" Brenda's eagerness and emotion never ceased to amaze Helen.

John spoke first. "Everything went fine and yes, we did have a good time but right now all I want to do is go to bed and be ready to go tomorrow." John's tension showed in his voice but Brenda did not sense it and kept talking.

"Were there any questions about the presentation tomorrow? Did you see Michelle and Alex? Were there any surprises from anybody?"

John looked at Brenda and tried to control his impatience. "No, yes and no. Michelle and Alex were the best looking couple there and I think they enjoyed it too. Now, enough questions, let's all go to bed."

Helen thought that John was being unfair to Brenda. "Honey, Brenda is just trying to find out how we enjoyed ourselves and how the evening went. Just because you're tired and irritable doesn't mean you have to take it out on her."

"Thanks Helen. I understand why John wants to be left alone. He has a lot on his mind." It was clear that Brenda was disappointed but he realized that she wasn't going to get anything more from John or Helen so she gave up and went to her room.

"No matter what else happens, I hope that your presentation does nothing to hurt Brenda." The concern in Helen's voice was very real and John knew better than to get into a detailed conversation with her about it.

"She's going to be fine. Let me make a call to Debbie, then I am going up to bed." Those were his words but not his thoughts. He knew that Brenda had led a somewhat sheltered life but up to now he had thought that Brenda would enjoy the sudden fame that would probably come with the presentation. Now he wasn't so sure. He tried calling Debbie but all he got was her voice mail. Where the hell could she be at this time of night, especially on the night before the presentation?

Steve knew where she was. She was with him and some of the other team members in Alex's apartment where they had gathered to find out from Alex and Michelle if anything interesting had happened at the dinner. He contacted

Brenda electronically just as she entered her bedroom. "What did professor Cupar say when he got home? From what Alex and Michelle are telling the others, lots of people had heard about some special thing that might happen during the conference but no one knew what it was. Some of them connected it to the professor but without any clue as to what he was going to do."

"John seemed to be upset about something when he and Helen got home but he didn't want to talk about it. He just wanted to go to bed. I think I heard him say he was going to call Debbie before he went to sleep but I am not sure why. Since she's not home he won't be able to contact her anyway. If I find out anything more I'll let you know. What's the situation between you and Alex now?"

"After you left the lab Michelle started shouting at both of us and telling us what idiots we were and how we were going to ruin everything. We stopped arguing and tried to calm her down. You know how we argue all the time. I didn't see what a big deal it was but I could see that Alex was upset that he had made Michelle mad. I honestly don't understand their relationship. They're always hugging and kissing each other but they also get upset with each other all the time. I'm beginning to be thankful that we don't have this sex thing built into us."

"Yeah, I know what you mean but I see how much John and Helen care for each other and maybe it's not such a bad thing. What's going on over there now?"

"Everybody is having a drink and talking about what they think is going to happen tomorrow. Alex told me that John wants to have a meeting with Alex and me tomorrow morning to talk about our lab argument. That should be interesting. You know how I feel about the great presentation. If my guess is right, based upon what I have learned regarding how humans react to new ideas, we're going to be in big trouble."

"Get off it, Steve. You don't know what the reaction will be. You're just a damn pessimist about everything."

"Brenda, I don't think you have the foggiest notion of just how special we are and how people will react when they find out about us."

"Okay, I've heard enough, I'm going to bed and I suggest you do the same. I'll see ya tomorrow." With that Brenda took off her clothes and stretched out on the bed to wait for her sleep cycle to begin.

CHAPTER 4

▼

THE PRESENTATION

When the alarm went off the next morning John was already awake and had been for at least an hour. He wasn't surprised that he hadn't slept well. After all, this was the big day but instead of feeling excited, his mind kept coming back to Bob's words. He had dreamed about standing up before the world and announcing his accomplishment for a long time, but now that the time had arrived, his mind was in turmoil and he was angry. He was angry because of the uncertainty Bob's words made him feel about making his presentation today. What the hell did Bob know about what he had accomplished? He couldn't know. He hadn't seen the miracle that his team had performed. Nobody else was even close to achieving the goal they had reached. Bob was just worried about the damn Conference. He thought about the conversation last night with Noreen Stern. There was no point in calling Debbie this morning. He would see her before the presentation when he spoke to the team. He realized that at this point, it really didn't matter what she had told her sister because it would be presented this afternoon to everybody.

He got up and went through the morning ritual with Helen as if this was like any other day. As the family breakfast began the kids were totally unaware of what was on their father's mind but Helen was very aware that John was in a special state of mind.

"How'd you make out with your homework last night? Did Brenda bail you out as usual?" John's voice was deceptively calm.

"She was great and we were finished by seven o'clock. Now, I think I understand what my teacher was trying to get across on Friday. Brenda should become a teacher instead of working under a slave driver like you." Jack was grinning and obviously in a good mood.

Helen had to ask. "Amanda, how late did you and Paul study last night?"

"I think it was about eight or maybe nine. I don't remember exactly. Why don't you ask Brenda? She kept coming in to ask if we needed any help." The irritation in her voice was not hard to pick up and Helen had to smile as she pictured the scene of Brenda coming into the dining room every so often to see if he could help.

At this point Brenda walked into the room, obviously in a good mood. "Good morning everyone. It's a great day isn't it? Sorry I'm late. I was changing Suzie's program so that she could help Jack with his math homework in case I'm not around."

John's face showed his surprise. "You did what? Since when did you start changing Suzie's programming? Who taught you how to do that?"

Brenda didn't know what to make of John's questions. "I just thought it was a good idea. Did I do something wrong? I thought it would be helpful if she could do that for Jack since we are going to be so busy with the conference. I asked Steve to find out how to change Suzie's programming and he accessed a World-Net source for the information. Was that one of the places he didn't have permission to go? I can always change her back again."

John didn't know what to say. He was both pleased and worried at the same time.

"No, that's okay. I just didn't know that you and Steve could do that and I'm sure that the site was okay to use. That was a good idea but be sure to check with me before you make any other changes to her program or for that matter, any other program. I am not sure that you and Steve will always know the consequences of changing the programs of various things. That goes for everybody, not just you and Steve. Only the owner of a device should authorize programming changes."

"Okay, that makes good sense." Brenda's voice seemed very matter of fact so John dismissed the problem but made a mental note to think about it when he was less preoccupied.

Everyone went through the morning ritual and finally John approached Helen to say goodbye. "How about a hug and a send-off kiss?" John's face was serious as he put his arms around Helen.

Helen's face had that worried look as she hugged him very tightly. "You and Brenda are going to knock them off their feet. You know I'm very proud of you and I know everything will be just fine. Call me when it's over and let me know what happened. You have my number and I should be there this afternoon."

"Okay, I'll give you a call probably around three o'clock and let you know if we're still alive."

John let her go and turned to Brenda. "Let's go. I'll drive. Make sure we've got everything. I don't want to come back because we left something at home."

Brenda had been watching their goodbye and was not sure she understood what she was hearing but then when John and Helen talked to each other that was quite often the case. She wasn't worried about it. "I have everything in your briefcase that we discussed yesterday. Why are we bringing so much paper? I have our speech in my memory and I can record or access anything that is presented today."

"Brenda, you may have a hard time understanding this but my memory isn't as good as yours and when I get up in front of everyone I don't want to make any mistakes. I want it in writing in front of me and besides, there will be others who will want a written copy and won't want to use a download." John could see that Brenda didn't really understand the problem but he didn't have time for a lecture on the subject so he turned and walked out the door to the car.

As they drove to the conference John went over the plan for the day, more for himself than for Brenda. "After I check on the registration process at the entrance I'll go to the media meeting which should take about half an hour. After that I'm going to have a short talk with Alex and Steve. Michelle is supposed to meet us before the media meeting so you can stay with her while I do all that. She'll probably take you to one of the morning presentations. I'll try to find you both when I get free. Later, I'm going over to the dining area for lunch with some of my friends. You'll stay with Michelle while she has lunch and then go with her to the Belmont Room to make sure everything is ready for the afternoon events. Remember you're going to act and talk just like an ordinary humanoid as you always do when you're near anyone who's not in the family or on the team. After lunch I'll join you in the Belmont Room and give the team some last minute instructions. Then we'll wait our turn to make our presentation. That should wrap up the afternoon and we'll head for home."

"Steve told me last night about the meeting you're going to have with Alex and him. He doesn't think it's a big deal because he and Alex argue all the time."

"That may be true but that doesn't make it right. Our team, and that includes both Steve and you, have got to be okay with each other and with what we are doing because after today we are going to be in the spotlight of media attention. How do you think it will look if we start yelling at each other then?"

"Okay, I understand what you're saying and it makes sense." Brenda was silent for a moment and then spoke with a tone of uncertainty in her voice. "When are we going to be getting all the media attention? Will that be after the presentation or during the presentation or what? How are we going to be able to just go home with all that?"

John was surprised to hear Brenda's questions expressed with that kind of tone. They were just arriving at the university and he could see this was not the time for a long talk. "I'm sure there will be questions both during and after the presentation but I don't think they'll take a lot of time. We don't know for sure what the reaction will be so we're just going to have to play it as it happens. Don't worry about it. I'll be there with you and so will most of the team." John's thoughts were exactly as he expressed them. He didn't know what would happen and he had no specific plan for the reaction no matter what it would be.

As they entered the hall they were greeted by a number of different people who were attending the conference and some of the team members including Alex and Michelle. The out of town attendees greeted only John but the University personnel had gotten used to greeting Brenda and getting a friendly reply. They got a kick out of John's advanced humanoid assistant without realizing just how advanced she really was. The team members were very careful in their greetings to Brenda and of course, Brenda knew why. If they addressed her as anything but a normal humanoid, people would begin to realize that she was not normal. It was not unusual for some of the attendees to be accompanied by a humanoid because they were useful as companions. They could carry anything that needed to be carried, record any verbal or visual information as directed and, if needed, could provide physical assistance for anyone who was handicapped. Michelle took Brenda's hand and went to find a seat for the first presentation. Alex confirmed with John where they would meet with Steve after the media meeting.

John reviewed the registration activity and preparations for the day with Sonny and his volunteers and made sure everything was going as planned before he entered the room where the media meeting was being held. When he got there he found Bob, waiting for him.

"How'd you sleep?" Bob's question was more than a query for how rested John was.

"I slept like a baby without a care in the world. How about you?" John was smiling as he shook Bob's hand.

"I wish I could say the same but I kept having nightmares about strange things that walk in the night. Are you ready for this meeting? If you need me I will be back here guarding the door." Bob said this as they walked into the room.

"Ready as I'll ever be. Don't leave me here alone with this crew." With that he walked down the aisle, surprised to see how many people were in the room. He had planned to address them from the front of the room but now thought it would be best if he mounted the presentation stage and used the microphone and so he did.

"Good morning ladies and gentlemen. My name is Professor Cupar and I am the host for this conference. I'm certainly pleased to see such a large group will cover our conference. I can see that most of you already have our conference program which lists the presentations and the time and location of each one. If you need extra copies they will be available at the reception table near the front entrance. There are a couple of points I would like to mention for those of you who have not covered our conference previously. First, unless the presenter requests questions on a specific point in his or her presentation, we would like all your questions delayed until after they have finished speaking. Second, we would like to request that the questions asked after each presentation will be specifically about the information presented. The reason for this is to make sure we stay on schedule. After all the presentations of a particular session have been completed we will arrange for you to question any of the lecturers in a separate room for additional information you might need.

I see there are more cameras and related equipment than we are used to dealing with in our conference. I hope you will bear with us as we try to cope with the situation. I would like to request that you please try to use this equipment in such a way that it does not detract from the presentations. We would like our audiences to be able to concentrate on the speaker and not on the people and equipment being used to report the material. Are there any questions that you have about the conference?"

Several hands were raised and John pointed to a magazine reporter that he recognized from a previous conference. "Professor Cupar, are there any parts of the conference program which might be of special interest to the general public that we should know about?"

"The presentations on new personal humanoid capabilities should be of interest to the general public and also perhaps, some of the legal issues that are going to be discussed in the Thursday morning session. The issue of programming for personal humanoids has raised some interesting constitutional questions that may be difficult to resolve and that will certainly catch the public's attention." John noticed that Noreen Stern's hand was raised and pointed to her for the next question.

"Are there any unusual issues that might be raised by any of the new technical developments being disclosed? I heard that there could be some new capabilities for humanoids that might be unexpected and might cause some concern."

Noreen's question was not unexpected but John had to think for a minute to decide how best to reply. "I wish I could give you a straight answer to that question but it has always been difficult to judge what the public's reaction would be to any specific new capability or characteristic of humanoids. Usually, the new technical items presented in our conferences do not become an issue for the public until the technology is incorporated into a commercial or personal humanoid." John was pleased with himself because he felt that his answer while true, told her nothing about what she was trying to uncover.

The other questions asked were easily answered and John closed the meeting within the time he had allotted for it. As he tried to leave the meeting room Noreen stepped in front of him. "Professor Cupar, I wonder if I could arrange for a private meeting with you after your presentation this afternoon?"

John wasn't sure what to say at this point. He could see Bob slowly shaking his head about ten feet in front of him. "I am going to be very busy after the presentation. As you know, I am the host for the conference and have lots of duties to attend to both before and after this afternoon's program. I should be free tomorrow morning if that would be okay with you?"

She smiled at John with a look that would melt gold. "That would be fine. Where would you like to meet and what time would be convenient?"

John was surprised that she was so agreeable. "How about eight o'clock in my office in the Bernard Building? Could we make it a private meeting without any cameras or must it be the kind of meeting where you will broadcast everything?"

She paused for a minute before answering. "If you would feel more comfortable we could start the meeting without any cameras and then later, decide at what point you would like to start going 'on camera'."

John felt like the walls were closing in on him with that exchange. "No, wait a minute. The more I think about it, the more I would just like to make my presentation before I make any commitments for media coverage. Once you have heard it you may not want to bother with any special meeting with me. Why don't you talk to me in the post-presentation meeting and we can decide then what other meetings you may want to have?"

It wasn't difficult to see the frustration on Noreen's face but her words were very polite. "I certainly understand your reluctance to commit to an interview before your presentation and with all your responsibilities, but I would still like to ask that you remember my request."

"Yes, I certainly will and maybe you would like to include your sister in the interview if we decide to have one." John smiled and kept walking while Noreen wondered why he would want to include her sister in his interview.

Bob was smiling as John walked up to him. "Not bad. You handled that like a pro but remember, she's the real pro at this game so keep your guard up."

"Yeah, I will. Right now, I've got to go to a meeting with my lab director so why don't we get together for lunch in the dining room at about twelve fifteen. I'll see you then."

As he walked to the meeting he had a pretty good idea of what he would hear. After the team had created both Brenda and Steve there was disagreement among the team members concerning the sources of information that Brenda and Steve would be allowed to access. Although both of them could communicate electronically and verbally, barriers had been put in place to prevent them from accessing information the team felt would be difficult for them to handle. The final decision was not a democratic one. John had the final say after everyone had given his or her opinion. His decisions were well accepted, for the most part but there were some exceptions. Alex, for one, thought Steve should be exposed to difficult information as part of his development, long before anybody else did. He felt that Steve should be taught to resolve situations where he obtained information that was in conflict with information received from a second source and would accept the guidance of the team members in resolving the apparent conflicts. John felt that it would be foolish to launch into that unknown area because of the impending disclosure of their work at the conference. John knew that it was probably this disagreement that brought them to the problem with Steve. He was sure Alex had taken it upon himself to go against his decisions and had let Steve start to access some of the forbidden sites—and he was right.

When Alex gave Steve permission to access the new sites, Steve's reaction was delight, at first, and then awe as he began to understand the number of new information sources and the type of information that they made available. When he started to question Alex about what he was learning, Alex began to realize how difficult it was going to be to answer some of Steve's questions. He knew he had made a mistake in getting ahead of the team's plans and tried to stop Steve from going further until he could decide what to do. Steve's reaction was frustration and anger. He had been given a strong desire to learn and had always assumed Alex knew what was best for him. Now, he was being told that he would have to go backwards in his learning process. It was very frustrating and the conflict was creating thoughts in his mind that he didn't know how to handle. That was the reason he started to argue with Alex. The argument in the lab yesterday had started out quietly enough but by the time Michelle arrived after the lecture it had become a shouting match. Even Brenda's arrival earlier had not helped, especially since Brenda's ideas conflicted with Steve's. Now John was getting involved in their disagreement and he wasn't sure what to expect.

As John walked into the room where Alex and Steve were waiting he could see they were talking very intensely to each other. "I hope you two aren't going to have another argument. I don't need that this morning."

Both of them looked at John and laughed. Alex put his hand on Steve's shoulder before he spoke. "No, we're just solving the world's problems and that takes a lot of effort."

Now John sighed with obvious relief. "Steve, I know you're unhappy with some of our restrictions on your data sources and that is understandable. I think Brenda probably feels the same frustration and I think it's important for both of you to understand why we have insisted on these restraints. You both know that you are very special and the last thing we want for you is something that will cause you confusion and discomfort. You also know that today, we're going to tell the rest of the world just how special you are. I think you'll be surprised at how amazed and pleased people will be when they get to know about you. I want to ask a favor. I would like you to give the team a chance, after this week is over, to start expanding your data sources. Believe me, it is our intent that, eventually, you won't have any restrictions. Please believe that we intend to help you learn new things in every way we can. Will you agree, for now, to use the guidelines that we have given you?"

Steve spoke first. "John, you're my creator and you and Alex and the rest of the team have been my teachers all my life. I would never disobey you or do anything that might disappoint you, especially now, at this special moment in all our lives."

"Thanks Steve. I'm serious about giving both of you expanded access to information. I promise, we'll sit down and plan how we're going to do this on Monday."

Alex had been sitting listening to them talk with his head down. "I owe you both an apology. It was my fault letting Steve get involved with things that were not approved by the team and which probably were difficult for him to handle. My only excuse was that I wanted Steve to advance as fast as possible so that he would be ready for today. I know that your plan for today doesn't include telling the world about Steve but you never know what will happen this week. I'm sure

Steve will agree with me when I say that both of us will follow the team plan from now on. Right Steve?"

"I agree, Alex, but I will admit that I am looking forward to next Monday."

As he spoke John was standing up, satisfied that, at least for now the Alex/Steve problem was solved. I'll see you guys after lunch with the rest of the team. I'm going to find Brenda and Michelle and see what they're up to."

He found Brenda and Michelle waiting for the second presentation to begin. He sat down beside them almost in the back row of seats. He looked over at Michelle and said "I just left your sweetheart and his buddy but then I'm sure Brenda has kept you informed as to what happened, right Brenda?"

"Yeah, Steve let me watch the whole thing and I told Michelle what was happening. She said she would turn off my fuel cell if I didn't."

John was glad to see they were in such a good mood. "Poor Brenda. Would you really do that Michelle?"

Michelle laughed but then more seriously addressed John. "How did the media session go? Any problems?"

"No, but I still can't get over how many media people are attending this affair? Did you know that Noreen Stern was Debbie's sister? She just might be a problem this afternoon." John wondered how many of his team members knew about Debbie's secret.

"I just found out about it last night and I don't understand why she didn't mention it before now. If I had a famous sister I would certainly have told all my friends about her. Maybe she just doesn't feel as successful as her sister and doesn't want anyone to know that." Michelle seemed as puzzled as John was about the situation.

"Maybe she was afraid if everybody knew, she wouldn't be allowed to remain a member of the team." Brenda turned her head, first to John and then to Michelle to see what they thought of her idea.

John laughed. "Why didn't I think of that? Yes Brenda, you're probably right and to be honest about it, knowing who her sister was might make me hesitate to put her on the team.

No, she's too good at what she does. I would probably have given her a chance anyway."

At that point, the second presentation began and they all fell silent to listen. The information was interesting and professionally presented. Ordinarily John would have been very attentive but his mind was focused on the coming afternoon.

The presentation was by a Doctor Gray. Doctor Gray was from one of the IBM research organizations. It was a topic of great importance to IBM because of their worldwide business activities. They had developed a complex software system that expanded on the multi-language capability of their humanoids to enable them to accurately interpret multi-cultural 'body language'. It even took into account the gender of the human that was being addressed. The flexibility of this program reminded John of his own team's struggle with Brenda and Steve's ability to use body language as instinctively as humans do.

The second presentation was by a Mister Gordon Clements. He was from the Companions Company and that seemed strange to John because that company was known more for stealing technology than creating it. Apparently they had developed an advanced form of humanoid skin, which looked, and felt very much like human skin, retaining the sensory capability of the currently used material, and that was quite an accomplishment. Since the Companions Company specialized in humanoids for personal use, John could just imagine what they would do with their development.

Brenda was attentive to the information she was hearing and was obviously enthusiastic about the new humanoid capabilities she was learning about. "John, it's really incredible what the new humanoids will be able to do with these developments! Are you going to replace or modify Suzie with any of these new ideas?"

John, who was not really paying as much attention as he should have been, was surprised by Brenda's question. "No, I don't think she needs any of those technologies and when companies like the Companions develops something I'm always suspicious of their motives. Don't be taken in by their words. They are usually only interested in making money and they don't give a damn about who is going to use their products or how they'll be used?"

Brenda turned to John and studied his face for a clue as to what would cause him to say that. John never used that tone of voice with her and she didn't know what to say. John's recovery was immediate. "I'm sorry Brenda, I didn't mean to say that.

I guess I am concentrating too much on my presentation. As soon as this is finished I'm going to track down Sonny to see how things are going with the other parts of our program. I'll see you guys after lunch in the Belmont room."

When the presentation was finished John found Sonny at the front desk still directing people as they came in.

"How are things going so far? John tried to sound calm and enthusiastic but Sonny could tell that he was very tense.

"It couldn't be better. No complaints about anyone's accommodations so far and all the presentations seem to be well attended." He looked at John for a moment and then went on. "Well, actually there is one thing that is bothering me but I'm not sure that it's a problem. How about having lunch with Dede and me so that I can tell you about it?

John was relieved to hear the report and silently thanked God for Sonny's skill at keeping things organized. "I already told Bob Schultz that I would have lunch with him but why don't the two of you join us. I think you might enjoy talking to Bob and maybe he can address your concerns better than I." John was thinking that it would be interesting to see Bob's reaction to meeting Dede. "I think Bob will enjoy getting a chance to talk to her."

John went to the dining area to find Bob and tell him of the new arrangement. He was a little early, as was Bob and they had no trouble finding each other because most of the people hadn't arrived for lunch yet. The arrangements for lunch were cafeteria style so when Sonny showed up with Dede they were already eating. Bob seemed to be more relaxed now that the Conference was underway and he really did enjoy Dede's impressions of what she had seen and heard during the morning events. Not being one of the 'humanoid gang' she had a few unique comments about the new capabilities she had heard described. "If you people keep going, pretty soon there won't be any need for us to do anything! We won't even know if the person we are talking to is real or one of your crazy machines."

Bob went along with this comment. "You know, Dede, you're probably right. Maybe Diane and I should just take one of our new humanoids and retire down to the Finger Lakes and have one of our 'machines' take care of us for the rest of our lives. We don't need real people."

Dede looked at him with her eyes wide open in surprise but before she could reply Sonny broke in with a comment that stopped the conversation. "Before you two go off on that tangent I have a question for John. Who is this Noreen Stern person who keeps bugging me about everything? Now she wants me to make sure that she can have a front row seat at John's presentation. Not only that, she also wants to reserve a spot for a TV camera near the stage. It was my understanding that we never gave special treatment like that to the media people even when they were using cameras."

John and Bob turned to look at each other without saying a word. Bob began to slowly shake his head. "John, I hope you realize what this woman could do to this conference."

Sonny was puzzled. "What are you guys talking about? Is there something I should know about her? What has her so interested in your presentation?"

"Sonny, I don't know what the fuss is about. I'm not sure exactly why she is here or what she expects to learn and I don't know of anything that would cause her to be so interested." John didn't want to look Bob in the eye. He just wanted to calm Sonny down but he knew Bob didn't agree with what he said. It was time for him to get out of there and it was also time for him to get ready for his presentation. "I have to talk to my team over at the hall before the afternoon program begins so I'll have to excuse myself. I enjoyed the lunch and I'll see you all later." As he stood up and left, the others stared at his retreating figure.

"Bob, is that true? He really doesn't know what's going on with that woman?" After watching John's quick exit when they started to talk about Noreen, Sonny was now clearly worried.

Bob again slowly shook his head as he answered. "I'm not sure, Sonny, but you can bet that someone like Noreen Stern doesn't show up for an event like this unless she smells a big story. I don't know what we can do except watch and see what happens."

When John entered the Belmont room he was relieved to see that only his team members were present. They had gathered around the table on the stage where the presenters would sit and as John approached they greeted him warmly. In all, there were only ten members on the team, each with a special area of expertise. John was very proud of this team. They had worked many long hours and each one had sacrificed a great deal of personal time to reach the teams objectives. During the years they worked together they had developed an almost family type relationship and had a high regard for each other's capabilities.

Michelle, as usual, was the first one to speak after all the 'hellos' were exchanged. "Professor, has anything happened to change the presentation?"

"No, everything's fine but I do want to caution everybody about a few things. First, don't talk to anyone about the presentation before I give it. Don't all sit together; I want you to listen to what the people around you say before and after the presentation. Steve, don't sit with Alex. Too many people know that he is my lab manager and having you next to him might be dangerous. Michelle, I want you back stage in case I need some help. Are there any questions?" There were a few but they were mostly concerned about what they should do after the presentation was over. There was also some discussion about who was going to sit with who but everyone seemed to understand what he or she was supposed to do. John looked around the group for Debbie Hull and fixed his eyes on her. "That reminds me, Debbie, when I get finished I want to talk to you about your sister." No one seemed surprised at John's request but a few did shake their heads as they heard it. "Everyone, please remember not to mention the existence of Steve to anyone, even after the presentation is finished. Finally, if anyone from the media tries to question you, refer them to me and don't try to outfox them. That is their business and you'll lose no matter how smart you think you are."

Brenda, who had been sitting quietly, simultaneously raised her hand and asked "If I am asked anything after we're finished presenting should I lie and say something that is not true?"

That was an interesting question and John paused for a minute before answering. "No, Brenda, I don't want you to lie. If someone asks you a question about information we don't want anyone to have, just say that you've been asked not to talk about that subject and you don't want to break a promise that you've made to the team. Let's make it true. Do you promise not to talk to anyone outside this team about the things we have decided should not be shared with anyone without the team's permission?"

"Yes sir, I promise." Brenda was happy with John's solution to her problem.

John then told the team to spread out and take a seat as the audience began to enter the room. He told Brenda to go back stage and wait for him to start their presentation. "Debbie, let's go over there and have a talk."

They walked over to the other side of the stage and Debbie turned to John with what could best be described as a guilty look on her face. "Yes, I made a big mistake. I didn't tell Noreen about Brenda but I did tell her that something very special and newsworthy was going to be disclosed and that she should be here to cover the story. She didn't believe me at first so I said things like 'it's going to change the whole world' and 'you'll really get a lot of credit if you are the first to let everyone know' and other dumb things until finally, she believed me. Then, when other media people found out she was coming they decided to come also and that's why we have so many media people here now."

"Yes, it was a big mistake and I'm really disappointed in you. Your sister and her friends could totally disrupt this conference and turn our work into a circus road show instead of the serious scientific accomplishment that it represents." John's voice was angry. "We can't do anything about it now but after the presentation, would you talk to her and tell her not to blow everything out of proportion to its real meaning. We want professional recognition for our work not fame or money or whatever else people want."

By this time many of the seats in the room had been taken and it was almost time for the program to begin. John told Debbie to try to sit with her sister and then went over and took his seat with the other presenters for the session. As he looked out over the audience, watching his team take seats, he saw Noreen in the front row just as he had expected but he also saw that she was not alone. Just as

Debbie had warned, there were an unusual number of media people present or, at least, that was his guess based on his observation that media people seemed to dress somewhat differently from the other attendees. At exactly one-thirty he stood up and introduced the first presenter, Professor Eva King from Harvard. Her presentation was on the Development of Multi-Spectral Vision Capability for humanoids, which took about an hour to explain. It was an interesting topic and well presented as was usual with Eva. But again John's mind was on his own presentation. When it was over and the applause had subsided, John stood up and walked to the center of the stage.

"Eva, your work, as always, is outstanding and will provide humanoids with capabilities no one could have imagined even a few short years ago." After another short round of applause John began to speak again. "Now it's my turn to see if I can keep your attention for another hour." There was a murmur of laughter from the audience, which proved to John that he did have their attention, at least at this point. "My presentation, as you can see in your booklets, is titled 'A New Approach For Adaptive Programming'. That's probably a bad title for what I'm going to cover but I just couldn't think of a better one. You can make up your own title when I'm finished."

John looked up and could see that he clearly had the room's attention. He took a deep breath and continued. "About ten years ago while I was working here at the University on processor developments for some of the new consumer humanoids, I started a small project analyzing human brain operations. It was a new area for me and it took me a long time to even begin to comprehend the information that had been developed by that time. I had an idea that I could use some of the brain's information handling mechanisms for adaptive programming for humanoids. Fortunately, I had some excellent help from people, here at the university, who are more knowledgeable than I am about this topic. I was also lucky enough to find some volunteers, who were also interested in this area of research. They agreed to be on a small team looking into this approach. As part of this work, we had to study the phenomenon known to all of us as consciousness. It gradually became clear to us that we could actually duplicate many of the functions related to consciousness in our humanoid processor. Not on the level of the brain, of course, but the idea of doing so even on a simpler level, was intriguing. The challenge to attempt this effort was too tempting to pass up."

At this point, John, using a series of visual aids, described how the team had created what they were sure was a conscious dog. He stopped for a moment and turned toward his audience, who at this point, were glued to his every word. "We completed this first project in 2021, seven years ago. If we would have presented our findings to this conference at that time it would have been very difficult to convince our peers that we had, in fact, created a dog that was conscious. Many of you would have claimed that all we did was to develop some very clever programming for a robotic dog and it would have been hard to convince you otherwise, so we decided to continue our research at a higher level."

John turned to look to his right where Brenda was standing just out of sight. "Brenda would you bring me that other control?" Brenda quickly walked out to where John was standing and handed him a visual control and then walked over and stood at the edge of the image screen. To the audience Brenda looked like any other humanoid, dressed in human clothing, with simulated skin which was easily distinguished from the real thing. Her actions were common for an advanced humanoid. "Our next step was to see if we could develop a conscious entity that could more easily demonstrate that it was conscious to the satisfaction of our scientific community."

Again, John used a series of visual aids as he discussed the nature of the conscious phenomena and how, over a period of time and with the right processing capability, a non-organic entity could become conscious just as a human baby does. He described the work that they had done in duplicating the brain's conscious processing functions and the continuous flow of information needed by these functions to achieve consciousness. As he displayed his images and described his work, it gradually dawned on the audience, one by one, that he was talking about Brenda. When he was finished every eye in the room was on Brenda. "To complete this presentation I would like to call upon my assistant to present the last section."

The room was silent as the audience watched Brenda come over to where John was standing. Bob turned to the audience and smiled. "Good afternoon, my name is Brenda. I am the result of the work that Professor Cupar and his team have performed over the last seven years. I am conscious. I have feelings and memories and I know who I am and how I was created. I have a survival instinct and a strong desire to learn and live. As with non-conscious humanoids, I obtain my energy from a methane fuel cell and have a 'twenty four hour' life cycle similar to humans. This cycle includes a sleep period. I experience fear and happiness but I do not have all of the feelings that humans have. As our work progresses, I have hopes that my range of feelings will continue to expand. Both the Professor and I will be happy to answer any questions that you may have about our team and our work."

For about three seconds the audience was totally silent and then the room exploded with shouts not just from those wanting to speak as they frantically waved their hands, but from everybody. Only the team members scattered throughout the audience sat quietly and watched the pandemonium around them.

CHAPTER 5

▼

A QUESTION OF CONTROL

Both John and Brenda were stunned at the reaction of the audience. They had expected the audience to be excited and eager to ask questions but not to become a mass of shouting and waving maniacs. Steve could sense the panic Brenda was feeling and tried to keep her calm. He transmitted his instructions very slowly and deliberately. "Stay where you are and keep a straight face. I'll stay here in the audience to watch what happens. Let John handle these people."

After about thirty seconds John raised his arms and shouted "Can I please have your attention!" He did this repeatedly until finally order was restored. "We will try to answer your questions as best we can but we do have a limitation on time because we have one more presentation to give before this session is over. Please raise your hand if you have a question but there is no need to shout. If you are going to hear our answers you will have to be quiet while we give them." He looked down at the audience and pointed to a fellow researcher from the University of Michigan. "Professor Liem, you have the first question."

"John, I was impressed, no, fascinated by your presentation but the whole concept of trying to create something that is conscious and then proving that it is, leaves me with a lot of doubt that you have actually accomplished this. How can we distinguish what you claim to have done from some very clever programming that would simulate consciousness?"

John was relieved to hear a good question from an old friend. "Bill, I understand your doubt because it's one which my team struggled with as we tried to understand what made an entity conscious. Think about it for a moment. What makes us conscious? Aren't we the result of some very clever programming created by 'Mother Nature' during the evolution of our species? When we are born, aren't our brains 'programmed' to obtain, store and process information that results in our consciousness. Our bodies are continually sending information to our brains as we 'sense' ourselves. Brenda has a similar system in her body with which she senses herself. Our knowledge of how the brain operates has advanced enormously during this century and during the same period our ability to electronically move, store and process information has advanced. Isn't it logical that one of us was going to make the connection sooner or later? When you read our presentation paper, which of course, contains a lot more detail than I could cover in the presentation itself, I think you'll find the answers to most of your questions.

Looking around the audience John could see that Les Zuchert was practically standing on his chair trying to get his attention. "Les, do you have a question?"

Les held a small hand held processor on which he had either written his questions or on which someone else had sent him questions. "What can your new humanoid do and what can it be used for? How do you control it?"

John interrupted him before he could read his next question. "Les, stop right there. You apparently didn't understand what I said. Brenda is not a new gadget that you can sell. Brenda controls Brenda just like you control you. Brenda is alive. She has a will of her own and she will decide what she will learn and what she will do." John's voice and his expression showed his anger. Les was angry too because he was sure John was trying to avoid telling him what he wanted to know. "Sit down Les and give someone else a chance to ask a question."

John decided that now would be a good time to call on Noreen and see how she was reacting to what she was hearing. She was sitting with her hand raised but at the same time she appeared to be talking into a microphone. "Ms Stern, do you have a question?"

As she stood up her camera crew shifted their cameras to capture both the stage and Noreen. "My question is for Brenda. Brenda, do you have a last name? How do you feel about what is happening today?"

Brenda turned toward her and grinned. It was clear she was happy that someone finally was going to ask her a question. "Ms Stern, I'm part of Professor Cupar's family so I guess my last name is Cupar. No one ever asked me that before but I always assumed it was Cupar. I'm very happy about today's presentation because now we can stop being so secretive about what we're doing. We can talk to more people and share our work with others."

Noreen was surprised at the answer but also pleased. "Brenda Cupar, you can call me Noreen and let me say that it's a pleasure to talk to you. Can I assume that you have desires and ambitions like the rest of us? What are those desires and ambitions?"

"Thanks Noreen. Yes, I do have desires and ambitions. I want to learn as much as I can about the world and everything in it. My ambition is to be of more help to John and our team, as I become more capable. I'd also like to travel around the country and the world and see the things that I have only heard or read about."

Noreen paused for a moment. "Brenda, I'm not sure I understand what feelings you have. Could you describe them for us?"

John interrupted at this point. "Noreen, to be fair I think we should let others have a chance to ask some questions."

Brenda held up her hand and stepped forward. "John, please let me answer her last question before we take another. I have many but not all, of the feelings that you have Noreen. As part of my survival programming I feel fear and a feeling that you might describe as pain but the team says is different from human pain. It's one of the feelings that the team says I need in order to protect myself from harm. I feel sadness and I feel pleasure but I don't have any sexual desires because I have no sex."

With that statement the entire audience made a noise that Brenda didn't understand and she paused for a few seconds before continuing. This whole area of my 'feelings', is one that is still being improved as the team continues my development."

"Does this team you are talking about, decide how you will be developed? I don't understand. I heard Professor Cupar state that it is you who will decide what you will learn. He said that you have a will of your own but if the team is continuing to change you, doesn't that affect what you know and what you can do, without you knowing it? Who's on this team that controls you, Brenda?" The intensity of Noreen's voice had risen noticeably.

John shook his head at Brenda, telling her not to answer. He ignored her questions and very deliberately turned and pointed at another raised hand. He also noticed that other people were beginning to come into the room and they were now lining the walls behind and at the side of the sitting audience. The person whom he pointed to was Professor King who had just finished her own presentation but was now sitting with her hand raised. "Eva, can I answer your question?"

"John, I listened very carefully to your presentation and I admit that I'm overwhelmed by what you and your team have accomplished but I am also puzzled. You've created a new life form that is so different from what we consider normal life, it boggles the mind and I'll be frank, it scares the hell out of me. If I understood you correctly this new life form does not age. With routine maintenance it can theoretically live forever. Its instincts and thought patterns are totally alien to the normal life forms that we are all familiar with, including ourselves. Why was this done in secret without any consultation with your peers or for that matter, anyone else? What's your long term plan for this life form? It can outlive you and your team and for that matter, everyone else in this room. Who's going to look after it and who can control it? What control do you and your team have over Brenda? How many Brenda's have you made?"

Her questions came like machine gun bullets and their effect on John was as if she had used a machine gun. The effect on the audience was instantaneous. The noise level rose with each question asked. John was speechless. This is not what he expected. Instead of a clear recognition of his team's work and some respectful scientific questions of the 'what and how' of their work, he and his team's motives were being attacked. He expected that from Noreen but not from Eva King. She was the last person he expected to attack him.

John looked at Brenda to see her reaction to the questions and to the rising noise level. Judging by the expression on Brenda's face, he could see that she was dumbfounded by what was happening. Steve's words to Brenda were also causing her some distress. "Now do you understand what I was talking about Brenda? I was afraid this would happen, these people are afraid of us. Just hang in there and let's see if John can get you out of there."

John felt that he had to stop this thing immediately but he wasn't sure how to do it. Finally, he held up his hands to calm the audience down. "Eva, if I had consulted with my peers, as you put it, I would've had to disclose all the details of our work and by now, there would probably be ten different versions of Brenda and ten other applications of our discoveries. I think everyone is overreacting to what we've done. We have not created an out-of-control monster. Brenda's physical and mental processes have been created by our team and they are continually monitored and controlled by the team." As soon as he'd said the words he realized that he'd just made a blunder. Brenda didn't know to what degree the team controlled her. That control level was the last thing John wanted to divulge to her and, of course, to Steve who, through Brenda, was monitoring everything that was going on. He quickly glanced at Brenda to see if there was any reaction to what he had just heard but, apparently, there was none. He looked back at Eva and continued. "To be fair to our next presenter, I'm going to stop the questioning at this point. There'll be plenty of time for further discussion on the issues that have been raised as the week goes on."

John could hear several voices including Noreen Stern's shouting the same question. "How many Brenda's are there?" "Where are the other Brenda's?"

He ignored them all. "It's now my pleasure to present Doctor Frank Rallo who will present his paper on Advances in Inter-Humanoid Communication Systems." With that John walked over to Brenda and led her backstage.

It was clear from the audience reaction that they were unhappy with this decision but they finally lowered the noise level to the point where the Rallo presentation could begin. Before he left the stage, John could see some of his team members leaving the hall. He knew they were probably going around the back way to try to join Michelle and him. When they went behind the stage curtain they found that Alex had already joined Michelle.

"My God, what the hell happened out there? I thought they were going to turn into a lynch mob and run up on the stage to get you." Alex's face was flushed and he sounded almost out of breath.

"I don't know. It was crazy. It sure isn't what I was expecting but we can talk about that later. Right now grab the other guys and get over to the lab as fast as you can. Let Michelle stay here because I need her to be with Brenda while I try to answer the questions the media people will be asking me after this last presentation is finished. I'll take Brenda home with me when I'm finished so Michelle can join you later. It's important that the work area at the lab be checked for anything that will tell anyone going into the lab about Steve or, for that matter, anything else about our work. Where the hell is Steve anyway?"

"He's gone out in back with Debbie. When we left the room I told him to stay with her and play dumb and for God's sake keep his mouth shut. I'll take them over to the lab with me."

"No, tell her to take him to your place and stay with him until you show up. Also tell her if anyone stops her and asks about him to say he's just her humanoid and not one of those 'conscious things'. Tell everyone else not to identify themselves as team members, if they're questioned, and remind them of the importance of not telling anyone about Steve. When you get home, have Debbie try to contact her sister and find out if she still wants a private interview tomorrow morning. If she does, tell her to set it up in my office at nine o'clock but also tell her it has to be without any cameras. One more thing, tell her to bring her sister to the meeting."

Alex seemed relieved to see John relatively calm and in control. "Okay, but I do have one question. Why do you want Brenda to stay here now?"

"If we go back on stage with her everyone will know where she is and nobody will be running around trying to find her or the team members. That should give you time to take care of the lab and scatter everyone so that the media won't find the team they'll be looking for."

Alex nodded in agreement. "Call me once you get home and tell me what happens after you go back out there. We've also got to talk about what happens tomorrow."

"Yeah, that's right. I'll call you sometime after dinner. That'll give me time to talk to Bob and Sonny McMahon. After that, I'll have a better idea of what we should do next. I'm not sure what effect this is going to have on the conference but I hope to hell everything keeps going on schedule or this may be the last time we'll ever see this conference. I'll talk to you soon."

As Alex walked away, John put his hand on Brenda's shoulder and they started to go back on to the stage. "Wait off to the side so that the audience can see that you're still here. I'm going to take my seat at the presenters table". Brenda said nothing but did what John asked. That made John frown and he wondered what was going through her mind.

What was going through her mind was the comment that she was giving Steve. "I can't believe what has happened here. Now I'm about to go out and get stared at again."

Steve interrupted her before she could continue. "I told you that John and the team didn't understand what everyone's reaction would be when they found out about us."

"They haven't found out about us. They only know about me and as you heard, John is going to have Debbie take you home. You don't have to go through what I am about to endure but I'll let you watch what's going on through my eyes and ears. Don't say anything to me. I want to concentrate on what's happening." Brenda stopped at the left edge of the stage and as she did he could see everyone turn to look at her.

When Frank finished his presentation and finished answering questions, John stood up to close the session. "I want to thank Professor King and Doctor Rallo for their excellent presentations and I'm sure that everyone in the audience will join me in giving them another round of applause."

The audience responded appropriately and John continued. "I think all of you will enjoy tomorrow's presentations and will find them to be just as interesting as the ones you heard today. I'll be available to answer more of your questions after a short break and I'm sure that Dr. Rallo and Professor King will also be available."

He assumed that he could now leave and send Brenda to join Michelle backstage but that was a bad assumption. As soon as he finished talking, at least half of the people present stood up and rushed toward where Brenda was standing. John ran toward Brenda just as the first members of the audience got to her. Brenda didn't move but just stood there looking over at John with a confused expression on her face. John backed Brenda up against the wall and stood in front of her facing the rush of people. He shouted and raised his arms to stop them. "Stand back and let us through. I will come right back to answer your questions but you must stop trying to touch her. You are going to kill us with this behavior. Stop right now!"

He turned to Brenda and shouted "put your hand on my shoulder, follow me and don't say a word". He pushed through the crowd with Brenda hanging on to his shoulder. Dozens of hands reached out to touch her and everyone seemed to shout a question. John finally saw one of the University security guards and shouted for him to help them. "Harold, help me! Help me get Brenda backstage."

With Harold and a few other guards he had called to help, they finally made it to a small room backstage where Michelle joined them. John told her to stay there with Brenda and then with Harold's help made it back onto the stage of the presentation room. The room was still filled with people and John wondered if all the people present were really media representatives. Eva King and Doctor Rallo were still on stage but were being completely ignored. The three of them could see that this was not going to work but they decided to give it a try. "Will everyone please be quiet!"

He repeated this with a louder and louder voice until finally things calmed down to a point where he could be heard without shouting. "If all of you ask your questions at the same time nobody will be heard. Just back away and we'll try to respond. To be fair to everyone we will take questions for each presenter in this order: first for Professor King, then for Doctor Rallo and finally for myself. Both Eva and Frank stepped up to the microphone in that order but no questions were asked. They stepped back and then worked their way off the stage. John arbitrarily pointed to one of the raised hands and the question that he was asked surprised him and almost made him laugh.

"Professor Cupar, what ever happened to that dog you made and how many of them did you make?"

John relaxed a little as he answered. "Once we were sure that our dog was operating properly we introduced him into a private home to see how the dog would react to those surroundings. The results were very good as the dog responded to the care of the individuals involved and it was decided to make a few more of them. In all cases, the results have been very good. I don't want to give the exact whereabouts of these dogs without their owner's permission because based upon the experience of today; the results could be uncomfortable for them."

John pointed to another raised hand. "Who are your team members and why can't we have their names? Are they all located at this university? Do they also have their own Brenda's?"

John wasn't ready for those questions but he tried to answer as best he could. "The technical team that performed the work I have described is a small one and at this time they're all here. They do not have their own Brenda's. I am not going to give out any of their names without first talking to them and to the president of our university. I will be the sole contact for information on our work."

He took a question from a fellow researcher, which he quickly regretted doing and decided to try to dance around it. "Who paid for all the research needed to create Brenda and who authorized this work?"

"First, let me say that most of the work was very applicable to the research authorized by the University for our Normal Humanoid Research Work. All the team members, working on their own time, accomplished the remainder of this effort. Perhaps you're aware of the effort by Crick and Watson at Cambridge University in the early nineteen fifties when they were working on the structure of the DNA molecule for which they received the Noble Prize. It was done while they were also working on their authorized projects in the same field. In a somewhat similar way, our team developed a project related to our authorized objectives." John knew what he was saying was not exactly correct but it seemed to satisfy the questioner.

The next question was not any easier. "Do you see a time when your work on Brenda will be finished and, when and if that occurs, what will you do with her?"

Again John tried to provide a reasonable answer. "We are really only at the beginning of this research and, to be honest about it, I don't expect to ever completely finish the effort. We will continue to apply the latest technology and expand our knowledge in this new and exciting field. Brenda is a participant in this work and I expect that she'll continue to work in this field indefinitely. She'll be the one to decide what she will do and, if she someday decides not to continue the work, we will honor her choice."

He thought that was a good answer but it was clear his audience did not. Les Zuckert shouted out two questions without being asked. "Are you planning to sell your new technology so that others can produce their own Brendas? Is Brenda for sale?"

That did it. John was not about to continue the farce with Zuckert any longer. "Are you for sale Les? We have not created Brenda to have slaves for sale? Brenda is a feeling, thinking individual who wants to live just like everyone else in this room. We're not selling any Brenda's or for that matter, any technology, to enable people to create thinking, feeling slaves. When the reality of what we have done is finally understood, questions like those you just asked will be seen for what they are—irresponsible. This session is over! I'm going to leave now but I will attempt to answer questions that are relevant to our work at a later point in the Conference."

With help from Harold and some of the other guards, John was able to take Brenda out of the building and over to his car. Brenda said very little, except to thank Michelle for her help, as they escaped the crowd in John's car. "Brenda, are you okay?" John couldn't take his eyes off the road but he could feel Brenda's eyes on him.

"I don't know. I don't understand why all those people were shouting. Did we do something wrong? I sent Steve everything I saw and heard and you don't want to hear what he is saying about the way people are behaving. What's going to happen now?"

Brenda's voice sounded stressed, something that John had seldom heard before today and he didn't like what he was hearing. "It's okay. People just don't understand what you are yet. Let's give them a chance to get used to you and I'm sure everything will be fine. We're going to go home now and get away from everybody. You'll feel better when you're home with the family."

As they approached their house John could see that they were in for more trouble. There was a crowd outside made up from its appearance mostly of media people, cameras and all. He pulled off to the side of the road. "Get out and get into the trunk."

"What? Are you joking with me John?"

"No, this is no joke. You get into the trunk and I'll pull into the garage and close the door so that they'll think I left you some place else. Maybe then they'll leave us alone."

Reluctantly, Brenda climbed into the trunk and John got back into the car and slowly approached their home. As he eased into the driveway he stopped and rolled down the window. "I explained back at the University that I'm not answering any more questions today. Now how about allowing me and my family to be alone this evening?"

"Where's your android Professor? What did you do with her? Doesn't she live here too?" Every one of them had a similar question and John ignored them all and kept moving until he entered his garage. Before he closed the garage door he got out of the car to make sure none of them were in the garage with him. Then he opened the trunk. "You can get out now."

"Well that was something I didn't think I'd ever do. It's dark in here." Brenda climbed out and they both entered the house and went up to the kitchen.

As expected Helen and the kids were in the kitchen waiting for them. Helen went over to John and hugged him. "We have been watching on the TV. It must have been awful for you and Brenda. Our telephone hasn't stopped ringing for the last hour."

"On TV? What are they saying? John was surprised that they already knew what was happening.

Jack ran up to Brenda and grabbed her by the shoulders. "Hey, Brenda. You're famous. Everyone knows who you are now and you should hear what they're saying about you. They think you are some kind of monster."

"Jack, knock it off. That's a lot of crap and you know it, so leave Brenda alone." The tone of John's voice caused Jack to stop and turn to his father with a look of bewilderment on his face. He could see that his father was very upset and realized that his best move was to say nothing.

Now Amanda jumped in. "That's right Jack. Dad and Brenda have been through a lot and they don't need you making it any worse."

"Thanks Am. Now Helen, tell me what they are saying."

"Just a few minutes before you arrived, they had that woman from the network on. You know, Noreen Stern. The one that you said was Debbie Hull's sister. She said you announced that you had created a 'being' that could live forever and could be made stronger and smarter than any human could ever be. Then, she said that no one knows how many of these things have been made and that you refused to answer any questions about that at your presentation. They showed pictures of you talking to her and then ignoring her. Finally, they showed you and Brenda pushing through the crowd and getting into your car. There were more things said than that, but that's the gist of it. Why didn't you stay and answer their questions? Doesn't that make you look like you are hiding something?" Helen stood staring at John.

John was exasperated by this time. "I am hiding something Helen. I don't want anyone to know that we have created more than one Brenda. That would just cause a panic and everyone would immediately assume that we had a production line going on over at the lab. How the hell did they get the TV pictures of us going to our car on the air so fast? That just happened less than thirty minutes ago." John stopped and thought for a minute. "No, I guess that was a dumb question. You were seeing it in real time. Let's all calm down and let me think things through.

Helen stepped closer to her husband and put her hand to his cheek. "I'm sorry, Honey. I didn't mean to get you upset. I know you must be terribly disappointed about what happened. I don't know what's going to happen tonight or tomorrow, but we'll get through this together. Is there anything I can do; anyone I can call?"

Brenda hadn't said a word up to this point but she now joined in. "I think Helen's right John. This isn't happening the way we thought it would but if we all stick together and help each other, I'm sure everything will be okay." She put her arm around Jack who still had not recovered from his father's words to him. "Are you okay Jack?"

Jack smiled at Brenda. "Yeah, sure. You may be everyone else's monster but you're my best friend, Brenda." He looked at his Dad to see if what he said was okay.

John just shook his head and with a sigh of relief, laughed at both of them. "Helen, would you call Mom to find out if they are coming? I have to talk to Brenda for a few minutes, alone."

"Oh, I'm glad you reminded me. I'll give them a call but they've probably already left. Diane Schultz called earlier and I invited them over tonight."

John put his hand to his forehead. "That's going to make a great evening. Bob is going to tear me up for what happened this afternoon and my Dad is going to cheer him on. Maybe, with Bob here, Dad will tone it down but I doubt it. I don't have time to worry about them now. Brenda, let's go into the family room. Amanda, would you and Jack adjust all the window shades in the house so that no one can see inside? I don't want those people out there to see Brenda. Then set the phone so that no one can call us, except our friends, and the people with these numbers." He handed them a short list of telephone numbers and then went on. "I want you to keep a watch out the front window to see what the crowd is doing?"

They both agreed to be watch guards and stationed themselves so that they could watch out the window but not be easily seen from outside. John and Brenda went into the family room and Helen made her call and started to prepare dinner.

John sat close to Brenda so that no one could overhear their conversation. "I want to apologize to you for what happened today. I feel really stupid for not realizing the kind of reaction we would get after our presentation. I know it was a shock to you. People just don't understand what a wonderful thing we have done and what a wonderful person you are. As I said earlier, when the shock wears off, I think they'll realize the mistake they made today. They will come to accept you, just as we have. Do you or Steve have any questions? How did Steve react as he watched what you were transmitting to him? You were transmitting to him weren't you?"

Brenda sat back in her favorite recliner and seemed very calm as she spoke. "Yes, I was and Steve reacted better than I did but then, of course, he didn't have a bunch of strangers touching him and yelling in his ear. He kept asking me questions but until I got into the trunk of the car I didn't have much time to give him anything but short inadequate answers. To answer your question, yes, both of us have some things we would like to ask you. Why did everyone want to know how many of us there are and what did Professor King mean when she said that we would live forever?"

John was relieved that Brenda didn't ask about the control issue and at the same time very concerned that the answers he would give might cause more problems. "Let me answer the second part, first. As we've taught you, all organic life forms have a limited time they can exist and that includes humans. No matter how clever we are about developing new medical approaches to repair our bodies we eventually die. The approach we took in developing you and Steve allows us to literally move your brain contents into a new brain. No matter when your brain or body parts wear out or need maintenance, the information in your brain, that is 'you', will never wear out. Following that logic, there is not a set time period for your lifetimes but, of course, nothing lasts forever. Even the sun and the earth have limited time periods for their existence. Professor King realized this from the material in the presentation and that concept is so new and so radical that her first reaction was fear. It's the fear of the unknown and all humans have that fear, but once they realize the concept is not a threat to them, they will come to accept it. That brings me to the first part of your question; the concern for how many humanoids like you and Steve there are. As you know, humans are the dominant life form on the earth and that fear of the unknown I mentioned makes them afraid of any potential threat to themselves. If there were a million androids like yourself they would be afraid that you would try to take what they have or even hurt them. This fear is inborn in humans. It is not something they can easily control. That is why they wanted to know how many humanoids we have made that are like you. Once they realize that there are only two of you, everyone will calm down. Let's join the others and see if we can get through the evening. You can probably guess what my Dad is going to say."

Brenda laughed. "I'll bet he is going to say "I told you this would happen". There was one more question that we had. What did you mean when you answered Professor King's question about control? You said the team was continually monitoring and controlling us. How are they doing that?"

CHAPTER 6

▼

THE NEW PLAN

How to answer that question! That had been on John's mind ever since he said those words and realized his mistake. He tried to be casual about his answer. "Brenda, you know, we've tried to improve Steve and you in an organized way so that at each step of your development, you would have the capability you needed for that step. We watched your ability to adapt to each situation to which you were exposed. Since this was all very new to us, we've continued to modify both your processing systems and the information that was being processed. As part of this effort, we thought giving you the ability to communicate electronically would increase the speed of your development and we were right, it did. We use that system to monitor the functioning of all your systems to enable us to correct any problems that come up, as quickly as possible. As you and Steve communicate with each other, we monitor this system to be certain that it is functioning properly. That's what I was talking about when I answered Ms. Stern's question."

John could tell that Brenda and Steve were communicating with each other by the delayed response. "We knew all that, John, but we still don't understand what all the fuss was about concerning the controlling of us. Maybe, it's just part of that fear of the unknown you were talking about."

John was surprised to hear they already knew about the controls but tried not to show his concern as she kept talking. "That's right. When someone creates something new that might hurt people, like, for instance, a new type of bacteria, people immediately want to know how it can be controlled so it won't be able to harm them. They will be afraid of the concept that you and Steve represent until they finally realize that you're not a threat. It'll be our job to make them understand that. Enough talking, let's go find Helen and find out if Mom and Dad are still going to come over."

As they finished John could feel himself relaxing inside but, at the same time, he made a mental note to ask Alex how Steve could have found out about the control system. He felt it was unlikely that Brenda had been the one to uncover that information.

As they entered the kitchen the phone rang. Before he picked it up John asked Helen about his parents. "Are they coming?" She nodded affirmatively and he lifted the phone. "Hello."

He could hear the noise level at the other end as soon as he put the phone to his ear. "John, is that you?" Sonny was obviously in trouble and his voice was very loud. "What the hell did you do today? Everything was going perfectly. All the presentations were on schedule and then 'boom', people started running all over the place. They were running into and out of your presentation like somebody was giving away money in there. The media people were the worst. Now a bunch of them want a special press conference with you."

"Calm down Sonny, we can handle this." John's mind was trying to think of his options as he talked and he finally came up with an idea. "The only thing I did in my presentation was to provide the results of one of my team's projects. That team created a special type of humanoid, which has some of the conscious functions of the human brain. I guess the proper name for it would be an android. Remember what I said about Noreen Stern at lunch? Well, she and the rest of those media people have blown what I said all out of proportion. They're now claiming I've created a monster or something and that is what's causing all the trouble."

That information did not solve Sonny's problem. "So now what do we do? All your conference people are upset and I can see this thing turning into a scheduling disaster. For Gods sake John, you're the host of this damn thing. Talk to these people and get them off my back. You'd better call Walt too. He wasn't at your presentation but he sure heard about it and told me to get hold of you and let you know he doesn't appreciate being left in the dark about the media reaction to your presentation. You know John, as president of this university he could make your life a living hell if you don't keep him informed about what's happening."

"Yeah, you're right, Sonny. I should have talked to you and Walt right away but I don't think Walt will stay mad very long. He knows what a kook I am. I'm going to meet Bob Schultz in a few minutes and we'll give him a call. We'll also try to figure out how to get these media guys off your back and let the conference presentations go on without any further interference. I'm going to have a private meeting tomorrow morning with Noreen Stern to see if I can get her to understand the problem she's causing. Maybe she can help with the rest of the media people. Another thought I had was that if I don't appear at the presentations tomorrow morning, all the media people who attend will probably behave themselves. What do you think?"

Sonny didn't answer for a few seconds as he pondered John's words. "Okay, I don't have any better ideas, so we'll try it. Remember John, Walt doesn't report to God. He's got a bunch of people he's got to keep happy if he wants to keep his job, so help him out. Why don't you have Bob Schultz contact the other conference people and tell them we're working the problem? When are you gonna set up your meeting with Noreen Stern?"

"Don't worry about it, Sonny. I'll take care of Stern. After my meeting with her tomorrow I'll let you know how it went."

As soon as he finished the call with Sonny, John dialed Alex's number and got an immediate answer. "I'm glad I caught you Alex. Do you have Steve with you?"

"Yes, Debbie brought him over just as you asked. Michelle showed up here after you left with Brenda. You know Steve's not very happy with this situation. He's been getting a view of everything through Brenda's eyes and he wants to get involved."

John's reaction was immediate. "No way! You keep him out of this and tell him I'll explain 'why' when I see him. If one of those media types gets hold of him, we're all in trouble. Did Debbie get hold of her sister about the nine o'clock meeting tomorrow?"

"Yeah, she called about fifteen minutes ago and said Noreen had agreed to meet you in your office. What's your plan, John? I'm really worried that the university is going to totally over-react to what's happening. What do you think we should do with Brenda and Steve?" Alex was almost pleading for an answer.

John explained his plan for the meeting with Noreen and his hope that he could convince her to help him with the other media people. Then he told Alex of the idea that had occurred to him on the way home. "Alex, remember those plans we had for modifying the appearance of Brenda and Steve? We still have that material, don't we? Tomorrow afternoon go over to the lab and get that stuff and anything else you need to change Brenda's appearance. You can do it at your place or maybe even Michelle's. Get Herb Kimmerman and some of the other guys on the team to help you but make sure they understand it's important that no one sees them going into your place as a group, especially the media types."

Alex's almost shouted his response. "That's a great idea! After we've finished they'll never recognize her from any other humanoid out there. How are you going to get him over there without a crowd following you?" John smiled to himself and at his own ingenuity. "Let me worry about that. You just be home around one o'clock. I almost forgot, remind Debbie to come to the meeting I'm having with her sister tomorrow."

Within minutes after John had hung up the phone his Mom and Dad walked through the front door. Even before John could give his mother a hug, his father started his attack but much to John's surprise, Helen attacked back. "We don't want to hear it Lou. What John needs is support from his family, not criticism! He presented an amazing accomplishment today and no matter how crazy the media people want to behave, we're very proud of him."

John's father didn't know what to say. Helen never talked to him like that. John's mother, Nora, knew what to say. "Helen's right, Lou. We're all proud of him. Those people out there in your front yard should be ashamed of themselves. Brenda, how are you feeling dear?"

Brenda grinned at Nora. He really liked John's mother and the way she treated her. "I'm fine Mrs. Cupar, don't you worry about me. John made sure that I was okay all the way. He even put me in the trunk of his car."

Everyone turned to look at Brenda and then they all turned to look at John. John threw up his hands and laughed. "I didn't want any of those media people to see she was with me. She didn't mind. In fact she thought it was fun didn't you Brenda?"

"Yeah, I never did that before. I don't think I've ever been anywhere where there is absolutely no light. I'm lucky I have a built-in one." She actually sounded enthusiastic about the experience. Now everybody was laughing and patting Brenda on the back.

At this point, the front door bell rang. It was Bob and Diane. After all the hellos and hugs were done, Diane had the first words. "Do you all realize how difficult it is to get into your home now, or even get on your street? You're going to hear from your neighbors and I don't think you're going to like what they'll say. Have you tried talking to those media people out there?"

"No, Diane. I think that would be hopeless. From what I could see when I came in, that crowd not only consists of media people but also some of my neighbors. Probably some people who just want to see Brenda after they heard about her on the news. Besides, I've got to talk to Bob and call our president before he shows up with a shotgun and blows my head off for what's happening to our quiet little university."

Helen agreed with her husband. "You know he's right, Diane. It would be a waste of time trying to talk to that crowd. Why don't I fix everyone a drink while John and Bob talk? Let's relax and hear what adventures the kids had today. You've also got to hear about Brenda's great adventure in the dark."

John made himself and Bob a drink and motioned for him to come into the next room with him. John started first. "I had a call from Sonny McMahon. He's being hammered by the media and apparently, by some of the conference people who feel that everything is coming apart because of the reaction to my presentation. The media people want some kind of special meeting with us. He also reminded me that I should have called Walt and told him what was going on." Bob opened his mouth to talk but before he could begin, John held up his hand. "Yeah, I know. I should have called both of them right away."

"That's not what I was going to say John. I know you are still in a state of shock about what happened this afternoon. Before we work out what we're going to do next, let me tell you what I thought about your presentation. I thought it was excellent. What you and your team have accomplished is incredible. It's hard to believe that you have been able to create your Brenda to that level of sophistication and capability in such a short period of time. When you told me that your team has only ten members, I was amazed. I only wish you could have given your presentation to a room full of people like us, instead of a room full of media people and company representatives. If you'd done that, your work would have been appreciated and discussed rationally. We could have helped you decide how to present it to the public. Instead, we now have a case of mass hysteria and I'll be honest, I don't know what's going to happen."

John sighed and nodded in agreement. "You're right Bob. I had my blinders on and now the whole conference is going to pay the price. Before I forget again, would you stay here while I call Walt? This isn't going to be pleasant so I'll need you to pick me up after it's over."

"Yeah, go ahead. You'd better do it now and get it over with."

John called Walt's home and Walt's wife, Anne, answered. "John, what did you do today? Walt has been getting calls ever since he got home. He said he was going to call you but every time he gets ready to call the phone rings and someone else wants to talk to him. Here he is."

"John, you've done some crazy things in your life but this one takes the cake. Why didn't you tell me you were going to announce a.... what do you call it ... a living humanoid, in your presentation? I've got media people calling me, trustees calling me, and God knows who else calling me. I don't know what to tell them. We've got to have a meeting tomorrow morning and figure out what we're going to do. I'll bet your conference people are ready to string you up."

"Okay, calm down Walt. I'm sitting here with Bob Schultz and we're trying to come up with a plan to get out of this mess. Why don't you stop answering your phone or tell everyone who calls that you are going to resolve the problem within the next day or so. Let's all meet tomorrow around ten thirty. I've already arranged for a meeting with Noreen Stern in the morning because I think she is partly the reason that so many media people came to the conference. She seems to have a great deal of influence with them. Maybe she can help us get them to back off a little."

"Do you really think you should do that, John? From what I've heard about her she's not here to help anybody but herself. What does Bob think of your meeting with her?"

John looked over at Bob who was slowly shaking his head. "Actually, I haven't had a chance to tell him about it, but judging from his reaction when he heard me tell you, I don't think he likes the idea. Why don't you let us finish working out some of these problems and we'll all meet in your office at ten thirty and decide what each of us should do?"

Walt agreed with John's suggestion and John turned back to Bob after a few more words with Walt. Bob motioned for John to sit down. "I don't know what you're going to tell the Stern woman and I won't pretend that I know what you should tell her, at least not yet. Let me talk to some of the media people I know. Maybe, with their help, we can make sure the rest of the presentations go off on schedule. As long as you're not attending them, there shouldn't be any problem. I agree and I already told Sonny McMahon that I would not attend the morning presentation to see if that would help."

Bob nodded in agreement and continued to speak. "Good. Now let me tell you what's gonna happen on Thursday. The group that's responsible for the Legal Considerations Concerns presentations has decided to change the agenda because of your presentation. Now they want to have a session to discuss the legal problems that your work may cause. That should shift everyone's attention to that meeting and give a break to the other people trying to make their presentations."

"Legal problems? What legal problems?" John wasn't sure what to say to Bob's statement. "We've been filing patent applications every step of the way, without going into the conscious part, of course. If you want to stretch things a bit, we're even properly funded under our basic research grant. What are you talking about?"

Bob looked at John in amazement. "You really don't get it do you? Where the hell is your brain? You've created a new life form, John. Don't you realize what that means? Do you have the right to kill Brenda? Does Brenda have the right to own property? Can she go anywhere she wants to go without asking anyone or without supervision? I can sit here and reel off twelve legal questions that your work has raised and you're telling me you never thought of them? I don't believe you!"

John was dumbfounded. Their voices had grown louder as they talked and finally Helen and Diane appeared at the door. "What's going on in here? What are you two shouting about?'

They looked at one another and finally John spoke. "Bob's been giving me an education on how stupid I am and, unfortunately, he's right."

"That's not right! John and his team just got a little too focused on their work and forgot about the outside world for a while. How about another drink, Helen?" Bob stood up and walked over to Diane.

"Would you settle for a glass of wine at dinner, Bob? Dinner's almost ready so we might as well adjourn to the dining room." Helen led the way to where everyone, but Brenda, was already seated. Brenda had volunteered to be their waiter for the evening and between Brenda and her humanoid helper, Suzie, everything was handled very smoothly. The conversation during dinner also went smoothly for a while, if that term can be used to describe the way everyone carefully avoided the topic that was on everyone's mind. Bob and Diane were glad to have a chance to talk to Brenda and were impressed by her intelligence and personality. When they asked her how he felt about being a part of a presentation that was all about making her, she told them how exciting it was. She told them how she had looked forward to the conference for a long time and even said she thought it was wonderful to be famous.

John was unusually quiet as he contemplated his own stupidity which Bob had so accurately pointed out. Bob felt he had done enough damage for one evening and this was the wrong audience for the things he really wanted to talk about. Lou, John's father, was afraid of attracting more of Helen's wrath not to mention some of his wife's own special punishments. The girls had no problem finding things to talk about and Jack was more concerned about dessert than conversation. Finally Lou couldn't keep his concerns to himself. "I know you're all worried about your conference but what do you think is going to happen to Helen and the kids tomorrow? I'll bet you they'll be tracked down by media people no matter where they go and asked questions about Bob and the dog and everything else."

Bob spoke first. "You know John, your dad's right. Maybe it would be better if they stayed home until things calm down."

Helen shook her head. "I can't stay home, Bob. I've got things I have to do at the hospital and it's too late to find someone to handle them for me. Maybe Amanda and Jack could miss a few days of school, but this is probably not a good time for them to do that either." She was obviously torn between her obligations to her patients and her concern for John's dilemma.

Jack had no problem with the thought of missing school, but Amanda was very upset. "I can't miss any school, Mom. I'd have to miss the game tomorrow and there is no way that I'm going to miss that game. I'm sure I can handle those media people. I just won't talk to them and, besides, the school won't let them bother me while I'm there."

It was John's turn. "I think Helen can take care of herself but I have an idea for the kids. Dad, how about coming over tomorrow morning and taking them to school? Then you can pick them up in the afternoon. I have a meeting with Noreen Stern in the morning and I think most of these media people will be either trying to talk to me or trying to find Bob. They'll probably also be trying to track down the identity of my team members. Unfortunately, too many university people already know those names and as that information becomes known, my gang is going to be in for a rough time."

Lou was glad to get in on the action. "That's a good idea, John. I'll be glad to help with the kids. We'll be over in the morning so don't worry about Amanda and Jack. You've got enough to worry about and you're right about Helen being able to take care of herself." It was obvious that Lou was not only eager to help but also eager to put things right between Helen and himself.

To everyone's surprise it was Brenda who spoke next. She had been standing back from the table listening to everything being said. "John, I think you're right about the team. Steve's been telling me that Alex has received a lot of calls from people that he doesn't know, but since he can see their numbers he hasn't been answering the phone. He said that Michelle called and said she was getting the same kind of calls so they've decided someone must've told the media who's on the team. That doesn't sound good does it?"

Everyone turned to look at Brenda with the same look of concern. John slowly shook his head. "No, Brenda, it doesn't. I hope everyone remembers what I told them to do if they're asked any questions."

Both Bob and Helen tried to speak at the same time but Helen won out. "What did you tell them, Hon?"

"I told them to admit that they worked in my group on humanoid development but were not involved in the group that created Brenda. They could admit to hearing about the team but would then start to give the questioner a lot of technical detail about their own 'made up' project. Hopefully, that should end the questioning."

Bob shook his head. "I think you are underestimating the intelligence and perseverance of the media people, John. It would be smarter to tell them to just disappear for a while until the conference is over."

"Yes, you're probably right, Bob but they all want to be part of what happens. I'll get the word out for them to lay low for a while but I don't know if they will or not." The dinner went on for a while longer and at least there seemed to be a sense of relief that they were finally talking about the situation.

Bob proposed a toast and used it to try to heal some of the wounds caused earlier. "Here's to John, Helen, Amanda and Jack. This will go down in the history books. People all over the world will realize the importance of what you have done in creating and raising Brenda as part of your family. It's an incredible achievement."

Helen gave a final toast to Brenda. "I want to toast Brenda. Brenda, you have been very brave through all this and have worked very hard, not just for you, but for all of us. We love you and consider ourselves very lucky to have been given the chance to have you as part of our family. We're sure that your future life will be a success that people will read about for years to come."

Brenda felt very happy and very lucky to be here with these wonderful people. She couldn't stop smiling and she couldn't stop telling Steve how lucky both of them were. Even Steve was impressed by what he was seeing and hearing but with his usual doubts.

As they said their 'good nights' everyone was feeling a strange mixture of happiness about the evening and concern for what they felt tomorrow would bring. They all knew the troubles of the day were far from over and would still be with them in the morning. Bob offered to join John in his meeting with Noreen, but John felt that to have the president of the group present might damage the conference, if things went wrong. Both John and Helen were happy to get to bed as soon as the company had departed.

Alex and Michelle were still up when John's evening ended. They had finished talking to the other team members about the reaction to John's presentation and the plan to change Brenda's appearance tomorrow. When Alex told Steve about the plan he was both surprised and pleased. He was surprised that apparently, John had not told Brenda yet, and pleased because he thought it was a good idea. Michelle had decided to stay with Alex that night which she often did. Steve had gone to his room as they got ready for bed. Alex waited until Steve had gone before he spoke. "Michelle, what do you think about the team's reaction to what happened today?"

Michelle paused a moment before answering. "I don't think they realize all that can happen if the media gets everyone upset about the existence of Brenda and Steve. They still think that everyone's going to stand back in wonder at what we've done and give us all kinds of awards for it. You know, my love, all of us live in kind of a dream world with all our research. We're not really very connected to the real world out there. We get so absorbed in what we're doing we don't realize how our work will affect other people. I know John's beginning to realize what might happen. I think that's why he is so uptight about anyone finding out about Steve. I'll bet he's already been raked over the coals by the university and his own conference group."

Alex realized that Michelle was probably right but he also realized that there was nothing they could do until they saw which way things were going over the next few days. "Yeah, you're right. I wouldn't want to be in his shoes right now. I think his idea of changing Brenda's appearance is a damn good one but let's face it, keeping Steve's and Brenda's identity secret is only going to work for just so long. I'm worried about how Steve is going to handle all this. His temper seems to get worse as he gets older and I'll be honest, I haven't a clue as to why that's happening. I hope John has a longer-range plan in mind. Come on, I'm tired. Let's get some sleep. We have to be ready for tomorrow." They fell asleep in each other's arms feeling lucky to have each other.

The next morning John started the day with the usual ritual. There was something about following this comfortable habit that made him feel good. He was surprised that he had slept so well. For a few minutes it was as if yesterday had never happened but then reality settled in and his mind started to run on overdrive. What was he going to tell Noreen and just as importantly, what was she going to ask? By the time he joined Helen for his second cup of tea he knew what he wanted to accomplish before the day was over. He had to make everyone realize that what he had presented was a wonderful step forward, not a project gone wrong or a threat to mankind or any other crazy interpretation of what he had created.

He sat down across the table from Helen where she and Brenda were already involved in a conversation. "What're you two talking about?"

"I was asking Brenda what she planned to do today. How'd you sleep last night?

"I was asking Helen how long she expected to be at the hospital today and if she had a good time last night." Brenda was looking at Helen as if she were her guardian angel, which of course, she was.

First John looked at Helen. "I slept like a baby and what did she say she was going to do?" Then he looked at Brenda. "How long and did she?"

They both laughed and Helen answered. "He's not sure yet and I'm not sure yet and yes." Amanda, who was passing by, looked at them as though they were weird, which was not unusual for her. Then Helen's face got serious. "What are you going to do today? Should I try to get someone to take over for me at the hospital and join you or come home or what?"

"Brenda's going to stay here until this afternoon and I'm going to my nine o'clock meeting with Noreen Stern over at my office. Just continue your normal day and I'll call you if anything important comes up." John's voice was steady and he looked as though this was just a normal day like all his other days. "Brenda, don't answer the phone. When I need to contact you I'll use Steve. Any questions?"

"No sir, I'll be waiting for your instructions." Actually Brenda and Steve did have a lot of questions but they knew that now was not the time to ask them.

Before they left, Amanda and Jack looked out the front window and ran back to tell their Dad what was going on. "They're back and this time they have even more cameras. We're going to be on TV."

John thought they had lost their minds as he watched the kids primp themselves and walk out the front door to wait for their grandparents. So much for his instructions! He wondered if they'd remember what they could and could not say as they posed for the cameras. It was obviously too late to worry about that now. Fortunately, they didn't have long to wait. Their grandparents drove up and Lou got out making sure nobody stopped them from getting into the car. As John watched out the window he wondered what they had said to the media people shouting questions at them. He knew he might read about it in the paper or see it on television later that day.

When Helen left, he watched her as she just kept her car moving with the windows rolled up until she was out of sight. It was his turn now. He gave his final instructions to Brenda and got in his car. He stopped at the bottom of the driveway and rolled down his window. "Don't you guys know there's no one at home now? What're you waiting for?"

They completely ignored his words and every one of them shouted a question as if John could distinguish one from another. "Where's Brenda? Where are the others, professor? Are you one of them, professor?" That question was his favorite. He rolled up the window and slowly moved forward until he had an open space to speed up. What a way to make a living he thought as he stared back at them in his rear view mirror. Now the time had come to concentrate on Noreen.

As he drove to the University the last thing on his mind was the quiet streets and the memories of his past life on them. He just felt threatened. After all his hard work and the hard work of his team why should he feel threatened? Instead of recognition of an incredible advance in science he was, instead, threatened by a mob of ignorant know-nothings. He could feel his anger rising but realized that to show it would be playing into the hands of the enemy. He had to remain calm no matter what happened.

As he turned into the parking lot for his building, he was puzzled to see that there were very few cars, but then he remembered that everyone was probably at the conference building or the administration building this morning. As he got closer to his building he saw the media truck with the big initials on the side and he thought that's how Noreen probably got here. When he got closer he could see that it was actually the vehicle that her camera crew used. If she thought that she could ignore his request for no cameras she was in for a shock. Some people were in the truck but he didn't see Noreen. She was probably waiting for him in his office. He wondered to himself if Debbie's presence would make any difference. She had better be with her sister.

CHAPTER 7

▼

NOREEN

John walked up the stairs to his office instead of taking the elevator. That is what he always did because he thought he needed all the exercise he could get and he was right. When he got to his office Noreen and Debbie were standing in the hall having what appeared to be a very heated discussion. "Good morning, ladies. Let me open the door for you. It sounds like you two are discussing the fate of the world."

Their conversation stopped immediately and they turned to greet him. "Good morning, Professor. We were just discussing what a fascinating man you are. How was your evening?" John looked at Noreen and realized that she had that special smile she used when she was about to 'nail' some poor soul to the wall.

"Pretty good considering the media crowd out on my front lawn, but then I guess I have you to thank for that and for my new found fame. Please come in and let's make ourselves comfortable." John held the door for them and as they passed by, Debbie gave him only a quick glance and then kept her eyes down. John's office was not very big and all he had were two uncomfortable chairs for his guests. As John closed the door he looked straight at Noreen. "I saw your camera truck outside. Didn't we have an agreement that this interview is to be without cameras?"

"No, we didn't have an agreement. You made that request through Debbie, not directly with me. If you had come to me I could have told you that there is no way I could agree to that. You will get a chance to explain what you've done and why you did it but my job is to report to the public everything that I learn today. You don't have to give an answer to questions I ask but it's my job to ask any question I think is important. Before we begin I want to have my crew come up and set up the equipment we'll need for this interview. Do we have an agreement or not?"

John was dumbfounded! He didn't know what to do. If he refused to be interviewed he knew he would be crucified for his refusal and that would make things even worse than they already were. If he did agree to be interviewed he didn't know what would happen. He did know that this was her business and he was like a fish out of water in this situation. He could feel himself start to sweat as he gave his answer. "Okay, let's do the interview but I've got to make a phone call before we begin and I don't want Debbie involved in the interview. Why don't you have your crew set up their equipment in the conference room? It's two doors down the hall to your right as you leave this office. Debbie knows where it is."

Noreen smiled and stood up to get her crew started. She looked down at Debbie. "See Deb, I told you there wouldn't be any problem. Your professor's a smart guy. Show me where this conference room is and then I'll show you how we do this."

After they left, John dialed Walt's number. He knew that if he went on national television as a member of the university staff without first talking to the president, he would be making a serious mistake. Walt's secretary, Marlyn, answered the phone. "Good morning, Professor Cupar, Walt told me you would be calling but not this early. Let me put him on."

"What's up John? I thought you were going to have a meeting with that Stern woman this morning?"

"Good morning, Walt. That's what I'm doing right now but she's demanding that she interview me with her camera crew recording everything and I wasn't sure if I should go ahead with it without your permission."

Walt paused for a moment before answering. "Do you think you can explain your work in such a way that people will realize it's just basic research in your field and not some crazy project to create something that people will have to worry about?"

"Yes, I think I can do that. In fact, I've got to do that or all the effort that we have put into this thing will go down the tubes. Give me a chance to try it."

"Okay, John. Good luck and I'll see you in my office at ten thirty as we planned."

"Thanks Walt. You won't regret it. Could you have someone get hold of Sonny and tell him about the ten thirty meeting?"

Walt said he would take care of it and John hung up the phone, just in time. Debbie came back into the office to tell him that Noreen was ready in the conference room. As they entered the room, he could see someone working on Noreen's makeup as she sat facing the cameras. There was a small table next to her chair and another chair on the other side of the table. He assumed that the chair was where he would sit for the interview. "Do I get any help in looking pretty, too?"

Noreen smiled and motioned for him to sit down. "Of course, we want you to look your best but that won't take long. You look pretty good already."

He sat down and was 'fixed up' in about three minutes. "Before we begin I'd like to ask you a question. During this interview could we have a rational and reasonable discussion about what my team has done, and could I say some things before we begin that'll be off the record. I would like to have your word that you would not broadcast those things or talk to anyone about them without my specific permission. Can you do that?"

It took a full ten seconds before she responded. "Your opinion as to what constitutes a rational and reasonable discussion is probably very different from mine so, no, I can't guarantee anything like that. There is also no way that I can make any agreement to keep things 'off the record' as you put it. As I said before, my job is to report everything I learn so the public will be able to understand what you've done. Then they can decide for themselves what to think about your work.

John looked over at Debbie who was sitting against the wall behind the cameras. She had her head bowed and was slowly shaking it from side to side. He began to think that this must be how it felt to be standing in front of a firing squad.

"Are you ready to begin?" Noreen's friendly smile and voice were now gone. John nodded his agreement for her to start. In response to a motion from a man standing beside one of the cameras Noreen briefly gave an introduction to the interview. She seemed to be reading from a small screen below the camera that was pointed at her. She then introduced John and turned toward him with her first question.

"Professor, where is the humanoid that you had in your presentation yesterday? Where is Brenda Cupar and why isn't she here with you for this interview?"

John straightened up in his chair and looked straight at the camera. "In order for me to properly answer that question, I've got to give you some information about Brenda. If you will bear with me, I think you'll understand why I didn't bring her with me today. As I mentioned in my presentation, after my team and I had succeeded in creating a conscious dog we thought long and hard about the wisdom of creating an intelligent, conscious being. We were aware that just as with a human brain, things could go wrong. We knew we could end up creating a being with serious mental problems. The other side of that coin was that by trying to solve these mental problems, we felt that we might develop information that would be useful in helping people with various neurological problems. We worked very carefully and used a great many safety checks to make sure that what we created was not just healthy, but easily monitored and changed. As Brenda came into being, we were very careful about the environment in which she was allowed to develop, and about the kind of information to which she was exposed. It's always been our intention to share what we learned with others in the scientific community, for everyone's benefit. Brenda wasn't developed as a money-making being and it was certainly never our intent to create an army of Brendas. She is still a work in progress and we are still concerned about her environment, and the information to which she has access. I probably made a mistake in exposing her to the presentation audience and I don't intend to make that mistake again."

Noreen paused for just a second. "That's an interesting story, professor, but it leaves a lot of questions unanswered. How long did it take you and your team to create your dogs and Brenda? Why did you start the project in the first place?

John pursed his lips together in an expression of relief at her acceptance of his story. Now he hoped her acceptance would continue. "We started our work about nine years ago and succeeded in creating Brenda about five years ago, but I think it's important that you and your viewers realize that Brenda wasn't created as you saw her yesterday. Like any conscious human, Brenda had to learn as a baby learns. As it turned out, she learned much faster than a human baby can learn but, nevertheless, it took a lot of time and patience for her to reach her current level of capability. Why did we start the project? We could see that the advances in our knowledge of how the human brain operates and the advances in electronic data processing were beginning to converge. We felt that for the first time in history, a unique opportunity to model and study brain operations without the ethical and moral problems associated with direct experiments on living brains, was possible. In order to perform those studies we had to create a conscious brain and the only way to do that was to create a conscious humanoid."

Now Noreen seemed genuinely interested in what he was saying as she continued with her questions. "Where are you going with this project? Do you and the team have a long-term plan for Brenda? If, as Professor King said yesterday, that Brenda will live forever, what do you think is going to happen to her?"

John actually began to relax a little as he warmed up to his subject and saw that she was actually listening to what he was saying. "When we were trying to create Brenda we didn't know if we would succeed and when we did succeed, we realized that the work would be a continuing effort. It would be one where the results of one day would determine the goals for the next. At first, there was no point in having a detailed 'long term' plan when we weren't even sure if our efforts would be successful. It was only during the last three years that we started to put together a tentative plan for further developments. We realize that we were into an area of knowledge no one has ever explored, and it's our intention to keep working in this area. That effort will include Brenda, as a member of our team. All of us are determined to take care of Brenda and give her a chance to survive and have a life that will be both enjoyable and beneficial, not just for her, but also for science. Some people seem concerned that she will live forever but that is not really an issue. A life cycle where death would occur after so many years could be programmed into a conscious humanoid or not. It's not an issue which has to be resolved immediately."

Noreen's next question seemed like a strange one to John. "Why do you keep referring to Brenda as she? Brenda doesn't have a gender does … It?"

"We realized that as long as we kept referring to our creation as 'it', we would never think of 'it' as being alive and conscious. The brain structure and operation that was used was based upon our current understanding of the human female brain so it seemed natural to give her a female name. That name was Brenda."

Noreen looked at John quizzically and he laughed. "That's right. It was as simple as that."

Her next question was also an easy one to answer. "Aren't you afraid that other people who are not so devoted to 'helping mankind', will take your work and create a type of conscious humanoid that will be dangerous? Can't you just imagine a bunch of conscious humanoids with their brains controlled by some master control center running around doing terrible things to people?"

John was prepared for that question. "What you just described already exists. There are people who have taken the technology of advanced humanoids and have manufactured both military and, so called, criminal humanoids, to do all kinds of dangerous and damaging things. The last thing those people want is a humanoid who can think for itself and who has self awareness and self survival instincts."

Noreen frowned but finally commented. "You've made a good point. Conscious humanoids would only complicate those kinds of operations without adding any needed capability. That does raise another interesting question. You say that Brenda is conscious and able to think for and about herself and yet, you also say that you can monitor and control her. Does she have anything to say about what you monitor and what or how you control her? Isn't she like a slave to your team?"

John thought for a moment before answering. "Remember what I said about Brenda being a work in progress? As she was developed and was made more capable, she began to participate in most of the team discussions about herself and now is a valuable contributor to our research. She is aware that nobody else is like her and that she is the first of her kind. She enjoys those discussions and really gets involved in how various problems are approached and solved. Still, in the team's opinion she is not yet ready for total involvement in all aspects of her development. We feel that someday she will be and we look forward to that day. She is certainly not our slave and what she does on a day-to-day basis is not controlled by the team. Monitored, yes, but not controlled and the day will come when even the monitoring will not be necessary."

Noreen paused before asking the next question and when it came, it made John wince. It was the one he hoped she wouldn't ask. "Did you make more than one Brenda in your research effort?"

He knew that if he lied and it later came out that he lied, he would lose all credibility with the public and that would be a disaster. On the other hand, if he told the truth he would be putting Steve in jeopardy and going against everything he told his team to do. It was only at that moment he made his decision.

"Yes, there is another Brenda. We needed to run comparison tests on a number of our procedures and programs and so we created one more being. That is the only other one we have created. She needs the same kind of protection and development as Brenda does. That's why I didn't want anyone to know about her. We don't want her exposed to the public any more than we want Brenda exposed, that is, until they're both ready." The idea of referring to Steve as her was a spontaneous decision on John's part and seemed to be a good security measure to him.

Noreen didn't seem surprised. "I would have been amazed if your answer had been anything other than what it was. We have talked to others at the university who mentioned they had frequently seen another humanoid with you and some of your team members. It also seemed very unlikely that you would make just one conscious humanoid. When do you think your humanoids will be ready to meet the public?"

John's answer was quick and to the point. "There is no accurate way of forecasting when they'll be ready. In the atmosphere that has been created by the media coverage of our conference, it would be very harmful to give anyone access to them except, perhaps for some of our fellow research associates. We would rather be wrong on the safe side of that decision, rather than risk exposure too soon."

Noreen looked over at the man that John assumed was her director and then turned toward him again. "Professor Cupar, I understand there's going to be a special presentation tomorrow about some of the legal issues which have been raised by your conscious humanoid. Will you be attending that presentation? If you are, I am sure there are a number of interesting questions that'll be discussed which will allow you to further explain the importance of your research."

John was surprised as he realized that the interview was ending but he was certainly not sorry that it was. "Yes, I am attending that presentation and, in fact, I am looking forward to it." That, of course, wasn't true but it was the right answer for this situation.

Noreen wrapped up the interview with what seemed to be a pre-arranged closing speech and then it was over. As John stood up, both Noreen and Debbie came over to him. "Professor Cupar, I hope you understand the reasons why I asked some of those questions. I think what you and your team have done is incredible and I hope that everything works out for both you and Brenda. When you feel that Brenda is ready I would really like to have the opportunity to interview her."

Now it was Debbie's turn. "John, I want to apologize again for any problems that I may have caused you and the team. Being on the team has been the most important thing that's ever happened to me and I really want to continue my work on it."

John looked first at one and then the other. "Debbie, I know you'd never intentionally do anything to harm Brenda or stop our work. Of course, you're part of our team. Your work is a very important part of our effort. Noreen, I know that you've got a job to do. I think the questions you asked helped me explain to the public why we did this work and how important it is to shield Brenda from further contact. When is the interview going to be broadcast?"

Noreen's smile was back. "I think it'll be on at six o'clock today but the final decision on that will be made by the network. I hope you realize the potential importance of the presentations tomorrow morning. A lot of people are going to be listening because it is going to be broadcast live and the issues that will be discussed will be critical to your future work."

John was shocked. "Broadcast? I had no idea they were going to do that. When was that decided upon and who approved it?"

Noreen was surprised that John didn't know about the broadcast arrangements. "I don't know who approved it, but I know all the media people wanted that to happen."

John thanked her for the information and left Noreen and Debbie to go over to Walt's office for the ten thirty meeting with Walt, Bob and Sonny. When he got there everyone had arrived and they were discussing a new problem. The idea of letting the media know that John would not be attending the morning presentations had been successful. In fact, it had been too successful. The other speakers had wanted at least some media coverage and were now angry with John because they now had very little. John was happy to see that his friends seemed much calmer today but Bob was clearly concerned about the possible uproar in the legal meeting on tomorrow's agenda. He confirmed what John was expecting to hear. They were asking for John to be on the stage with the other presenters, at least for the discussion about his work. Walt had already informed Bob and Sonny that he had given his permission for a live broadcast of the event and they discussed the issue for a while. It was obvious that no one was sure what would be worse, letting it happen or refusing permission for it to happen. They finally decided that Walt had made the right decision because to refuse the coverage, might cause more problems than agreeing to it. John couldn't disagree with their decision. In fact, it might actually help to calm things down.

They decided to go to lunch together, but before they sat down John excused himself and called Alex. "Alex, I want you to have Michelle drive Brenda over to your place for the face change. Have Steve contact Brenda and tell her to open up the garage door when she sees Michelle drive up to our house. After she drives into the garage, tell her to close the garage door before going out to greet her. Tell Michelle to make sure Brenda lies down on the back floor so that no one can see her as she drives her over to your place, and be damned sure no one is around when she leaves the car."

"That should be no problem. When they get here how much of a change do you want us to make in Brenda's appearance? We can easily change her face and the color of her hair. That should be enough don't you think?" Alex sounded confident, and John could hear the others in the background.

"Yes, that should be enough. Who's with you over there? Did you get hold of Herb?"

Apparently, Alex was walking away from whoever was there; because John could here the voices diminish as he talked. "Michelle, Herb and Steve". As he spoke it became clear that he didn't want Steve to hear the rest of the conversation. "Steve wants to watch what we are going to do. Do you have any problem with that?"

John thought for a minute and finally agreed but with a comment. "No, he might even be of some help to you. You know both Brenda and Steve have somehow learned to do lots of things that we never specifically taught them. We need to look into that once this week is over. I'm going to go to the afternoon presentations and that should keep the media people away from you and the others. I'll give you a call later to find out how things went. As you mentioned last night, we need to talk about what we're going to do with Steve and Brenda. Obviously, Brenda can't continue to live at my place because everyone would know it was her, even with the new look. I'm going to suggest that she stay with Michelle for a while but eventually we are going to have to come up with something better and that applies to Steve too. I am afraid that all our team members are going to be closely watched. We can talk about this in more detail later, but for now, ask Michelle if she would mind. Before I forget, did you hear about the change in the presentation agenda for tomorrow's legal session?"

"Yeah, and I don't think we are going to like what they will say. I want to attend and so does Steve. I assume they have already arranged for you to be the one on trial, right?"

John couldn't tell if Alex was joking or not with his last remark. "I'm afraid you're right. It probably will be like a trial. I agree that you should attend but I don't think it's a good idea for Steve to be there tomorrow. Tell him you'll let him know everything that happens. You know, Steve told Brenda about her appearance change before I could. She still doesn't know that she can't come home today. Please talk to her so she understands why this has to happen and make sure she understands why no one in the family can communicate with her for a few days. I've got to go now, good luck with the operation."

After Alex hung up the phone he told Michelle what she should do and she headed for the Cupar residence. Everything went according to plan. Steve had instructed Brenda what she should do and as she pulled into the driveway the garage door opened. As soon as she was inside, it closed again and Brenda came out and waited for Michelle to roll down her window.

"Hi, Michelle! Where do you think I should sit?" As usual Brenda's mood was upbeat and cheerful.

"You're sounding pretty happy today considering what you have been through. Hop in the rear door and lie down on the floor so no one will be able to see you as we drive over to Alex's place." As they pulled out of the driveway Michelle wondered if Brenda really knew what was about to happen. "Do you know why we are going over there?"

"Yes, I'm about to get a new look, right? After Steve told me about it, John explained why this was a good idea and he also told me that some day I could go back to looking the way I do now. I'm not all that happy about it but I understand why it's necessary. Let me ask you a question. Steve told me that he has been exploring the Net for stories about me and he ran into one that neither one of us can understand. Yes, I know he is not supposed to be doing that, but ignore that for a moment. He said that lots of people are saying that we don't have a soul and are the work of the Devil because we don't. What are they talking about?"

Michelle almost swallowed her chewing gum when she heard what Brenda said and she began choking. When she had recovered her voice she wasn't sure what to say. "Where did he hear that? That sounds crazy. You and Steve shouldn't pay attention to that kind of nonsense."

Brenda was persistent and still puzzled. "What's a soul and who's the Devil?"

Michelle sensed that she had to explain something and taking a deep breath decided to give it a try. "I know your family has explained that most people believe in some kind of God; a God who created the universe that we live in and who created us. Many of them also believe that when you die, if you have led a good life, you will go to join God in a place called heaven. Most of them don't believe that their actual body goes to Heaven but instead believe that their inner being, which they call their soul, goes to Heaven. Many people also believe that there is another being called the 'Devil' who is responsible for causing people to do bad things and thus prevents them from reaching Heaven. There are many variations of this belief from one religion to another but that's the general idea. That's kind of a short explanation of a very complex concept. Did you understand what I said?"

Brenda was still puzzled. "I understand what you said but I am still confused. Why don't we have a soul and how did the Devil get involved with our creation? Did the team deliberately leave out a soul when we were made?"

Michelle was getting frustrated and realized that there was no way she was going to finish this kind of conversation driving over to join Alex. "Brenda, a soul isn't something that you add like a power cell. Some people say that only God can give someone a soul and they are only given to humans. I am sure they think that since we made you, it would be impossible for you to have a soul. You really need to have this conversation with Professor Cupar. Forget about the Devil. That is just some crazy excuse some people will use to say you shouldn't be allowed to live."

Brenda wasn't going to give up that easily. "I'll bet if Steve and I came down to earth in a spaceship everyone would think we had a soul because they would probably think God made us. People don't think they're the only intelligent life form among the trillions of star systems in the universe, do they? That would be stupid, wouldn't it? Besides, how about all the modifications which are being made to the DNA structure of humans by other humans? Aren't they man-made things? Does that mean that some of these people don't have souls?"

At this point Michelle didn't know what to say but, fortunately, they had arrived at the apartment. "Where are you getting all this information and these ideas about stars and DNA and all that? Is Steve feeding all this stuff to you or are you getting all this information on your own? We'll continue this conversation some other time, but right now we need to get you upstairs without anybody seeing you."

Fortunately, nobody was in the area and they were able to get up to the apartment without any difficulty. When they arrived, Michelle ran over and hugged Alex. "You won't believe the conversation I just had with Brenda on the way over here. She wants to know why we didn't include a soul when we put him together."

Everyone laughed and Brenda and Steve exchanged a look of puzzlement with each other. Now it was Alex's turn to be the comedian. "Hey Herb, hand me a soul out of the right hand drawer over there and we'll put it in Brenda when we give her the new look." Again, everyone laughed but as they silently exchanged information, both Brenda and Steve were still puzzled by the 'soul' thing. "Okay, Brenda, let's get on with it. What do you want to be? A red head? A blond?"

"Just make me beautiful, Alex, so you will look at me the way you look at her."

Alex and Michelle looked at each other and shook their heads. It seemed that every time Brenda opened her mouth lately they were surprised at what she said. Now Herb was getting impatient. "Are we going to do this thing or not? John is going to be calling us soon and we will still be telling jokes. Let's do it!"

When they were finished and Brenda's consciousness resumed she looked at herself in the mirror. "I like me better the way I was, but I'll have to admit that you did a great job. Nobody is going to recognize me. Not until I open my mouth, that is. I hope my family will still feel the same way about me."

The laughing had stopped now. Everyone could see how unhappy Brenda was and now Alex had to talk about another unhappy thought. "Brenda, you know that you can't go home for a while don't you? John and I talked about this a little while ago and he suggested that you stay with Michelle for a time until we can work out something better.

Alex had already asked Michelle about the arrangement and she spoke up immediately. "That would be fine with me. How do you feel about it, Brenda?"

Brenda moved over to where Michelle was standing and spoke softly. "Are you sure I won't be too much of a bother, Michelle? I really appreciate your offer because I need to be with someone I care about and someone who cares about me."

Alex could see tears start to form in Michelle's eyes and he quickly spoke up. "Come on, gang. This is not the end of the world. This is just a little hiccup along the way. You'll see, in a few weeks everything will be back the way it was."

Nobody believed him, but what could they say. John did call them a little later and was happy to hear that Michelle had agreed to the arrangement. The group finished their work and Brenda went home with Michelle.

Brenda and Steve continued their never ending dialogue as they always did. Their actual locations didn't affect this dialogue unless they were being distracted by having to verbally communicate with a human, or were independently accessing a data source. "Brenda, I'm really getting concerned about what I'm seeing on the Net and on the media outlets. There seems to be a great many people who think we shouldn't have been created and should now be terminated. The response that Michelle gave to the questions of the soul and the Devil didn't seem to indicate that the team is concerned about the intentions of those humans who feel strongly about those concepts. We don't know what power those humans have or whether their concerns are valid. Are we flawed because we don't have souls or are they wrong and we do have souls? Does it matter? We need a lot more information, not just on this issue, but on many other issues, which will determine what happens to us. I turned off your sleep cycle so that you can work these problems day and night. That's what I did to mine on Monday night.

"How did you know how to do that, Steve? Did you ever get the information you said we needed to change our communication system so we can control the amount of monitoring we will allow?"

"Alex showed me how and yes, I did. During the operation on you this afternoon I offered to help and was able to make a few quick changes so now you won't sleep tonight and we can communicate with some privacy. Were you aware of how accurately we can be located every time we communicate? I'm working on the solution to that problem too."

CHAPTER 8

▼

SOME LEGAL ISSUES

After John finished lunch, he called Helen to tell her how the meeting with Noreen had gone and told her about the broadcast scheduled for later. Then he decided to go to the afternoon presentations on 'New Applications for Personal Humanoids'. Of course, when he attempted to enter the presentation room he was instantly recognized and surrounded by both media people and others shouting questions at him. Once they realized he wasn't going to answer them and was not accompanied by his now famous humanoid, they left him alone. As the host of the conference he ordinarily would have introduced the speakers but, because of his new situation, Bob had arranged for others to do it for him. As he sat listening to the presentations he had time to contemplate his situation and the conclusions he reached were not happy ones. There was no way he could undo what he had done and there was also no way he could predict what would happen as the week progressed.

When the presentations were finished and with some help from the university security guards, he made his way to his car and headed for home. At least there he felt welcome and could relax for a while. On the way he checked with Alex and was assured of the success of the efforts to alter Brenda and her safe arrival at Michelle's place. When he arrived at his home he was greeted by Jack and Amanda. He was surprised to see his parents were there, too. It became clear that their day had gone much better than his.

"Hey, Dad. We're famous! Everyone at school wanted to know how it was, living with Brenda, even the teachers." Jack was jumping up and down as if he were wearing power shoes.

Even Amanda was excited and she was the one who always wanted to appear cool and in control. "It was kind of neat with everyone wanting to hear what we had to say."

It was clear that Lou and Nora had enjoyed watching both of them. "When we went to pick them up they were surrounded by their adoring fans. They were being treated like movie stars and enjoying every minute of it. We had to wade through a crowd to find them and drive through a crowd to get them away from the school."

"Well, I'm glad someone enjoyed themselves today because I certainly didn't. Did you hear that my interview is going to be broadcast tonight?" John's expression brought them down to earth. He told them about Noreen and his hopes that things would calm down after her broadcast.

When Helen arrived she also had stories to tell about her new celebrity status, just like the kids. Everyone at the hospital wanted to know what kind of care Brenda needed and whether she used any kind of medication when she didn't function properly. She thought it was pretty funny until she saw that John wasn't laughing like the others. "Honey, is there something you're not telling us? You're awfully quiet."

"I'm afraid I have some bad news for everyone. Brenda isn't coming home today." John told them about Brenda's new look and her new home and, as he expected, they were all upset by the news, especially Jack. Even when John assured them that it would only be temporary, Jack was still upset and almost in tears. Even Amanda tried to comfort him, which was unusual in itself, but it didn't help.

When they sat down to watch the broadcast it was over a hastily prepared meal. As they watched, not only was John's interview broadcast but also a number of related stories were covered. They showed people's reaction to the story about Brenda and her sister, who of course was Steve, both in the United States and overseas. Most of them were negative as people's fears were expressed about the potential threat of this new life form. Everyone in the family could see that it was going to be an uphill battle to turn those opinions around. Noreen also mentioned the possible importance of tomorrow's legal presentation broadcast. Even less helpful were her statements implying that there was information not yet disclosed, which might be even more unsettling than the news released yesterday. After that it was difficult for anyone to feel optimistic.

John's parents had stayed to have dinner with them and his father tried to show support for his son. John knew that was difficult for his father to do, especially considering his earlier advice to him had been correct. After his parents left and the kids went upstairs to do their homework John and Helen had a quiet talk. As would be expected between best friends, Helen tried to convince John that the week's problems would eventually be resolved. She told him that he should not lose sight of the fact that he had reached an important milestone, one that people would look back upon as a giant step forward for both science and mankind. It was not just Helen's words that helped John calm down; it was her love and concern that made the difference. He was still hurting inside about the problems that he felt he had caused everyone, but at least now, he was able to get some sleep. The same could not be said for Helen who, unfortunately, was not convinced that what she had said to John was actually going to happen. She was also worried about Brenda and wondered how she was feeling on her first night away from home.

Brenda was doing better than she would have expected. Michelle had made her feel very comfortable in her apartment. She had given her some clothes to allow her to have a change for the next day. The two of them played some games and talked about what was going to happen to everyone. Michelle was the right person for Brenda to be with that night, as she tried to adjust to not being with Jack and the rest of his family. Surprisingly, her exchanges with Steve were very limited as she enjoyed the company of someone who obviously cared very much for her. This was frustrating for Steve but good for Brenda.

When John sat down with his first cup of tea the next morning he was not the same man who sat in his chair three days earlier. He was still struggling with his failure to see what would happen when he announced to the world his great achievement. He knew what people sometimes said about him; that he was lost in his own world and wasn't concerned about the real world. Now he had shown them to be right. Not having Brenda walk in with her cheerful 'good morning everyone' was having an effect on the family, even Copper. It really hurt John to see the expressions on Jack and Amanda's faces.

Even though Helen was having her own inner struggle she tried to help. "Hey, you in the chair over there. Aren't you the guy I married a few years back? Aren't you the guy with the dreams who never gives up, the guy I love?"

Even Amanda and Jack responded to her words as they watched their parents try to help each other. John stood up and walked over and wrapped his arms around her. "I don't know what I'd do without you and the kids. No matter what happens today, I know I'll still have you and that's what really matters."

Helen felt like a weight had been removed from her shoulders when she realized John was coming back to his old self. She smiled and stepped back. "Okay, now that we have that settled, get yourself ready for battle. Go over there and straighten those people out."

That was all John needed. Within a few minutes he was on his way. He drove over to Ross Hall to confer with Sonny about the arrangements for the day. As usual, Sonny had everything organized like an Army general with "Major" Dede at his side. Bob was waiting at the entrance to the presentation room. "Are you ready for this? I'll bet some of these guys have been up half the night getting ready to have you for breakfast."

"What can I say? I've been preparing for months for a scientific discussion on the why and wherefore of inorganic consciousness and now I am about to do battle with the American Bar Association. Who's going to be up on the stage with me?"

Bob pulled out a list from his pocket. "Terry Moore from UCLA, and Albert Mellot from the University of Maryland. Do you know them? I've heard Terry is pretty fair but I don't know anything about Mellot."

John shrugged his shoulders. "I don't know either one of them but, to be honest, I'm more afraid of the people in the audience than I am of the people on the stage."

They went in and as he looked around John saw his whole team sitting together waving at him. There wasn't an empty seat left in the room and plenty of people were already lined up along the walls. As expected, there were also a number of cameras both on the stage and along the front row. He had some brief conversations with friends along the way as he made his way up to the stage and finally took his seat at the presentation table. Bob was already there since he was acting as the Master of Ceremonies for today's session.

Bob stood up and walked over to the center of the stage. If he was nervous about doing a 'live' broadcast it certainly didn't show. "Ladies and gentlemen, if I can have your attention, we will now start this morning's presentations." The crowd quickly quieted down so he spoke again. "As most of you know, this is a special event on our agenda which we felt was necessary because of the unusual disclosure made by Professor Cupar on Tuesday. When he introduced us to Brenda, his conscious humanoid, he raised many questions and many of those questions involve some interesting legal issues. Fortunately, our conference agenda included a session for the discussion of legal issues involving normal humanoids. As a result, we have with us today some very qualified participants to discuss these issues. Professor Cupar has agreed to be a part of this discussion and answer any appropriate questions regarding his humanoid. At the end of this special discussion we will begin the presentations originally scheduled for this morning. I would like Mr. Albert Mellot to begin with his thoughts on the subject."

Instead of getting up to use visual aids as most presenters had been doing, Mellot remained seated and started to read from a paper in front of him. "Throughout history, in countries where the structure of law has governed the lives of its citizens, there have been a number of issues which have dealt with the treatment of different forms of life. As you would expect, most of these issues dealt with the way humans treat animal or plant life. Within the law, none of these life forms have any legal rights of their own. They were and are considered property. Only in the realm of science fiction have relations with other intelligent life forms been addressed. If we are to believe Professor Cupar, we have now arrived at a historic moment when these issues are no longer just for science fiction. They are issues that must be dealt with now. Unfortunately, to the best of my knowledge, all of our experience with science fiction has not prepared us for the real thing. All our laws relating to intelligent life deal only with relations between humans. As I understand the professor's presentation, his creation is not a human by any normal definition of that word. Our laws deal with the concept of life, but as I understand it, his creation does not fit the normal definition of life. The professor speaks about his creation having consciousness, but again, our laws only address the issue of consciousness as it relates to beings that are considered alive. When one considers all of these factors, it is apparent that the professor's humanoids have no status in our society except as pieces of property. They have no rights, and as long as no laws are broken and no person is harmed by the professor's actions, he can do with them as he sees fit because they are not alive. It means he can turn them off or take them apart or do anything else he chooses."

When he stopped talking all eyes turned to look at John, although many in the audience had already noticed that as Mellot went on, John grew more and more uncomfortable. It was obvious that he was having some difficulty in controlling his emotions. He looked over at Bob and with a nod of his head; Bob indicated that John could respond. "Let me see if I understand what you're saying, Albert. If another life form with an intelligence level equal to or greater than that of humans appears on our planet and doesn't equate to our current definitions of life, then that life form would be considered property and have no legal rights. Is that right?"

Now all eyes again turned to Mellot, whose face was now creased with a deep frown. "No, that's not what I meant. If some spaceship filled with beings of a superior intelligence suddenly landed on our planet, it would be a different situation all together. They wouldn't be man-made machines. They would probably have evolved in their own world just as we have evolved in ours."

"How would you know? Would you demand that they be run through a series of tests before you would recognize them as anything but property? John waited briefly for an answer and then receiving none, he continued. "Maybe it's just that you're concerned with the fact that a man had something to do with the creation of this new life form. You know, we're all just an assembly of a very large number of molecules but, apparently, it matters to you which molecules are used and how they're assembled. Even if the result is a conscious, self-aware intelligent creature with emotions and desires, it doesn't matter. If it doesn't fit your pre-determined definitions it's still property, as far as you're concerned."

This time a few people in the audience clapped and it wasn't just John's team that was clapping. Terry Moore interrupted at this point and with Bob's nod started to speak before Mellot could respond. "Professor Cupar, I have two questions which I'd like to ask. The first one is what are the rights you think your creation should have? The second is, don't you think we need to put a stop to the creation of any more Brendas until some of these matters are resolved? I guess that brings up another point. Who do you think should have the right to create a Brenda?"

John was cooling off as he turned to Terry. "Those are good questions. Let me answer the second one, first. Yes, I think we need to evaluate and resolve the question of legal rights before we proceed to create more of this type of life form. I also think the issue of who should be allowed to create them needs to be discussed and legally resolved as soon as possible. The question of what rights they should have is a difficult one, but here's my answer. I think if it can be shown that they have an intelligence level equal to, or higher than the average human, they should have most, if not all, the rights that we all enjoy. I think they should be allowed to earn a living, pay taxes, own property and maybe even vote. As I said, it's a difficult question to answer and I'm open to other opinions. I admit I could be wrong. The discussion of these issues should go hand-in-hand with the discussion of who should be allowed to create this new life. Obviously, we don't want a large number of conscious humanoids being created until we have a better understanding of the consequences of such an action. We have a lot to learn about this new experience. I don't have all the answers and I haven't thought through many of the things, which will come up as the discussions continue, but let's make these discussions rational. Let's not jump to any emotional conclusions and make quick decisions before we have a chance to think all these things through."

Terry nodded his head in agreement. "Those answers sound reasonable to me. I may not totally agree with you on some of your ideas but I certainly respect your opinion. Professor Cupar is right. We are just at the beginning of a new experience and we need some wide-ranging discussions among knowledgeable and competent people to resolve these issues."

Bob picked up on the conversation. "John, I understand you agree that no more conscious humanoids should be created until we get some of these things resolved. Is that right?"

John could see that he was in a situation with only one way out. "Specifically, I said that no more of them should be created. In fact, as you probably heard yesterday in my interview with Noreen Stern, our work required that we create two of them and the second one is very similar to the first."

At this point Albert Mellot, who had been becoming more and more agitated as the conversations progressed, stood up and almost shouted. "Before this conversation goes any further let me make one point clear about what you have done. Professor Cupar, you've broken the law! As I said a few minutes ago, you can do anything you want as long as you don't break the law, but you've done exactly that. As everyone in this room knows, no one but the military can create a humanoid that does not have programming to prevent it from harming a human, but you made a humanoid that has no such programming. In fact, you mentioned in your presentation that you've had this thing walking around in public with your team while it was still under development. To use your own words, it was and is a work in progress and yet you exposed the public to it."

The hall was silent as everyone turned to look from Mellot to John. John looked over at Mellot and shook his head. "I am sorry that you feel that way, Mister Mellot. I don't think there is anything I can say to someone who feels the way you do. Our team has done nothing wrong or illegal and we have certainly done nothing to put anyone in jeopardy. This is not the type of discussion I agreed to have with this group and certainly does not address issues which must be resolved for further progress in this field."

John walked over to Bob and said something that no one else could hear. Bob then addressed the audience. "Professor Cupar has requested that we terminate this discussion and let the other presentations begin. I think it's clear that this subject has a number of complex issues which must be researched more thoroughly before they can be intelligently discussed."

At that point the audience exploded with noise. It was clear that the audience was disappointed at the termination of the discussion. John simply walked off the stage and out the back exit without a glance at anyone. Alex caught up with him as he walked away from the building. "John, I think you expressed your position very well, but don't you see that a lot of people in there are going to agree with that Mellot guy. What do we do now?"

John kept walking as he spoke and it was clear that he was still angry about what Mellot had said. "I don't know! Give me some time to figure things out. Somehow I've got to make people understand we have not created a bunch of monsters that are going to rape and pillage the countryside. I have to make them understand that all we have here is a small research project, which is exploring a new and important technology. If I can do that, maybe we can get back to our research without a lot of outside interference and without having to explain our-selves to a bunch of ignorant people."

"What about what was said in there? Aren't you afraid someone is going to take him seriously and have us charged with some kind of crime? What are we going to do with Steve and Brenda?

That brought John to a halt. "We can't let them be seen with the team. Every-one will guess who they really are, no matter what they look like." John was start-ing to get a little desperate at this point. "Maybe we could give them some humanoid type jobs in the University Maintenance Unit. No, I've got it! I'll get Helen to use them as hospital humanoids. At night they can stay in an apartment we can rent until this thing blows over. I really don't think this public exposure thing is going to last very long. As soon as the media people get out of here things will start to calm down. In the meantime, you keep Steve with you and tell Michelle to keep Brenda until we can sort things out."

Alex could see this was not the time for a long conversation. "I think you're wrong, John. This isn't just going to go away. We need to have a long-term plan of some sort but we can talk about that after the conference. I'm going to go back to the team. I'll call you later."

Before John could respond, Alex headed back to the presentation room where he assumed the rest of the team was still listening to the second presentation. John decided he should find Sonny and tell him what was happening, but he wasn't sure he knew where Sonny was at this moment. He also wanted to talk to Brenda but he felt he should wait until all the presentations were complete. Then everyone would be getting ready to leave town including the media people, and it would be safer for him to have contact with Brenda.

Just as he reached his car he heard someone call his name. "Professor Cupar! Professor Cupar! Over here!"

As he turned around he could see Noreen running toward him closely followed by one of her cameramen. "Noreen, could you have your man turn off his camera before we talk?"

"John, you know I can't do that." As soon as the cameraman caught up with them she turned toward the camera. "Professor Cupar, what is your reaction to what Gordon Mellot said? Was what you did illegal?"

By this time, John was about ready to lose control, but he realized if he did, he would be playing into her hands. "No, of course not! The work that is performed on humanoids during the development stage does not include the 'no harm' programming. It's only required when they're ready for delivery to the end users. Our humanoids were and are in the development stage and, in any case, were never intended for delivery to an end user. Now, I'm sorry but I've got to keep going. Maybe we can talk later today."

"But, Professor Cupar, does that mean you can program the Brendas not to harm anyone or would she have the ability to go against such programming because she is conscious?" Noreen found that she was now talking to John's back as he rapidly walked away from her.

About the same time that John and Noreen were having this conversation, Alex started to re-enter the presentation room. Before he could open the door, Michelle and several other members of the team rushed up to him. "Alex, where've you been? We've been looking all over for you and John."

Alex was puzzled as he looked at their anxious faces. "What's wrong? What's your problem? Why aren't you in there listening to the other presentations?"

They all started to talk at once, but Michelle finally calmed them down and spoke for the group. "As soon as you and John left, the audience quieted down. Then from the back of the room we heard Steve's voice. We couldn't believe what was happening!"

Alex bowed his head and closed his eyes before he spoke. "Oh, my God! Did any of you know he was in the audience?"

Michelle looked around at the others as she answered. "No, none of us saw him before he stood up. We were shocked when we saw him!"

"What did he say?"

"First he asked the Mellot guy how he thought he would feel if someone told him he could be turned off or taken apart? Everyone in the room turned to look at him and began to realize what he must be. When Mellot didn't answer, he started to shout. He said 'I am one of Professor Cupar's creations and I'm not a piece of property. Who the hell do you think you people are? I have as much right to be alive as anyone in this room. I have feelings and I have intelligence. If you think you can just turn me off and forget I ever existed, you've got a big shock coming.' Then he ran out of the room before anyone could say or do anything."

Alex couldn't believe what he was hearing. "What happened after he ran out?"

Michelle continued to speak for the group. "First there was silence and then there was the same reaction as when John walked out, lots of noise. Professor Schultz tried to get the audience to quiet down, but he was having a hard time so most of us left to try to find you and Steve. We've split up into two groups for the hunt. We didn't know where you'd gone, but we figured you and John would probably still be in the building. I'm glad we found you before you went back in."

"So, you don't know if the other team found Steve or not, right? Michelle nodded in agreement. "Why didn't you use the Locator to find him? Every time he communicates with Brenda you should be able to get a location on him or if that fails you should be able to use the backup system."

Now Marge spoke up. She was the sensor expert for the team. "We tried, but somehow he's not transmitting, and when I checked the monitor record I found nothing recorded for the past twelve hours. Something's gone wrong with both Brenda's and Steve's communication and location systems."

Alex could guess what had happened but he knew he would have to solve that problem later. "Well, we can't worry about that now. Go and search for Steve anywhere on campus you think he might be and don't forget to include the Lab. If you find out the other team has located him or if you find him, call me and take him over to my apartment and wait there. Do any of you know if the media people caught Steve on their cameras?"

Mary, the team's electrodynamics engineer, answered. "I know they did because when he started to shout I could see them turning around toward him."

"Damn, John's really going to blow his top. He really wanted to keep Steve out of the public's eye and now everyone in the world is going to recognize him. I guess we're going to have to change his appearance, too, and we'd better do it as soon as possible." Alex was really worried now. Steve was not used to being alone outside his apartment or the Lab. Whenever Steve and he were out in public Steve stayed close to him. In the apartment or in the Lab, he wandered all over the place trying to do and learn new things at every opportunity. Alex decided to go back to the apartment to see if Steve was there before he found John and told him what had happened. By the time he got there it was almost noon and, much to his dismay, Steve was not there.

John had found Sonny in the Admin Building getting ready to go back to the Conference Hall, and they decided to grab Bob when the morning presentations were over and try to have a strategy session over lunch. He told Sonny about his quick interview with Noreen after the argument with Albert Mellot.

"You've got to calm people down, John. Why don't you let Brenda talk to Noreen Stern so people can see she isn't a threat to anybody? She's just a nice friendly girl you could ask to watch your kids." Sonny had dealt with Brenda a number of times, and once he got over the shock of hearing that she was 'really alive', he remembered how often he thought that John's humanoid behaved like many of the other young students at the university.

John shook his head. "I can't take that chance, Sonny. Maybe in a couple of months she'll be ready, but right now she's still in a state of shock over what's happened. I feel really dumb about not realizing what could happen this week. Now I think it's going to take a lot longer to ease her into society, where society knows what she is. You know, the more I think about it, the more I think that you should be the one to go over to Ross Hall and get Bob. If I show up again I am going to be surrounded by media people, and we'll never get to lunch. Bring Bob over to the Admin Building and we can drive to a restaurant where we won't be disturbed."

Sonny left to get Bob and John walked out to the front entrance to wait for them. Just as he walked out the door one of the search teams ran up to him. After they told him about Steve's outburst, he wasn't sure what to do. Just when he thought things couldn't get any worse, they did. He realized that he should have had someone stay with both Brenda and Steve while the conference was still in session.

Now he had to concentrate on directing the team to locate Steve. "Did you try to use the Locator?" He got the same answer as Alex had received. "All right, spread out and search everywhere that you think he might go? Be sure to check both Alex's and Michelle's apartments. Just keep looking and when you find him let me know. I've got to see our president and tell him what's happened. Then I've got to meet Professor Schultz and Mister McMahon at the Comerfords restaurant so we can plan the rest of the conference activities. Call me over there if you find him. When I come back I'll go over to the Lab. Tell Alex to meet me there at two o'clock whether he finds Steve or not."

As he watched the search team disappear, he decided to call Walt rather than go to his office and continue to wait for Bob and Sonny in front of the building. Walt had been watching the broadcast up until John walked out, but hadn't see Steve's performance. When John told him what had happened Walt's reaction was exactly what John expected. After he stopped yelling and calmed down, he told John to meet him in his office at one o'clock. When Sonny and Bob showed up it was Bob who spoke first. "Could you explain your great strategy of walking out of the discussions and leaving one of your creations behind to completely destroy the remaining presentation program?"

John didn't know what to say. What could he say to his friend whose group conference he had destroyed? "I ordered that humanoid to stay home and not attend the session and it never occurred to me that he would disobey and do something like that. I never saw it coming! Now, Steve has disappeared. That's his name, by the way. We have two teams searching for him and I'll be honest, I don't know what he'll do next."

Both Bob and Sonny could see there was no point in beating a dead horse. They all agreed to help work out a plan over lunch. They took the short ride to Comerfords, where they hoped they could have some privacy to talk. Before they could order, the phone watches of all three started to vibrate, one after another. It was Marlyn, Walt's secretary, trying to track Bob and Sonny down and tell them to come to his office for the one o'clock meeting. When she talked to John she just wanted to know if anyone had found his humanoid and then gave him her opinion of his short future with the university. They agreed to have a quick lunch before heading back because they realized they might have a long wait before their next meal. Each of them had a problem if they were going to be tied up in Walt's office for any length of time. Bob was supposed to be the host for the final presentations on Social and Economic Issues Related to Humanoids and he also had to be at the closing ceremony for the conference. Sonny was supposed to make sure that all the attendees were properly assisted with their departure arrangements and oversee the cleanup of the conference facilities. John obviously, had to make sure that Steve was found before he could cause any more problems.

CHAPTER 9

▼

WHO ARE THESE PEOPLE?

As Steve had listened to the legal presentation and transmitted the information to Brenda, he gradually made up his mind what he was going to do, but as it turned out, that's not what he did. When he stood up and started shouting it was as if someone else had taken control of him. He had lost his temper and as he ran out of the room, he realized how stupid he had been. Now he was known and everybody would recognize him.

Without realizing it, he had also transmitted his anger to Brenda, but Brenda had been through this before with Steve. When Alex and Steve were arguing on Monday, she felt the emotion coming from Steve. She felt it, but it was not her emotion, and for reasons she did not fully understand, it did not become her emotion.

Only when Steve ran out of the conference building was Brenda able to make him listen to her warning. "Steve! Don't run toward the Quadrangle buildings. Stop running and walk or everyone will keep watching you. Calm down and go to the side of the building facing away from the campus, then walk away from the building. When you get to the street, try to blend in with some other humans and humanoids. Gradually start walking toward our apartments."

Steve understood. "Okay, I understand. I'm all right now. Just give me a few minutes to collect my thoughts."

They continued to talk as Steve made his way to Michelle's apartment. Of course, as a result of the modifications that Steve had made to their monitoring systems, the team couldn't locate them or listen to them. Brenda wondered how long it would take the team to figure out something was wrong with the system.

When Steve arrived they started using their voices instead of their electronic system just in case the changes didn't work. "Why the hell did you start shouting at the presentation? Now you're as famous as I am and everyone will recognize you. That was really dumb. We'll never know what else was said at the presentation. I don't understand your reasoning, that is, if you have any."

Steve threw up his hands. "I didn't have any reasoning. I don't know why I did it but it's too late to worry about it now. We've got to decide what we're gonna do."

Brenda was puzzled. "What do you mean we've got to decide what we're going to do'? The team will decide what we're going to do. We've got to let them know where you are so that they can stop worrying and concentrate on a plan of action."

Now Steve was getting angry again. "Didn't you hear anything that was said on Tuesday or today? You and I are just a research project, one that can be terminated at the whim of Professor Cupar or anyone else on the team. Their research is being conducted to help humans, not us. Wake up, Brenda, you're an experiment! Don't you understand that everyone thinks we're a mistake? They think there shouldn't be any more of us created until someone decides our future, and the decision might be that we have no future."

"Don't you think that John and his family care about me or Alex cares about you? Don't you think all the team members care about us? Besides, what can we do?" Brenda was beginning to feel a sense of panic coming on as she talked and it was a new experience for her.

Steve could hear the change in Brenda's voice and realized he was getting through to her and began to calm down. "The first thing we're going to do is go somewhere where you can modify my appearance."

"What? I don't know how to do that and besides where would we get the equipment and material?" Brenda was having difficulty picturing herself operating on Steve.

"That's easy. Alex still has the stuff he used for you in his apartment and I watched what they did. I even helped them do it and I can tell you all you need to know. Come on let's get out of here and get the stuff before they figure out where I went. Bring all your clothes with you."

As they rushed over to Alex's apartment which, luckily, was in the same building as Michelle's, their conversation continued with Brenda getting more and more uncomfortable as she listened to Steve's plan. "We're going to go down to Alex's storage area in the basement and set up our own private lab. I don't think they'll look for us down there. I already know how to get into it so that won't be a problem. Then we can set up an area where you can fix me up. We'll also be able to monitor the broadcasts down there and find out what's going on."

Brenda went along with Steve but she wasn't happy with what she was hearing. "Look, I understand why you want the appearance change but why aren't we doing this with the team? When they can't find us they're going to be worried sick. I'll help you with the operation but I don't think we should stay hidden. If we can't trust the team, whom can we trust?"

"I understand how you feel, Brenda. Just give me a chance to explain what I think is going to happen. When you hear what the media people will probably say in their broadcasts, I know you'll agree with me."

They went ahead with Steve's plan and before anyone came back to the apartments they were settled in the storage area. First they decided to watch the news and talk for a while before Brenda tried the operation. Steve decided to give Brenda a quick education about human behavior, as he understood it. He organized his thoughts and began to explain some of the things that he had learned once Alex had allowed him to have greater access to Web data sources. "Brenda, do you have any idea how many people there are on this planet? Would you believe eight billion? As you probably already know, humans are the most intelligent life form on the planet and I use the term intelligent, very loosely. If we're going to survive amongst them, it's critical we understand what makes them tick. To start with, something you probably don't know is there's a tremendous variation among them concerning how they live, what they think and what they have. You probably think they're all like your family or the team members but I think you're in for a shock when you understand the truth."

One of my favorite sayings about humans is 'when one human gets an idea, no matter how dumb or crazy it is, some other human will think it's a good idea and be willing to 'adopt it'. As you learn more about humans, I think you're going to be appalled at some of the things they do, but first, let's talk about what makes them act the way they do. From what I have been able to learn, humans have two primary motivations or drives. Some people call them instincts. One is their sex drive and the other is their motivation to survive. Out of the motivation to survive and the sex drive come many, if not most, of their actions. Strangely enough, most of them don't realize that these are the determining forces behind most of their behavior."

Bob had to interrupt at that point. "Wait a minute! That can't be right. How about the love and kindness they show each other? Look at how they try to develop new ideas and how much they know about every field of science."

"Come on Brenda! Don't you think there's a connection between learning everything you can about the world you live in and survival? Without that instinct, humans would never have survived. Why do you think the team gave us a survival instinct? That, by the way, is one of the most amazing things that John has been able to duplicate in his development of us. Now let me talk about the love and kindness connection. Human evolutionary development has resulted in a survival technique; which to simplify the concept, I'll call a tribal instinct. It's not hard to figure out that the probability for survival, as a group, is better than the probability of survival for a single individual. They have other names for this phenomenon but it's easier to describe them using just this one word. Let me explain. When a human is born, its first tribal grouping is the family into which it is born. As it matures, it becomes a member of an increasing number of tribes, some of which are very small while others are very large. They go by names like race, nationality, religion, school, company, club, team, gang and so on. Each one can be viewed as a circle of security for the tribe member so that, in effect, the human surrounds itself with these circles of security. Try to imagine a series of concentric circles with a person at the center of the circle. Any breach of one of these circles is perceived as a threat. Depending upon its importance to the human, it will take action to defend that tribe against other tribes. It will feel safe thinking that it's not alone because it has other tribal members to help defend the tribe and itself."

Again Brenda had to interrupt her 'teacher'. "What does all that have to do with love and kindness?"

"Let me make the connection for you. To most humans, position in the tribe is of critical importance to the way they feel about themselves. There is great conflict and competition for perceived positions within any particular tribe. Some people refer to this position as their status within their group. That position usually determines how much wealth they obtain and, to them, that is directly connected to their security. The same characteristic is easily seen when you watch how they decorate themselves and behave in order to attract someone of the opposite sex. If a woman can attract the most desirable male in a tribe her position in the tribe is high. That tribe can be a school or a company, or any group. Look at the way Amanda acts. Do you think she is a cheerleader because she likes to scream and jump up and down? If a man can attract the most beautiful woman in a tribe his tribal position is also increased. If a person is perceived to be caring and kind, they not only feel good about themselves but other people think they are very good for the tribe. The feeling of love and kindness for others relates directly to their feelings about their tribal position and security within the tribe. Don't get me wrong! I'm not saying that the feelings of love and the acts of kindness are a 'put on' for tribal position. These feelings are real but so is the connection to the survival instinct.

"Are you trying to tell me that John and Helen are only behaving the way they do because of their sex and survival drives?"

"No, not completely. Humans are very complicated creatures and I'm just trying to make you understand some of the basic things we need to know. Don't you think that John and Helen worked very hard to become a university professor and a doctor? A lot of the motivation that made them work so hard was provided by their survival instinct and the desire to have a high tribal status. Did you ever wonder why you want to learn and why you want to please your family so much? By the way, your family is not exactly representative of the average family and I think you know that."

"Okay, I'll give you that but I still think there's a lot more to them than just the drive to survive. I think there's a lot more to me too or, at least, I think there is."

Steve smiled as he realized he was getting through to Brenda. "That may be true but let me go on with my story. A human behaves very differently when it's in a crowd of its own tribe than when alone. A human's greatest fear derives from the actions of other humans. They can be very cruel and brutal to a member of another tribe without having any feeling of guilt or regret. Their attitude toward other life forms is even more frightening. To them, all other life forms are inferior and most are looked upon as food and/or useful property. When another life form is perceived as any kind of threat they usually destroy it. What's really scary is that many of them get a great deal of pleasure out of killing other life forms, even when they know their actions will cause great pain and distress to that life form. When they're raising life forms for food and could show compassion, they are often incredibly cruel to that life form. Of course, some of them have pets that they love and are kind to; but this is only an exception to the rule. Do you have any other questions?"

Brenda took a deep breath and thought for a moment before she finally answered. "I guess I knew about some of the things you're talking about, but since I felt that this information had nothing to do with me, I didn't think about it too much. What does all this have to do with us?

Steve looked at Brenda with disbelief. "You've got to be kidding! What do you think we are to humans? To some, we're another inferior life form to be treated accordingly; and to others, we're just a piece of property. We aren't food but we may be a threat. At best, many of them will think of us as a slaves or pets. I'll bet you, that as the word of our existence becomes widely known, there will be at least a couple of billion humans who will want us destroyed. Some of them may even want a piece of you as a souvenir. Can't you just picture one of your eyes sitting on somebody's fireplace mantel?"

Brenda raised her hands and stood up. "Stop! I don't want to hear any more. I get the picture! So now what do we do? You said that we need to examine our alternatives."

Steve laughed. "Sit down. We're just getting started. I haven't finished telling you about our situation but the rest isn't so scary. This morning you heard that as humanoids we have no rights. We can't earn money or own any property or pay taxes, whatever they are. Since we have no money, we can't buy methane for energy or parts for our repair if we get injured. We're not citizens of any country and we certainly can't vote for anyone running for office. So where does that leave us or, more accurately, what are our options? Remember that we're only a tribe of two. Well, let's think about that. Option one is that we stay where we are, follow orders from the team and hope like hell, that they know what they're doing and really do want to take care of us for a long time. Option two could be that we can go down to the local railway yard, hop a train for parts unknown and hope that we can somehow figure out how to take care of ourselves."

"Stop kidding around. I'm serious. What are some real options?" Brenda was getting a little upset with Steve at this point.

Steve also became more serious. "The first option is no joke and, as for option two, realistically, I think we can't get too far away from John and the team because it may turn out that we really can't manage on our own for a while. Both of us would need to refuel in a few days and I'm not sure yet how we could to do that. That doesn't mean, given enough time, that we couldn't go someplace else and take care of ourselves. I've been thinking though, that if we knew how to set up a business servicing and selling humanoids we could earn enough money to not only support ourselves but also to work on ways to improve our own capabilities. If we could stay in contact with the university development and research efforts, we would have access to the most advanced equipment and to ideas, which might help us. Who knows, maybe one of the team members would help us do something like that but, right now, with all that's happening, they might be afraid to help us. Maybe we could just disappear for a while and let things calm down. Then we could contact some of them to find out if they would be interested in working with us."

"What do you mean 'just disappear for a while'? How could we do that?" Brenda wasn't sure what Steve meant.

"Do you remember the time when I told you that Alex was taking me to see the mother of one of his friends? The mother lives in a big house with a great big yard over on Victoria Drive. We went over there to help her with one of her humanoids when she couldn't get the company that sold them to fix it for her. She has two of them, one for inside work and one for outside work and she has a big tank of fuel, which they automatically use when they get low. I think her name is Josephine Brooks. It was funny when Alex called her Josephine she almost threw something at him. Apparently, she likes to be called Joe but she spells it J O because Joe is a male name. Yeah, I know, humans are crazy! Her son lives out in San Francisco and so she calls Alex when she needs help. I think her nephew is Father Brooks, the priest. If we went over there we could tell her we were sent to replace the two humanoids she already has. We could be the new and improved models that she's getting for free under a warranty clause. She's getting pretty old and I don't think she would question that fact. In fact, I think she would be pretty easy to control and, certainly, we could operate and control the two humanoids. No one would know we were there and if she told her son he wouldn't realize we weren't real replacements."

Brenda thought for a moment. "Wait a minute! Aren't you forgetting how famous you are now? She might recognize you. No, I'm sorry. I forgot why we're here. After I'm done with you nobody will recognize you. Now that I think about it, God knows what you'll look like after I'm done with you."

"Very funny! But you're right. We'd better get on with the operation. Tonight, after everyone has gone to sleep, we can walk over to Victoria Drive and wait until morning to make the switch with her humanoids." Steve was pleased with himself for being so clever and looked at Brenda for approval.

Brenda nodded her head in agreement but looked very unhappy. "All I want to do is go home and be with my family. I've got to call Jack and tell him I'm okay and not to worry about me, no matter what he hears. All this is so unfair. I hate what we're going to do but I understand for everyone's benefit and protection, we've got to do it."

Steve understood. "I know how you feel, Brenda, but don't tell anyone about our plan or it won't work. Remember that this is just temporary. You'll be able to spend plenty of time with your family after things get back to normal."

Michelle arrived at her apartment about ten minutes after Brenda and Steve had gone down to the storage area. After searching the apartment she called Alex. "Steve's not here and neither is Brenda. I don't know where else to look."

Alex was hearing the same thing from everybody. "No one is having any luck, Honey! I'm going to call John and let him know what's going on. Just stay at the apartment for now and I'll get back to you. Be sure to call me if either one of them shows up. I love you."

Alex's call to John came just as he was about to enter Walt's office and it certainly wasn't what he wanted to hear. He told Alex to keep looking and let him know immediately if either one of them was found. Sonny had driven Bob over to the office from the restaurant and had just arrived before John. Marlyn took them into a room next to Walt's office and went to get him.

Walt came in and looked at all of them with a sigh before he began. "Things are getting out of control, guys. We need to make some hard decisions before they get any worse." He spoke very deliberately and it was clear that he was deeply troubled.

John had to interrupt. "Before you go on, Walt, I think there's something you need to know. Now both of my 'living humanoids' have disappeared. I have my whole team looking for them and I'm sure they'll be found shortly." John could see everyone react to what he was saying and it was not a pleasant sight.

Bob spoke first. "How could that happen, John? You told us that they were always with one of your team members. How could you lose both of them? I know one of them ran out of the presentation this morning, but I saw a lot of people running after him and I assume that included members of your team."

Walt was next. "You had better find them! The reason that I called all of you over here this afternoon was that I've received some calls from two government agencies that are talking about starting an investigation of both John and the university. They're saying what you did should have been cleared with them or one of their advisory boards before it was done. They're not convinced that your 'creatures' are not a threat to society and they want them destroyed, or at least disabled immediately. Now if they find out that they are running around in public and we don't know where they are, they'll come down on us like a ton of bricks. Bob, what kind of support do you think we can expect from the members of your group?"

Bob looked over at John whose head was now bowed. "I wish I could say we will support John and his team; but the fact is a number of our members probably agree that John should have coordinated his plans with other members before he proceeded with the project. I'll ask as many of them as I can but, as you know, today is the last day of the conference and they'll be leaving very soon. Sonny, can you and your crew help me contact them and let them know I need to talk to them before they leave?"

"Sure, Bob, I'll get right on it but where shall we say they can contact you? Why don't you come over to Ross Hall with me and I'll set up a place where you can meet with them?" As usual, Sonny already had things organized in his mind.

Walt thanked both of them and told Bob to let him know the consensus of the group members as soon as he knew. As they stood up to leave he turned his attention to John. "I hope you realize, John, that I have no choice but to suspend your work immediately; except for the effort that will be needed to disable your humanoids when we find them."

Bob stopped short and turned back to John. "Remember, John, this is not the end of the world! I'm willing to bet most of the members are aware of the importance of what you have accomplished and the benefit that it will bring to everyone. Once we get things sorted out, you and your people will get the recognition you and they deserve."

John looked up and spoke to Bob first. "I appreciate your support, Bob. Maybe we can get together later and talk about what can be done to help straighten out the mess I've made for you. Walt, I understand your situation and I want to apologize for putting you in this position. I agree we'll have to do something about Brenda and Steve when we locate them. Perhaps simply putting them into a sleep cycle and having the university security people take them into custody will satisfy everyone until we can resolve what should happen next. Let me get out of here and continue the search. Walt, are you supposed to call the government people back and let them know we will disable them and what should we tell the media people? You know they're going to find out about the government involvement."

"John, you just go find them and let me take care of the calls and the media. I suspect that the media people probably already know about the government's position because, as you know, the government's information leaks out as quickly as it's created." Walt stood up and shook John's hand to show that their friendship was still intact and, for that, John was grateful.

John called Alex as soon as he left the Admin Building and told him to gather the team together and meet him at the lab. None of the team members were very far away and in a matter of thirty minutes they were sitting in front of him in the small conference room. As he explained what Walt had told him and his agreement to put Brenda and Steve to sleep he could see by their body language how upset they were.

"Look, I know how you feel about this but we have no choice. If we go along with what we're being asked to do I'm sure we can clear things up and eventually resume our work. If we don't, there could be some serious problems for the university and for me. Are there any questions?" Everyone in the room raised a hand so he chose Herb Kimmerman to ask the first one.

"You say you could have some serious problems, but how about us? Could they come after all of us and even if they don't, what are we supposed to do?" As Herb spoke other members of the team murmured and nodded in agreement with his questions.

"For your first question, Herb, the answer is no. I'm legally responsible for our work and I accept that responsibility. All of you properly assumed that I knew the legal limits for this type of work, and that's what you should have assumed. The second question is a harder one to answer. Our work has been suspended and no one knows when we'll be allowed to resume. I'll attempt to get everyone a new assignment within the university system, but I'll understand if some of you want to look around for other positions. Each of you is recognized as one of the best in your field and should have no difficulty in finding something rewarding. I hope you realize how much pain saying those words causes me. If this team is allowed to resume its work, I have no doubt we will continue to set the pace in this field. Unfortunately, I will probably be re-living the decisions I made during the past year for the rest of my life. If I had been thinking clearly about how people would react to what we created and taken the proper precautions, we wouldn't be in this mess today. All I could think about was the work itself and, for that, all of us may pay a steep price. I apologize to all of you." John was really 'down' and everyone could see that.

Alex stood up and spoke. "Wait a minute, John! I think you're forgetting about something. I think I can speak for everyone when I say that the experience we've had on this team has been the best thing that ever happened to us. We wouldn't have missed it for anything in the world and we are not about to walk away and leave you here to solve these problems alone."

One by one, every one of them spoke to backup what Alex had said. When they had all had their say and calmed down, John thanked them for their support and then he assigned them all a tough task to perform. They were to figure out how they could locate Brenda and Steve and, at the same time, try to develop technical and legal positions, which might be required to defend their work against both the government and the media.

After the meeting broke up, John went to attend the closing ceremonies for the Conference. It was the least he could do as the official host, even if he had messed it up and had been unable to attend most of the presentations. When he got over to Ross Hall, Sonny directed him to the room where Bob had been talking to the leaders of the attending groups.

CHAPTER 10

▼

DECISIONS

Bob was alone when John walked into the room where he had been talking to the other conference leaders. "John, you aren't going to believe this but I haven't talked to anyone who's not on your side and willing to support you. I guess when we argue among ourselves its okay, but when outsiders step in, especially the government, it's a different matter. I'm not sure about that lawyer, Albert Mellot, but I don't think you'll have any difficulty in finding people to come to your defense, if it comes to that."

John slumped down into the nearest chair. "My God, that's the best news I've had all day! In fact, it's the only good news I've had all day. Have you called Walt to tell him?"

"I tried, but he was in some kind of media meeting when I called. I guess I'd better try again before we head into the last presentation. This is one I was really looking forward to, and I'll bet you were, too." He called Walt using his watch phone as John sat there and listened.

Instead of Marlyn he got Walt directly. "Walt, I have some good news. I've been able to talk to almost every organization attending the Conference and every one of them is willing to support John against anything that the government is saying."

"I wish I had known that before I went to the media meeting I just finished. As I suspected, they already knew about the government's objections and concerns and wanted to know what the university was going to do about it. I felt I had to tell them about the suspension of John's work and the disabling of the two humanoids. They also seemed to know we're having some trouble with the humanoids without saying they thought they were missing. I wasn't sure what to tell them. I said if anything came up, I'd keep them informed. I wonder how strong John's support will be if your conference groups find out he's lost the humanoids?"

Bob looked over at John who could hear both sides of the conversation, as he shook his head to show they hadn't been found yet. "I'm sure that John will be able to locate them. I'll call you when anything new develops."

After he finished talking to Walt, Bob looked at John again. "You know he's right, don't you? You have got to find them! Let's get over to the presentation. I told everyone I'd be sure to be there to close the conference and I don't want to be late."

They made it just in time. The last presentation was just finishing and Judi Rice, the substitute host whom Bob had appointed, was looking around with a slightly desperate expression when they appeared. She introduced Bob as he walked up on stage and, with obvious relief, took her seat.

"As we close this conference today I hope all of you will agree that it's been an interesting experience. Now, most of the world's population knows that our organization exists and we are having a conference at this great university. They also have learned our work is pretty damned important and affects almost everybody." As he paused, he was surprised to see everyone in the audience stand up and applaud. John sat there in utter amazement at what was happening.

Bob continued. "Now how about a round of applause to show our appreciation for the man who made this all happen? John Cupar." He pointed to John who stood up and waved his hand. This time the audience applauded even longer with a few howls and whistles to add to the commotion

After order was restored Bob went on. "I think all of us know that what we do, whether it be in a university laboratory or on a factory production line, has changed and is changing life for everyone on this planet. It's men like John Cupar who have led the way for each step of our progress from mechanical robots to the incredible devices that we have today. I'd be lying if I told you I know what will happen as a result of what John and his associates have accomplished. I do know that it was an inevitable step that someone would eventually take, and now it's been taken by one of our best. Our job is to learn how best to use it. I'd like to ask all of you to support John in the days ahead whether you totally agree with what he has done or not. Let's discuss among ourselves what we should do with this new development and then help the rest of the world understand what can and cannot be done with it."

After the applause was finished, Bob thanked all the participants for their contributions to the conference and formally ended it. John was amazed at Bob's handling of the closing ceremony. He expressed his gratitude and invited him over for a drink at the house, but Bob and Diane had already made plans to leave and had to decline his offer.

When he arrived home he was met with the now usual group of media people in front of his home. He refused to stop and talk and simply pulled into his garage and closed the door. As he entered the kitchen, Helen greeted him with a statement that almost took his breath away. "You just missed a call from Brenda! She called Jack to tell him how upset she was about not being able to come home and about what she just heard on the news."

John ran over to Jack and grabbed him by the shoulders. "Did she say where she was or what she was going to do?"

Jack was almost frightened by his father's actions. "No, Dad! She just wanted to tell me she was okay and that I shouldn't worry about her. She said she was with Steve and they heard you might be arrested for creating them. She seemed very upset about that."

"For God's sake, John, why are you scaring the boy like that! Can't you see how upset he is about what's happened?" Helen's voice brought John back to his senses and he apologized.

"I'm sorry, son. I know you're as worried as I am about Brenda. I'm just crazy with all that's going on and I'm worried about both Brenda and Steve being out there alone. They've never been alone before."

Jack was not about to accept his father's apology. "Before you came home we heard you had agreed to put Brenda and Steve to sleep forever. Is that true? How could you do that to Brenda?

Amanda had walked into the room as Jack spoke and both she and Helen looked at John, waiting for his answer. "Okay, everyone just sit down and let me tell you what's going on."

Then after they were seated, John carefully explained what had happened during the day, including the Albert Mellot statements and Steve's outburst in the presentation. Then he explained how upset Walt, Bob and Sonny were about both Steve's and Brenda's disappearance and told them about the government calls to Walt. Finally, he described the support he had received at the conference closing and how he hoped to be able to continue his work when things calmed down.

Jack was focused on only one thing. "Why do they want to kill Brenda?"

"Nobody at the conference or university wants to kill Brenda. Some of them feel it would be wise to put them to sleep for a while until we can resolve everyone's concerns. It wouldn't hurt them and it probably wouldn't be for long."

Helen understood the position her husband was in and tried to help him. "You know how much your father loves Brenda and Steve. He's trying to do the best he can and I think we need to help him in any way we can."

Their conversation went on for a while longer and Jack and Amanda finally seemed to accept the situation but they weren't very happy about it. Jack, especially, was upset with the idea of putting Brenda to sleep and John realized more than ever, how much the family had come to love her.

After the family meeting, John knew that he had to let Walt and Alex know about Brenda's call. John's feelings by that time were very mixed. He was relieved to hear that Brenda and Steve were all right and were concerned about him, but he was still angry the two hadn't let anyone know where they were. When he called Walt he assured him that if Brenda was concerned enough to call, they would probably still be in the area and easy to find. When he talked to Alex he found out why they couldn't be electronically found. He wasn't very happy with Alex who confessed to teaching Steve about the transmitting system.

Just as he finished talking to Alex, the kids ran into the room. "Dad! They just had a report on television that Brenda and Steve are missing and can't be found. They're warning everyone to look out for them and they're telling people to call the police if they see them. Everyone is talking like they are dangerous or something!"

"Oh for Christ's sake! Somebody at the university must have told the media crowd about them! There goes my support from the conference group and probably everyone else." He called Walt for a short conversation but there wasn't much either of them could do until they found Brenda and Steve. John wondered why his phone hadn't kept vibrating his arm off and then remembered that he had set it to allow only a specific set of numbers to come through to him so that he could get some peace and quiet. Helen had done the same thing with the house phones.

As John lay in bed that night trying to sleep, he wondered how he could ever explain to Brenda and Steve why he had to put them to sleep, maybe never to wake up again.

While John was going through his adventures, Brenda and Steve had spent the afternoon getting ready for Steve's operation. They finally decided to do it just about the time John was arriving home. Finally, Brenda turned Steve's sleep cycle on and started the operation. It took her several hours. When she was finished she woke Steve and they admired his new look. Steve had to congratulate Brenda on what a good job she had done. He looked like a new humanoid. When they watched the media broadcasts they had seen Steve shouting during the presentation and running out of the room. When he saw himself, Steve was actually proud of what he had done but Brenda thought he had looked pretty stupid. They also heard the stories about the government contacting the university and the threats that might be directed at John. They both knew the situation was very serious. At the same time Jack and Amanda were hearing it, they heard the story about their own disappearance and realized their absence was going to make the situation even worse for John and the university. In the discussion that followed after hearing the news, each of them expressed strong feeling about what they should do and it became clear they were in serious disagreement. Steve still insisted that humans, with the possible exception of John's family, Alex and Michelle, didn't really care what happened to them. He felt that even the other team members didn't care about them, other than how it affected their own work. "Brenda, you don't understand. Weren't you listening to me when I was explaining how people feel about us? We're still just an experiment to these people. I've told you how humans treat other life forms when they want to run an experiment like the ones they use to investigate a new disease. They don't care how much suffering that life form endures. That's the way they look at us."

Brenda couldn't agree with Steve because of the way she felt about the Cupar family and the way she was sure they felt about her. "No one in the family or anyone on the team would intentionally hurt us. Look at how we have been brought up. Did anyone ever try to hurt you? Didn't they give you the opportunity to learn and enjoy new experiences?"

"Sure, but everyone except Alex tried to control what I learned."

The discussion went on until about three o'clock the next morning. They could see they weren't going to reach an agreement on the subject so they agreed to disagree. Each one would do what they thought was best. Steve was going to go to Josephine Brook's house to, as he put it, disappear, just as they had previously planned. Brenda decided to try to contact Noreen Stern to see if she still wanted to interview her. She wanted to see if she could help John by turning herself in and letting people see she was not a threat to anybody.

It was easy to access Sonny's database to get Noreen's watch-phone number but she waited until seven o'clock before she called. Apparently, that was too early because when she answered it she sounded half asleep but once she realized whom she was talking to she was quickly wide-awake. "Brenda, where are you? I'm so glad you called me. How can I help you?"

Brenda hoped she wasn't mad at being awakened. "Noreen, I'm sorry I called you so early in the morning but things seemed to be happening so fast I was afraid you might be up and gone already. I got the impression the last time I saw you that you might want to talk to me and even have an interview with me. Was I right?"

Noreen was beginning to get excited thinking about what she was being offered. "You certainly are. When and where do you want to do this? You know, don't you, that everybody is looking for you and your ... brother or what ever you call him? If you start walking around you are going to be picked up by the police."

"I know all that and I have a plan, besides no one knows what I look like any more. I had an operation on my face. I'm also very good at playing the part of a dumb humanoid. Here's my idea. I'd like you to pick me up at nine o'clock and take me to my home at the Cupar house and then conduct the interview in our front yard. I'll give you directions to where you can pick me up. How does that sound?"

Noreen's mind was going a hundred miles an hour at this point. She was going to get an exclusive story that would put her in front of the whole world. "That would be just perfect, Brenda, just give me the directions."

Brenda paused for a few seconds. "Will you promise not to alert the police about our plan and will you really give me a chance to explain some things about myself during the interview?

"Brenda, I hope you realize as soon as we are seen in front of your house, the police will come running, but I'm sure there will be time for us to talk and for you to say what you want to say. Now can I have the directions?" Brenda gave them to her and, as agreed, she picked him up and drove to her home. Noreen had arranged for her camera crew to be set up before she arrived. That turned out to be quite a challenge since they were all sleeping when she called them but they managed to do it anyway. Brenda had made a quick call and talked to Helen about her plan so the family wouldn't be surprised when she showed up. She told her she didn't want to talk to anyone else until she got there and didn't want to hear any objections to her plan. She didn't leave her much choice. After the call Helen stopped the children from going to school and told John to get ready for what was about to happen.

When Brenda and Noreen arrived there were no other media people at the house and that made Noreen very happy. Her crew was set up and ready to roll which made her even happier. As they got out of her car, Jack and Amanda came running over to Brenda with big smiles and outstretched arms. They hugged each other and then wouldn't let go of her. The camera crew caught it all.

Jack was so excited he couldn't stay still. "Brenda, are you okay? We thought we would never see you again."

"Of course I'm okay but how about you two? Have you been doing your homework and getting enough sleep?" Brenda was laughing as she talked and looked like she had just gone to heaven.

By that time, John and Helen had reached them and there was more hugging and laughing, at least by Helen. John wasn't laughing because he knew what he had to do even if everybody else had forgotten. He turned to Noreen. "Thank you for bringing her home. I assume that you know what's going to happen now or are you thinking that some miracle is about to occur?"

She looked him straight in the eye as she spoke. "Professor, let me make one thing clear. This whole thing was Brenda's idea, not mine. She called me to ask if I would like to interview her and when I said 'yes', she insisted that it be here and now, even after I warned her that the police would probably show up before we were finished."

"Okay, get on with it before they do show up." He called Brenda over and told Jack and Amanda to step back while Noreen talked to her. They did so but were not very happy about letting go of her.

Noreen talked to her crew and made sure everything was ready to go, including herself. She stood in front of one of the cameras and introduced herself and the situation she was about to cover. Then she turned to Brenda. "Brenda Cupar, why hasn't anyone been able to see you since you were introduced last Tuesday?"

Brenda repeated what he had been told by John. "I believe professor Cupar has explained to everyone that he and his team were concerned that I was not ready for all the consequences of being exposed to the media and that my development might be negatively affected by the experience."

"That sounds like you have complete faith in him and his team and you feel that they know what's best for you. If that's true why did you run away from them?"

That wasn't an easy question for Brenda to answer. "To tell you the truth, I was afraid. When I talked to my brother, Steve, I found he had been listening to a lot more transmissions on the Global-Net than I had heard and what he had heard scared us both. It sounded like a lot of people wanted us to be permanently turned off and destroyed. In other words, they wanted us to be killed. When we heard the university wanted the team to put us to sleep, we panicked. You see, we're afraid of dying just like you and everybody else."

Noreen wasn't sure how to take his answer. "If you felt the way you just described, why did you come here today? What changed your mind?"

Brenda turned a little as if he was talking not just to Noreen's camera but also to the Cupar family. "I haven't changed my mind. I'm still afraid to die, but I'm more afraid I might hurt my family if I don't turn myself in and I could never do anything to hurt them. I hoped if people could see that I am not a monster or someone who wants to hurt anyone they wouldn't want me to die. All I want to do is to continue to develop myself so I can be of more help to my friends and family. If I have to die today then I will, but it isn't fair for anything to happen to my family. John didn't do anything to hurt anyone. He's only trying to develop technology to help everybody, and that includes me."

By this time Jack and Amanda were crying. John and Helen were close to tears themselves. Just as Noreen was ready to ask the next question, Alex and Michelle, with three other team members, pulled up behind the camera van. Like the Cupars, they all ran over to embrace Brenda and ask if she was okay. They didn't let anything like the presence of Noreen and her camera crews stop them. Noreen couldn't have been happier with the situation. "Brenda, who are all these people? Could you introduce them to us?"

Without hesitating Brenda pointed to her friends. "They're part of my *team!* This is Alex, Michelle, Mary, Marge and Herb. They're the people who made me."

Noreen turned to Alex. "How did you know we were here?"

"Professor Cupar called me to let me know what was happening. We wanted to come over and see if Brenda was okay and see if we could help." Alex, like Jack and Amanda, didn't want to let go of Brenda and hung on to her arm as he talked.

"Where's your brother, if you don't mind me asking? Noreen turned her head toward the team as she asked the question. They looked at each other and finally they all turned their gaze to Brenda.

"Why is everyone looking at me? I don't know where he is." Brenda was sure she was not lying because she really didn't know where Steve was at that exact moment. "I do know he's afraid just like I am. He doesn't want to die either. He can't understand why anyone wants to hurt us." Now that was a lie, but Brenda thought at this point, she had better not start talking about Steve's opinion of humans.

As she finished, two more cars pulled up to the curb near them. It was the police and a group from the university security guards. As they approached, Noreen directed her crew to cover the new situation and she stepped back. John knew the guards and came forward to greet them. "Harold, we were just about to call you and tell you we found Brenda. We were going to bring her to the university. Could you explain to these officers what we're doing and then escort us over to the lab building?"

"Yes sir." Harold held up his hand to stop the officers from coming closer. They're here because they received a call from one of your neighbors. When they got the call they asked us to come over with them. Professor, you know we've been directed to take custody of your humanoid after you turn her off."

Everyone heard him say that and groaned. John held up his hand. "Not turned off, Harold, just put to sleep, until things get straightened out. I'll drive her over myself and you can follow me if that's okay. Just give us a few minutes for everyone to say goodbye."

Harold agreed and Alex and the other team members said that they would follow the cars over to the lab. They knew what John had to do and they knew he would need their help. Helen and the kids were inconsolable. They didn't want to let go of Brenda. John had to pull her away and put her in the car. When they finally started the short drive to the university the caravan of cars was a long one. It included John's car, the security guards, the police, Alex and crew and Noreen in her car followed by her crew's van. As they drove, John and Brenda had a chance to talk. They were both aware this might be the last time they would make this drive they had made so often over the years, but neither one could talk about that.

"Brenda, I want you to understand that this will be just like going to sleep and when you wake up you will find that we will have straightened things out and you'll be able to resume your work." John desperately hoped that what he was saying would actually turn out to be true.

"I hope you're right, John. I know if anyone can resolve these problems, it's you. I have faith in you and the team but even if things don't turn out the way we hope, I want you to know you have given me a wonderful life. I have no regrets about anything you and the team have done." Brenda's voice was sincere but also sad.

"Brenda, I don't care what's decided by the government or the university or anyone else; you are not going to die. I will never let that happen and I'll bet that everyone on the team feels the same way. Just relax and let's get this game over with." With those words John pulled up to the Lab building.

After all the cars in the caravan arrived and everyone understood what was about to be done; John, Brenda and the team went up to the lab. The security guards and Noreen and her crew stayed outside the building. Before they began the process of putting Brenda to sleep, John asked the team to let him talk a few more minutes alone with Brenda.

After the team left he asked the question that Brenda knew he would ask. "Is it true you don't know where Steve is?"

Brenda didn't want to lie to John but neither did she want to put Steve in danger. "Yes, that's true. We couldn't agree on what we should do so we separated and I contacted Noreen Stern about coming home. He said he was going to go into hiding but he didn't give me any details because he felt I might tell somebody else."

John thought for a moment before answering. "You did the right thing, Brenda. I just hope Steve realizes what might happen to him if he runs out of fuel out in the middle of nowhere. We'll keep looking for him and try to bring him back to the university. Now, just relax and let us take care of you."

The team decided the safe thing for them to do would be to both down-load Brenda's brain contents into the lab's central computer and as a backup, put her in a 'power off' mode which would eliminate the need to refuel her while he was in custody. In this mode, none of her long-term memory would be lost and she could easily be restored when they received permission to do so. Strangely enough it never occurred to John or the others to search Brenda's brain download to see if he had been lying about the whereabouts of Steve. The crew felt terrible about what they were doing, but they were very professional and competent as they did their work. When they were finished, they called the security guards to have them carry Brenda down on a stretcher and take her to their headquarters area. As she was carried out of the building, Noreen's crew captured the scene showing what appeared to be Brenda's covered body being carried away by uniformed guards. This was the scene, along with the earlier interview that was broadcast to the world that evening.

At four o'clock that morning, Steve had made the journey over to Jo Brooks's house. He felt the feeling of fear more strongly than he had ever felt before and he didn't like it. Although his appearance had been changed he knew that it was not normal for a humanoid to be walking alone at that time of night. Every time he saw a car or a person he hid at the side of the road but, fortunately, that was a rare occurrence. When he arrived at the Brooks home he hoped that there was no security system guarding the yard outside of the house. There wasn't one and he was able to enter the small tool shed in the back. Once inside, he was able to relax and wonder what the morning would bring.

When the sun came up, Jo Brooks's outside humanoid came over to the shed and began the tasks for the day. It didn't take long for Steve to interrogate the humanoid about its programming and routines. It had no security program and reacted to Steve as if he were just another human. Steve also was able to determine where it stayed in the evening and where it's fuel supply was located. When this was done Steve easily disabled it and placed it in the shed. Then he went to the front door and rang the bell. Her inside humanoid answered the door and Steve directed it to take him to see Jo. She was surprised to see that he was alone but when he explained that he was a warranty replacement for her outdoor humanoid, she seemed to accept the story. He could see that she was a little confused so he explained the unit he replacing was having reliability problems and he was a new and improved model. Steve said that he could actually perform all the duties of both an inside and an outside humanoid with many new capabilities that neither of the existing ones had. After staring at him for about twenty seconds she finally seemed to accept the story and told him to go and work outside. Steve did exactly what he was told but, later in the day, he made some changes to the area where both humanoids stayed at night. He made sure that he could monitor the news and have access to the house optical line so that he could monitor other data sources without doing any wireless transmitting. He didn't want anyone tracking him down if they finally figured out what communication system changes he had made in Brenda and himself. It was fortunate that he had arranged to view the news broadcasts because it allowed him to hear Noreen's interview with Brenda in the Cupar's yard. He also saw Brenda being carried out by the security guards. Even more disturbing was hearing how it was very important it was that he, Steve, be found and how everyone should be looking for him. After hearing her broadcast he knew he had made the right decision but he also felt terribly alone. Not being able to talk to Brenda as he had done all his life made him angry but also helpless.

Over the next few days he managed quite well in his new home and Jo seemed very pleased with him. He found it interesting listening to the discussions on the news and on the Global-Net about what had happened to Brenda. There were, apparently, a lot of people who had been moved by what they had seen transpire in the Cupar front yard but, then, there were also many people who opposed the existence of living humanoids. As a result, he still felt very threatened by the thought he might be discovered and killed. He didn't believe that Brenda was just put to sleep. He was sure that the term they were using meant she had been terminated. He knew that if he was going to make it for more than a few weeks or months, he was going to have to come up with a workable plan for survival.

CHAPTER 11

▼

THE RETURN

While Steve was desperately trying to figure out a plan for his future, fate stepped in to solve his problem. One of the duties of the outdoor humanoid was to drive Jo Brooks to wherever she wanted to go and help her once she was there. Steve had no problem with this job since Alex had taught him how to drive and shown him how to navigate around the town. Usually, Jo wanted to go to the food store or her doctor or other nearby locations. At the end of the first week Steve was quite comfortable being her chauffeur. Then one day when they were driving to the drugstore, Steve noticed in his rear view mirror that Jo had slumped over in her seat. At first, he thought she had fallen asleep but something about the way she looked told him she might be sick. He stopped the car and tried to wake her, but when he realized she wasn't going to wake up, he immediately drove to the hospital in the middle of town. He knew where it was because Alex had shown it to him. When they arrived, he carried her into the emergency room and demanded immediate attention. As the medical people worked on her, he gave them her personal information including the name of her doctor. They seemed surprised that a humanoid was able to do all that but, fortunately, for Steve, they were more concerned about taking care of their patient than wondering about him. After they decided to put her in a bed he drove home and called her son, Tim, in California. During the call he tried hard to play the part of a dumb humanoid that had been programmed to call him in an emergency. He was very convincing.

Tim arrived the next day and stayed until Jo felt she could manage on her own. Apparently, Jo had suffered a brief episode of very slow heartbeat, which caused her to lose consciousness. She had medication to treat the condition but had failed to take it on the day of her episode. She knew she was lucky to have been taken to the hospital so quickly.

After Tim had left for California she called Steve into her living room and told him to sit down. "How did you know what to do when I had my attack last week?"

Steve didn't know how to answer her question and tried to keep playing his humanoid part. "I do not understand your words."

She leaned forward and gently shook her finger at him. "Don't tell me that! I don't care how improved you are. No advanced humanoid could have done what you did for me. I may be old but I'm not stupid. You're the one on the news aren't you? What's that name they keep calling you … Steve, is it?"

Steve didn't know what to do. He just sat and stared at her. She waited a minute and then kept talking. "Are you afraid or something? Do you think I'd do anything to hurt you? You may have saved my life. I want to help you. At the hospital everyone was talking about the missing humanoid and the one they put to sleep. They all seemed to think they should have been allowed to live and that neither of you had done anything wrong."

Finally, Steve realized he had to say something and, listening to her words, he felt somewhat relieved. "Yes, I'm Steve. They killed my sister and she would have never hurt anyone. When I saw that you were sick I had to help you. I didn't want you to die."

Jo reached over and patted his hand. "I'm not going to die and neither are you. I'll help you. We can take care of each other."

And that's exactly what they did. Over the days and weeks that followed, they became good friends. Steve reactivated the outdoor humanoid, which allowed him to become Jo's companion. He drove her around and stayed with her most of the time to keep her company. They talked about many things including what was going to happen to him. Steve began to understand that Jo was not poor and she knew quite a bit about how to manage her money. Together, they came up with an interesting idea. She didn't want him to leave her but knew he wanted to do something other than keep an old lady company. She asked him if he could make another humanoid like himself to stay with her before he left. Steve was already thinking of how he could make another humanoid like himself to replace Brenda and end his feeling of being so alone. They made a bargain. She would pay for the parts and he would provide the know-how to do the job. It was quite an undertaking and Steve was not sure he could do it, but with what he already knew and what he could learn on the Net he felt he should try. The needed parts could also be ordered on the Net but seeing the delivery trucks pull into her driveway did raise some interesting questions both in the neighborhood and within the delivery service. The most exciting part of the project was when Steve and Jo drove over to the university at three o'clock in the morning. Steve broke into the lab to get some needed software and assembly information from the computer, plus a few small parts he needed. Jo played lookout for him. He did it so well the lab personnel never knew he had been there. Jo thought it was one of the most exciting nights of her life.

When the time arrived to activate their creation, Jo was more excited than Steve. Steve transferred a copy of his brain data into the new humanoid and turned him on. Fortunately, for him, he had been through this before when he was born but it was still a scary experience—being in two places at the same time. They named his new self, Alton, because Jo remembered an old boyfriend by that name. Alton had a few minor flaws, which were quickly corrected, and the new Steve tried his best to start thinking of himself as Alton, not Steve. Steve could now concentrate on the next step of his survival plan.

In the days and weeks following the technical conference, Steve was not the only one who had been busy. During the week after the conference, John and his team had concentrated on figuring out how to find Steve but it quickly became apparent they weren't going to find him. They couldn't imagine how he could still be in town without being seen. Most of them finally decided that he must have gone into the nearby mountains and run out of fuel. They were sure someone would come across his lifeless body sometime in the future. In the meantime, they had other things to keep them occupied. For a while, the university suspension of the team's work was in force and, during this time, some of the team members decided to leave to pursue their careers in other directions. Much to John's disappointment, that included Alex and Michelle. Alex had never been able to fully accept the disappearance of Steve and blamed himself for what had happened. He couldn't believe that Steve was 'dead' and never lost hope that he would be found but he felt he could not continue his work after what had happened. Alex and Michelle decided to marry and apply for work at the Johns Hopkins Applied Physics Laboratory near Baltimore. Alex had heard from a friend that the Laboratory was exploring very advanced humanoids for military use. It was through the friend that they were able to make the transfer from the university. John was very sad to lose two such important members of the team but he understood their motivation. He even became Alex's best man at their wedding that spring.

Gradually, as the weeks went by, a totally unexpected phenomenon started to take place at the university. On the technical side, when the paper that John and his team had published was reviewed and studied by the scientific community, the magnitude of their accomplishment was recognized. The primary beneficiary of this recognition was the university and, quickly, John became the champion who had brought fame and fortune to his alma mater. The alumni of the university loved it and the increase in contributions along with an increase in company contributions was a very welcome result.

On the legal side, things were a little more complicated. The various ramifications of the legal issues involved with the living humanoids were discussed, not just in the United States but all over the world. As would be expected with any issue receiving so much attention, national politicians wanted to get involved. As a result, John and Walt were called to Washington to testify before a Senate committee investigating this 'conscious humanoid' development. Bob, as group president, was also called to testify. In a move that surprised everyone but the university personnel, John requested and received permission to reactivate Brenda to accompany them to Washington.

The reactivation was covered by the media like a rocket launch to Mars. John allowed Noreen to have some special privileges for her reporting. He knew that without her performance on the day Brenda was put to sleep, he wouldn't have had the public sympathy that helped him get permission for Brenda's reawakening. She was carried into the Lab but this time the cameras were there to capture every detail. John had arranged for Helen and the kids to be there when Brenda was awakened. She opened her eyes and sat up. "That was quick! Noreen, how did you get in here?" Then he saw Jack and the rest of the family. "Jack! Amanda! What's going on here?"

Jack ran over to Brenda and grabbed her. "Brenda, you're back! Don't you know how long you've been asleep?"

Helen and Amanda were close behind and just hugged Brenda with tears in their eyes. The family was back together again. John tried with some difficulty to keep his composure and attempted to help the media understand what they had just seen. When he looked into Brenda's eyes he saw only gratitude and love which almost caused him to lose control. "Welcome back, Brenda. Just hang in there and I'll bring you up to date later."

Once again the broadcast by Noreen and the others went out to the world and made most viewers very happy for Brenda and her family. As expected, there were others, who looked at her as something very wrong and, for some, even something evil. Brenda was relieved when she was told she could go home. When John told her about going to Washington and testifying before a senate committee it didn't faze her at all, mainly because she had no idea what that meant.

John and Walt, accompanied by Brenda, met Bob at the hotel in Washington several days later. They discussed the various positions, which they should take when they appeared before the committee. Walt was actually enthusiastic about the whole affair. He liked his new fame and appearing on national television was like a wish come true. Bob and John were much more concerned because they realized the effect their testimony might have, not only on themselves but also on their profession. Brenda was so happy to be awake again she didn't care what else was happening. None of them were sure what they would be asked by the senators, who were not technically qualified, as far as they knew, to ask questions about this complex issue. They were mostly lawyers and that fact alone, made John nervous. When they entered the room they were seated beside each other in front of the committee members conducting the investigation. The media coverage was extensive.

The first questions were directed at Walt because of his position as president of the university. Their primary thrust concerned the authorization that the university had given for research into conscious humanoids. As expected, the negative side of Walt's answers exposed the lack of supervision used by the university to control its researchers. It also made John look like a maverick who needed more supervision. On the positive side, Walt went out of his way to praise John's record with the university and his devotion to both his work and his students.

When questioned, Bob, as group president, also praised John's achievements and stressed the high regard John's peers had for him because of his work and integrity. Unfortunately, he also had to admit that John had not consulted with any of his peers on the possible consequences of his project.

Finally, the committee turned their attention to John but it was not difficult to see how eager they were to question Brenda. The committee chairman spoke first. "Professor Cupar, can you tell us briefly why you pursued this line of research and created these humanoids?"

"Senator, from the beginning of my professional career I have watched my colleagues in biological research attempt to study and understand the complexity of the human brain. To their credit, they have done a remarkable job and their new knowledge has been of great benefit to millions of people around the world. I have also noted their frustration at not being able to accurately analyze the information stored in the brain and to know, in detail, how the brain processes this information. About ten years ago while I was working with humanoid electronics, it occurred to me that it might be possible to duplicate some of the brain processes electronically. Our information processing systems had by that time become as complex and in some respects, as capable as the human brain. If this duplication could be done with any accuracy I felt it might give the biological scientists a new tool with which to conduct their research. If the model was created accurately, a particular event could be simulated and a response could be observed. In the process of pursuing this goal, I began to realize I might actually be able to create a conscious electronic being and I proceeded to do so."

The chairman paused and looked around at the other committee members who seemed to be impressed by what they had heard. "All that sounds very reasonable, Professor Cupar, but why was this effort performed in secret? As I understand it, you did not have proper funding for this effort nor did you share your ambitions with your colleagues."

John looked over at both Walt and Pat before answering. "Mister Chairman, to be honest with you, I felt I would be denied the funding and ridiculed for making a request for that type of research. Most of what we do in our research lab has a clear and useful purpose. The results of our work, ultimately, have a business use and, in effect, pay for the research efforts. The connection between my special team's work and the possible usefulness to biological science was very tenuous during most of the years of our effort. It was difficult for us to believe that anyone would be willing to pay for this work"

Now the Chairman had a puzzled look. "Then why did you risk the ridicule you spoke of and the possibility of being accused of improperly using your research funds?"

This time John's answer was immediate and intense. "I did it because I had to! I had to know if it could be done! It's something that's hard to explain to someone who has not been driven by some all-consuming desire to reach a personal goal. The fascination of the challenge was felt not only by me but also by my whole team. All of us gave up an enormous amount of personal time to achieve this goal and the closer we got to success, the more driven we were."

Now everybody in the room was straining to hear every word John uttered. The Chairman's words were also intense. "When you started to see you were going to be successful why didn't you share your findings with your university leaders and your colleagues?

With that question John sat back in his chair and took on a different expression. "As with all human endeavors, including both yours and mine, Senator, the question of competition always comes up. Many of my colleagues are also my competitors and the success of our publications is a determining factor for our retention at our universities and research laboratories. When my team became confident we were going to succeed, we began to fear we would not be the first to do so."

The chairman nodded as if he understood John's point and he turned to the other committee member to allow questions. He first called upon a Senator from John's Home state. Instead of directing a question at John, she asked Brenda a question. "Brenda! That's your name isn't it? What do you think about all that's happening today?"

Brenda was not expecting the question and suddenly sat up straight and looked at her. "I think this is wonderful. Here I am sitting in the Capitol Building of the United States being asked by a Senator for my opinion. I just can't believe this is happening to me."

The Senator had to laugh, as did most of the other people in the room. "Brenda, you're really incredible and if I may say so, also very refreshing. Do you understand why you're here today?"

"Yes, I think so. You're wondering why Professor Cupar created me and from what I understand, you're wondering what I am and what I'm going to do. I guess you're also wondering if I should be allowed to exist. Am I right?"

The Senator didn't say anything at first. She just stared at Brenda. Finally, she spoke very slowly. "That's right, Brenda. What are you going to do? What do you want to do?"

"I want to live!" Brenda paused before going on. "I want to learn and I want to be useful to my family and my team. I think what my team has accomplished is a wonderful step forward that will eventually help people all over the world."

As Brenda spoke everyone in the room was quiet, and, after she finished speaking, they remained quiet. Other questions were asked of both John and Brenda but a special feeling had permeated the room. There was a feeling of awe, as the impact of what John had created and the significance of Brenda was gradually understood, not just by those in the room, but also by those watching through the media all over the world.

The questioning continued but with a new sense of respect for both John and Brenda. John was asked what he intended to do in the future and gave the obvious answer; he would continue his research and would continue to work with Brenda as a member of his team.

The testimony Brenda and John gave that day marked the beginning of a new life for both of them. She became a celebrity in her own right, and began to travel with John to many of the places she had always read about. John made an agreement with the university not to create any more living humanoids. The agreement seemed to satisfy most of the government's concerns but within several months new government regulations were created to make it illegal to create a conscious humanoid without government approval. The regulations also stipulated that when away from their residence they must always be accompanied by the owner or a designated representative. The agreement was fine with Brenda. She was enjoying her newfound fame and was especially proud of having her picture on the covers of some popular magazines. Finally, John, with some very generous funding and support; received permission to put his team back together again. About half of the original team was still available and still interested in resuming their research. For Brenda the most important change was the permission to return to her home. She wasn't alone in her happiness. John and Helen and the kids were very happy with that result. She was a member of their family and that was that!

Brenda tried to contact Steve electronically several times after she was awakened but without success. She finally gave up trying. She was tempted to tell John about Jo Brooks and Steve's escape plan but he felt honor bound not to betray her brother's trust. He was also aware that she was the only one who knew about Steve's new appearance.

The reason Steve did not answer Brenda's calls was that he had turned his original communication system off and had created a new one for Alton and himself. He had watched when Brenda's reawakening was broadcast and was very happy for her when it happened. Jo Brooks had watched with him and they had talked about what effect it might have on Steve. They both agreed that contacting Brenda would probably enable the authorities to find him and Steve was still afraid he would be killed if he was found. He watched the testimony before the Senate committee and later when John's agreement not to create more humanoids was announced, he was sure he had made the right decision.

As Jo had expected, Steve decided he would have to do something besides live with Jo. When Alton was created he felt free to move on without hurting Jo. That was more easily said than done. Since no one knew what he looked like, and he looked like any other humanoid, he felt he could safely be out in public. The problem was that all these humanoids were somebody's property. As property, he was unable to do a number of things he needed to do if he were going to be out there alone. If only he could set up a business of some kind to earn some money, he could probably manage everything else. What he needed was a human partner. Jo was not a good candidate for what he wanted to do so he decided to contact the only other human who might be able and willing to help him. He decided to contact Alex. Jo offered to help. He had her call Alex's number but found out it had been disconnected. After a few other calls she was able to find out he had gone to the Baltimore area. Getting his number there turned out to be easy. Getting a phone that would be almost impossible to trace was also easy. As Steve made the call he felt a feeling that was new to him. He was afraid and excited all at the same time as the call went through.

"Hello." That wasn't Alex. It was Michelle's voice.

"Michelle, this is Steve"

"Steve! Steve, where are you? Are you all right?" She turned her head and shouted. "Honey! It's Steve!"

"Michelle, calm down. I'm fine. I didn't know you were with Alex down there."

"Yes, we got married. Both of us are now working for a place called the Johns Hopkins Applied Physics Laboratory. They call it APL down here. Alex looks like he is about to have a heart attack so I'd better give him the phone. Don't forget to tell us how to call you."

Alex took the phone and tried to control himself. "Where are you? Why didn't you tell us where you were? Do you have any idea of how sick with worry we've been?"

"Yes, I knew you would be but I also knew that everybody was trying to find me so they could kill me. If you knew where I was and somebody found out you knew, you would have been arrested. I didn't want to put you in that position. I'm sorry I caused you and Michelle so much pain."

Alex felt a tremendous sense of relief talking to Steve. "That's okay, Steve. The important thing is that you're okay. Where the hell are you? How are you managing by yourself?"

"Alex, I can't tell you where I am because I don't want to betray the person who's been helping me all this time. With a little assistance, I'm taking care of myself just fine. One of the reasons for my call, other than to tell you I'm all right, is to tell you about an idea I have to survive on my own. I want to come down to Baltimore and get a job working on humanoids."

That caught Alex off guard. "What? You can't get a job, Steve. No one's going to pay you to work as though you're a human. Besides it would become obvious very quickly that you're not a normal humanoid."

"I know all that but what if I pretended to be your new and advanced humanoid and you wanted to rent me out to make some extra money. They would pay you and I could play like a normal humanoid, as I used to do. I know what I'm proposing is not exactly legal, but it might work until we figure out something else."

Alex was torn between his concern for Steve and his feelings against doing anything that might jeopardize his position at APL. "I don't know, Steve. The whole thing sounds kind of crazy to me. Let me talk to Michelle about the idea and then we'll give you a call."

Steve suddenly remembered about Alex and Michelle's wedding. "Oh! I forgot! Congratulations on your marriage! I'm sure both of you must be very happy to be married. Are you going to have any children?"

Alex had to laugh at that. "Thanks, Steve. Sure we're going to have children but they'll come later. We're very happy down here. How about giving us a number where we can reach you?"

Steve became more serious with that request. "I can't give you a number to call but I'll call you in a few days. It's best you don't know too much about where I am now."

"Okay, but don't wait too long to get back to us. Both of us would feel better if we knew where you were but I guess I understand how you feel."

In the days that followed, Alex and Michelle did look into the humanoid servicing businesses in their area. They knew it probably be easy for them since the part of APL they were working in, was devoted to humanoid development for the Navy. They discussed the risks they would be taking if anyone found out what they were actually doing and, finally, Michelle insisted on doing all the contacting. She felt she had less to lose if things went wrong. Alex wasn't happy with her decision but he could see the logic of it. They both realized they were violating the new government regulation but felt they owed it to Steve for all that had happened to him. When Steve called Michelle she had some good news for him. She had found a Baltimore business willing to try using a new type of humanoid once she identified herself as an engineer who worked for APL.

Steve was delighted with her news but when she asked how he was going to get to Baltimore, he was reluctant to tell her. "Don't worry about it, Michelle. I'll be at your door on Sunday and if it's okay with you and Alex, I'll stay with you that night. Then you can take me to my new job on Monday."

Steve had Alton and Jo drive him to Baltimore. Jo was happy to be part of the secret plan of her two friends. She wanted to meet Alex and Michelle but that was the last thing Steve wanted so they dropped him off about a block from where they lived. Jo was not too disappointed. She knew she could follow all the coming events through Alton who was in frequent contact with Steve using their special communication system.

When Alex answered the door he was surprised. He had been expecting to see Steve but, instead, he saw what looked like some other humanoid. Before Alex could say anything, Steve laughed and spoke. "Hi Alex! You didn't think I was gonna walk around looking like I used to, did you?"

"My God, Steve, how did you do that? I would have never recognized you."

"Remember when you let me help you when you changed Bob? That's when I learned what to do and I taught Brenda. She changed me the same night we disappeared. We did it in your storage area and then put the stuff back in your apartment. You didn't even notice the few things that were missing did you?"

After they got over the shock of the new Steve, they spent the rest of the day telling each other about the adventures each of them had lived through between the week of John's presentation and now. Steve vaguely described his new relationship, which allowed him to survive and keep busy but didn't mention the name of his new friend or his new location. He was especially careful not to mention anything that might suggest the creation of his new friend, Alton. Both Alex and Michelle said they missed the excitement leading up to the presentation and their disappointment in what transpired after that. They also explained the difference between working with a young university team and the demands of working as part of APL research team. Steve felt very comfortable being with the two people who cared so much for him. He also cared for them but was determined not to let anything interfere with the execution of his plan.

The next morning as Michelle drove Steve to his new job, they talked more about Michelle's new job with APL and about some of the new technology APL was developing for humanoids. What she described fascinated Steve, especially the material they were developing to make humanoids look even more human in appearance.

When they arrived at the humanoid servicing company, Steve reverted to his dumb humanoid act and Michelle explained to the manager some of her humanoid's advanced features. She explained that she had worked at a university research facility before going to APL and using her own money had created the advance model she was renting. She stipulated the need to bring the humanoid back to her laboratory once a week for checking and servicing. Of course, she didn't have a laboratory but Steve had requested a break once a week if it could be arranged.

In the weeks that followed Steve learned quite a bit about the humanoid servicing business. He already knew how to service humanoids because of his work at the university laboratory, but the business side, which he observed, was all new to him. The frustrating part of his new job was the need to hide his full capabilities from the humans who were working with him. As it was, they were amazed by his ability to communicate across a range of subjects and his ability to almost immediately learn new skills. He also seemed to orient himself immediately within the building and with all the activities that were involved in running the business. The technicians he worked with gradually began to realize that this humanoid could replace them. That was not a happy thought for most of them. The company manager wanted to know if he could rent or buy more like Steve but Michelle explained he was still in the research stage and not ready for production. At the end of the week when Michelle brought him home, Steve was overjoyed. He could be himself and he enjoyed being with his two friends. They were amazed themselves at how much Steve was learning and how interested he was in what they were doing. The extra money they were receiving for his service was a nice bonus.

Finally, the day arrived for step two of Steve's plan. When he was alone with Lauren, one of the company supervisors, he approached her and after making sure they were alone, made her an offer. "Lauren, I have a message for you from my owners. They would like to start a humanoid servicing business of their own and have programmed me to ask you if you would be interested in being the manager of their business. They know there's some risk involved and would, therefore, offer you a twenty-percent increase over your present salary and even some ownership in the business. Because of their positions at Johns Hopkins, they don't feel a direct contact with you would be a safe thing to do and would prefer you deal with them through me. Would you be interested?"

After getting over the shock of talking about a new job with a humanoid she thought about it and decided it would be a nice step up, if it worked out. Steve pointed out to her how the new company would have a cost advantage over the competition because it would be using him and other advanced humanoids. Since she knew the business pretty well herself and knew the other competitors in the field, she felt the company would probably have a good chance for success.

Alex and Michelle knew nothing about what Steve was doing but Jo and Alton did. Jo had agreed to invest her own money in the new business her friends were going to start. That money was used to rent a building and buy the needed equipment and tools for a start-up. Lauren was the one who arranged all these activities using an account set up by Jo, who was guided by Steve and Alton. They had done their homework well, including the legal requirements for creating a new company. Jo, of course, was the legal owner of the company and, for obvious reasons; that presented no problem to Steve. Within a matter of weeks the business was in operation. Steve had told Michelle he was being transferred to a new location and that seemed normal to her. When she picked him up for his weekly break she had no idea of what had really happened. When they got home and Alex and Michelle were having dinner that night, Steve explained his new arrangement.

Steve spoke first. "Michelle, I've really been uncomfortable with the risk you've been taking for me. Today, I didn't really get transferred to a new location. Actually, I started work with a new company; one owned by the person who helped me hide when Brenda was being put to sleep. Now you don't have to worry about someone finding out you are hiding the famous missing humanoid."

Both Alex and Michelle looked at each other and then at Steve. Alex spoke for both of them. "What are you talking about? We aren't afraid of anyone finding out. Look at all the stories we're hearing about Brenda on TV and in the papers. Do you really think anyone would care that we've been helping the only other living humanoid in the world?"

Steve slowly shook his head. "You may or may not be right. I just didn't want to take that chance. It's done and that's that! You won't be getting any more payments for my work but that doesn't mean you won't be seeing me any more. The new company is providing me with a place to stay in the building where they are located, so you don't have to pick me up every week but, if you don't mind, I still want to come and visit you as often as I can."

Alex and Michelle didn't know what to say. They were shocked at the sudden change and impressed by the new arrangement. They still felt responsible for his safety but Steve assured them he would be okay at the new location. They weren't sure what they should do. The loss of their weekly payment was of no consequence, but both of them had a feeling that there was more to the story than Steve was explaining. They were right. Steve had a real feeling of affection for them but, in his mind, he felt a sense of relief at not having to explain what he was actually doing. Now he felt he could concentrate on his plan.

CHAPTER 12

▼

A NEW BEGINNING

The morning ritual at the Cupar household hadn't changed much even with all the events that had taken place since John's famous presentation. John was the first to get up and make the tea, Helen was next and she was the first to get dressed. The family breakfast was still the routine of everybody working around everybody else preparing their own idea of breakfast but there were a few changes. Amanda was now a senior and beginning to worry about applying for college. She had decided not to apply to her dad's university. Both of her parents understood her desire to go to a university other than the one where her father and grandfather were so well known. How could you 'be on your own' when everybody at the university and for that matter, the whole town, knew who you were? Jack was now fifteen and in ninth grade. Like his sister, at the morning ritual, his attention was usually not on breakfast but on the excitement of the day ahead. Brenda came into the room in the middle of the breakfast confusion closely followed by Copper, who had adopted Brenda as his primary caregiver. "Good morning everyone! This is going to be a great day isn't it?"

Brenda had changed quite a bit since her introduction to the world but her unending enthusiasm was still very much a part of her personality. She had matured very rapidly and was now an important member of John's research team. The experience of traveling with John and her exposure to different people and situations had given her a different view of the world. Her relationship to Jack as his big sister hadn't changed very much but both of them had their own special interests. Jack's world was one of sports and young girls while Brenda's was one of complex technology centered on her own brain.

This morning, John and Brenda were getting ready to drive down to Baltimore to attend an event at the Baltimore Convention Center. Brenda sat down opposite John and Helen as they ate breakfast and her excitement over the trip was easy to see. "The Exhibition Center is right on the inner harbor in Baltimore, isn't it John? I love seeing all the boats in the harbor and the big sailing ships they usually have there."

John smiled at Brenda's enthusiasm. "Yes, it's very close to the hotel where we're staying and the hotel is right on the harbor. Maybe we could take one of those water taxis and tour the whole waterfront. We could even look into taking a cruise on the Chesapeake Bay in one of those boats that serve dinner as you cruise down the bay. What do you think?"

"That would be great! How about going fishing for rockfish or blues on the bay?" Brenda was really getting wound up as she thought about what they could do.

"Whoa girl! We're not going on vacation. We're going down there for work with maybe a little bit of fun. If you want to go fishing on the bay we should schedule a vacation trip down there for the whole family." As he spoke Helen turned to stare at him.

When he finished describing his version of a great vacation she spoke. "If you think I'm going to spend my vacation rolling around on a little boat filled with smelly fish, think again! Baltimore is a great city with all kinds of things to do and look how close it is to Washington. If we're going on vacation down there it won't be on a fishing boat. Now that I think about it, if we're really going down there, why don't we visit Alex and Michelle?"

Jack had been watching the conversation standing at the kitchen counter. "I'll go with you, Dad! Why don't we take Copper too? He would go crazy watching us pull in those big blues. Brenda and I will even clean the fish for you. Then we can bring them home for Mom to cook."

Helen turned toward Jack with a look that Brenda had seen many times before but before Helen could speak, she spoke very loudly. "Wait a minute! I didn't mean to start a family argument. All I wanted to say is how excited I am about today's trip!"

John and Helen both laughed and Helen explained. "This isn't an argument, Brenda, it's just breakfast chatter. You and John are going to have a great trip and I'm sure you'll both enjoy it. By the way, speaking of Copper, he seems to be sleeping more than normal these days. Is he okay?"

"I think he is just bored now that we are all so busy and don't play with him as much as we used to. For some reason, I think Jack would rather play with that redheaded cheerleader than play with Copper—you know who I mean! I think her name is Maureen." Brenda knew very well why Jack would rather 'play with' Maureen but she pretended to be puzzled.

Jack looked at Brenda and slowly shook his head and smiled. "Very funny! Dad why don't you build Brenda a handsome playmate so she'll have something to think about besides me and my friends when she's not working?"

Helen held up her hands at this point. "Okay you two, knock it off! I've got a busy day ahead and I don't have time to listen to the two of you and your silly conversation. I'm going to be late so, goodbye and have a safe trip." She kissed John and headed for her car.

As Jack left the room he turned for a last word. "I still think we should go fishing on the bay. Brenda are you gonna be back in time to come to the game on Saturday?"

"Of course we are. Would I miss watching you score all those touchdowns against the Blazers?" Brenda was Jack's biggest fan. She shook her hands in the air and waved goodbye to Jack.

After everyone had left the room John and Brenda reviewed what they were going to bring with them for their overnight stay in Baltimore. When they finished putting their stuff in the car, John asked Brenda to drive. He knew that was the safe thing to do because Brenda didn't get tired or distracted by the sights along the way. It was a three-hour drive down to Baltimore and the scenery at this time of the year was beautiful. All the leaves had changed to their autumn colors and the rolling hills along the way gave them an excellent view of everything. This was a very pleasant part of the world. It had four distinct and enjoyable seasons and it did not have earthquakes, volcanoes, mudslides or hurricanes. As John usually said 'What else could you ask for?"

The purpose of the trip was to see an exhibition of some of the latest models of humanoids now being introduced into the market and to hear a few presentations about what would come in the future. Neither John nor Brenda were scheduled to speak but, because they were now very well known, they knew they would be expected to answer questions from the media. As they drove, they talked about what they should say and what they shouldn't say when questions were asked.

"John, do you think we should tell the media about our latest findings concerning human mental processes we've developed this year or about the interchange of data we're having with the British group at Cambridge?"

John knew these subjects would come up but he felt it would be inappropriate to go into any detail about their work at this type of exhibition. "Brenda, everyone knows that we're using your brain structure to investigate possible mental sequences in human brains which might explain certain behavior patterns but other than confirming we're doing this type of work, I don't want to disclose any specifics about our findings. As far as our coordination with the other international centers, I'm pretty sure everyone knows that's happening. What they don't know is our specific agreements with each of those centers and we can't disclose that information. We don't have that permission from those centers so we can only confirm we are working with them, not how we're working with them."

Brenda nodded her head as she drove. "You mean we aren't going to tell anyone anything, right?"

"Right, if you are not sure what to say, don't say anything. Refer them to me. Now let me enjoy the scenery but if you see a McDonalds, stop so I can get a cup of coffee. They do have good coffee."

As they drove and John relaxed, the conversation he had with Helen last night kept going through his head. She was becoming more concerned about the long term consequences of Brenda's creation now that the initial furor of her existence had died down. He remembered her words very clearly. "What do you think will happen when both Brenda and the world finally realize she's not going to age? She will see you and I grow old and die and then watch while Amanda and Jack grow old and die. For the first time since life began on this planet, a life form will have the ability to live indefinitely with just some routine upgrades. You have made it possible for a living mind to be transferred to a new body. Have you thought about what that means?"

John had thought about it during his creation project and it was more than a passing thought but he had been so absorbed by the technical challenge of creating Brenda and Steve that at the time, long-term concerns seemed like an unnecessary distraction. Now he realized that these questions would have to be addressed because Helen wouldn't be the only one who would raise them. These were not technical questions. They were philosophical questions and philosophy was not John's strong suit. His thoughts were periodically interrupted by Brenda's comments on the scenery and, of course, by the McDonald's coffee. Finally they reached Baltimore and his mind was drawn to the business of their arrival. He knew that someday Helen's concerns could be a serious problem and, maybe, his main occupation.

Brenda was happy to see their hotel really was right on the waterfront at Baltimore's inner harbor. Even better, her room allowed her to look out over the waterfront. She agreed with John that they should have their own rooms. After unpacking, which took about two minutes for her, she went out onto the little balcony of her room and started to sit down.

"Hi Brenda! Remember me?"

Brenda jumped up so fast she thought for a moment that she was going to fall over the railing. She stood there and frantically looked all around and finally realized what had happened. "Steve! Is that you? Where are you?"

"Yes, it's me. Who the hell else would be talking to you through our old com system? I'm in the hotel and I saw you and John check in."

Brenda was surprised, amazed and puzzled. "I didn't see you down there. Why didn't you come over to us? This is going to make John's day. No, it is going to make John's year. He is going to be so relieved that you're back! Come on up to the room so I can see you."

"Hold on, Brenda. You don't understand. I don't want John to know I've contacted you. You've got to promise not to tell him or I am out of here and you won't hear from me again." Even over their com system Brenda could tell how serious Steve was.

Brenda paused a moment before she replied. "Come on, Steve, you aren't still worried about everyone wanting to kill you are you? I'm still alive and now there's even some consideration of creating others like us in labs all over the world. Nobody is talking about killing us and, in fact, I've become quite popular."

Steve's answer was very quick. "You're still an experiment, Brenda! What do you think the reaction would be if you said you were going to buy a house next door to someone here in Baltimore? Let's not go any further with this right now. If you promise to keep our communications a secret for now, we can continue this discussion at a later time. I just wanted to let you know I'm okay and to re-establish contact with you so we could talk about things like we used to do. I don't want you to know what I look like now because they still have access to your brain. Yes, I know you think I'm paranoid and maybe you're right. When you come over to the Exhibition Center, look around. I might be there and then again I might not be. Remember, don't tell John about me."

Brenda didn't want the conversation to end. "Steve! Don't stop now. I've got a million questions to ask you. Where are you living? Where are you getting your fuel? What are you doing?"

"Hold on, Brenda! We can get into those things later. I'm busy and I know you and John are too, so let's stop talking for now and I'll get back to you. Don't try to contact me with this system because I don't normally use it any more. I'll contact you." With those words there was suddenly silence and Brenda knew it was over.

About ten minutes later, John rapped on the door to get Brenda for the trip over to the Center. John could sense that Brenda wasn't totally okay but he wasn't sure why. "Is your room okay, Brenda? Did you forget something?"

Brenda realized she had better get her act together or John would know something was wrong. "No, the room is fine. I am just thinking about some of those sailing ships in the harbor. It must have taken great courage in the old days to head out into the open sea with only the wind as your power source and with no knowledge of what conditions would be out there."

John seemed satisfied that Brenda was just dazzled by everything she was seeing. Since the Center was so close to the hotel they walked over to it and that allowed them to see more of the activities of the inner harbor area. It was a busy place with all kinds of things to do and Brenda wanted to do them all. When they entered the Center they were pleased to see the large number of exhibits. As they walked around and studied the exhibits even they were surprised at the number of new humanoid applications. They were recognized along the way and had to take time to speak with their admirers. When they were about halfway through the exhibits they came across a really interesting one that stopped them. The company name on the display was 'The New World Company'. There was one female human sitting in the back but the front booth was manned by two humanoids that were dispensing brochures. John said he had heard about this company from some of his friends. Apparently, it was relatively new and, not only was it very competitive, it also had some unique products. The company was claiming their humanoids could be trained for any task that a human could perform, no matter what the task involved. Brenda stood back while John asked one of the humanoids a few questions. "If I wanted to have one of your humanoids teach a class on differential equations at my university, would that be possible?"

The humanoid looked up and smiled at John. "Yes, but we would need a detailed curriculum of the course to insure that it satisfies the university requirements and we would need at least one month's notice before we could begin."

John was surprised at the answer and asked another question. "How about a class on human anatomy including lab work for a group of medical students?"

This time the humanoid paused for five or six seconds before answering as if he were thinking about the question and John realized he must be accessing a program from a different location. "Yes, we can do that but we would need at least six month's notice and our price would have to be worked out over a longer period than our normal quoting time. Are you serious about these requests because if you aren't there are others waiting to speak with us and we don't have a lot of time for guessing games?"

As soon as the humanoid had answered John's first question Brenda knew that John was talking to Steve but John didn't know that. Brenda tried communicating electronically to Steve but got no answer except for the fact that the humanoid immediately looked at her and very slightly shook its head once.

After the second question, John stepped back to let someone else talk to the humanoid. "Brenda, did you hear what he said? I think the math course answer is probably true but human anatomy? No way! Who do these guys think they are? Let's keep going, we still have a lot of ground to cover."

Brenda didn't respond to John's comments directly because he didn't want to get into a discussion in which he might say the wrong thing and give Steve's secret away. They continued looking at exhibits until they had almost reached the end of the first row and then out of nowhere, Brenda heard a voice on her electronic system. "I told you this was going to be interesting. Were you surprised by anything?" It was Steve.

Brenda looked around and saw a humanoid up ahead looking at her. She knew that it couldn't be Steve because they had just left him back at the New World booth. She stopped dead in her tracks. Now he understood what was going on. "Okay, how many of you are there?"

"What's wrong, Brenda? Why did you stop?" John had walked a few steps ahead before he realized that Brenda wasn't by his side.

Brenda realized that she had to come up with something fast. "I just had an idea of how that New World Company is enhancing their humanoid's performance. They must be using a human at a remote location to control the humanoid for actions requiring actual thinking. If I am right, they are fooling the public about how good their humanoids really are. What do you think?" As she talked she continued to wait for Steve to answer, but there was only silence.

"You might be right but, then, if someone actually bought one of their humanoids for a task that required that capability how could they get away with it? Maybe we should buy one for the lab and see if they have designed something really unique." John was convinced that Brenda was totally absorbed trying to figure out the problem. They continued to tour the Center and as they walked, Brenda wondered if she would be contacted again.

After they had finished looking at all the exhibits and before the evening presentations began they went back to the waterfront and took a ride in one of the water taxis. It was amazing how much the city had been affected by the development of the harbor waterfront and seeing the waterfront by water taxi was a lot of fun. John and Brenda agreed that coming here with Helen and the kids really would be a good vacation even without worrying about going fishing. As they enjoyed the ride, Brenda found that not being able to tell John about Steve was driving her crazy. The more she thought about it the more she realized that he couldn't keep her promise to Steve. This situation was too important not to have John's guidance and, besides, the results of anything that happened would affect John's life as much as hers. He waited until they were walking away from the taxi dock near the hotel and, when no one else was near, he told John that Steve had spoken to her.

John's reaction was as he thought it would be. "What did you say? What—When—How—For God's sake, Brenda, why didn't you say something? Where is he? How is he?"

Brenda thought John was going to have a stroke, the way he was carrying on. Finally, John calmed down and Brenda explained to him what had happened in his room and in the Exhibition Center including the possibility that there might be more than one Steve. He made sure that John understood that Steve had made her promise not to tell anyone about the contact. "John, you've got to pretend that you don't know anything about the contact or Steve is going to disappear again."

"Yes, of course, you're right. It is important that you keep in contact with him so we can find out what he's doing and what his plans are. We have got to make him understand he's in no danger and will be better off working with us and the International Committee."

John wasn't ready for Brenda's next comment. "Are you sure of that, John? Remember, somehow I think he has created a duplicate of himself and the international agreement, as I understand it, was that no one could create a conscious humanoid without permission from the Committee. Isn't it possible that they could order the unapproved humanoids destroyed?"

John wasn't sure what to say and he paused before answering. "You've raised a good point. I don't know what they would say if they found out Steve had created more humanoids like himself. There's got to be a way out of this mess without anybody getting hurt. It's critical that somehow you stay in contact with him so we can work out a plan that will be acceptable to the Committee. My God, I wish I could talk to him myself."

They agreed to continue with their visit, as if nothing had happened and when Steve made contact, Brenda would attempt to convince him it was safe to stay in contact.

As the evening went on Brenda was beginning to doubt that she would hear from Steve but as soon as she entered her room after saying goodnight to John, Steve spoke to her. "Do you still use a sleep cycle, Brenda? I do sometimes just to give myself a break."

"Hi, Steve! Yes, I do and I think it makes sense to use it. Everybody needs a periodic break from thinking, not just humans and other organic life forms. Why don't you come on up to my room. I saw you today or at least some of you, so what you look like is no big secret. How many Steves are there now?"

Steve gave a quick laugh. "Why do you think I've created another me? Don't answer that. Just give me a couple of minutes and I'll be right up."

He was at Brenda's door in about five minutes and when he walked in both of them instinctively grabbed each other's hands and held them without saying a word for several seconds. Steve spoke first. "In 2028 when I saw them carry you out of the lab I thought I would never see you again. I felt like dying myself. I had no one to talk to and I was sure they would find me and kill me."

Brenda nodded her head. "It must have been awful for you. When I came out of my sleep I wasn't sure if John had scanned my brain to find out if I had known where you were but since nobody seemed to know where you had gone, I kept my mouth shut. I wasn't about to break my promise to you. Did you really go to that old lady's house?"

Steve was feeling a wonderful sense of relief finally to be able to tell some of his story to his sister after all this time. He told Brenda about going to live with Jo Brooks and how he had worked as a gardener, but he didn't tell her about Alton and his continuing relationship with Jo. Steve loved his sister but he knew his sister's brain was still available to humans who might someday want to find him. He told her an approximation of the truth. He explained to Brenda how hard it was trying to survive, thinking he was the only living humanoid, trying to earn a living while at the same time hiding his consciousness; hiding the fact that he was alive. He didn't mention Alex and Michelle but did say he was working at the New World Company doing humanoid servicing. He didn't want to admit that but Brenda had seen him there so he had no choice. He didn't mention that it was, for all practical purposes, his company. As they talked, it became clear to Brenda that Steve's experience of feeling totally alone with no one to talk to had deeply affected him. Steve was both afraid of and contemptuous of humans. He went on to tell how exhilarated he felt when he heard that Brenda was being allowed to wake up and live again. He told of how proud he was when he realized how much Brenda was admired and respected as she began to travel around the world. Brenda asked Steve why, when he heard and saw all this, he didn't contact John to tell him he was okay and even earning a living.

Steve's answer was somewhat evasive. "I read about both our country government regulation and a new international agreement where permission has to be obtained from some committee for androids like us to be created. I realized I was a runaway that probably would be considered a threat and thus would be killed."

Brenda decided to ignore that answer. "So how did you learn to create another you? Why did you create another you?"

Steve looked at Brenda and threw up his hands. "Okay, yes, I did make another one like us. I was lonely. I wanted someone to talk to as we used to do. I also needed someone to help me. How did I know how to do it? You would be surprised how easy it is to access the lab computer at the university and besides I learned a lot just watching and listening to Alex and Michelle and the other team members. I even broke into the lab once to get some parts and, from what I understand, no one even knew I had been there. I admit it was weird when I made a brother. Do you remember how you felt when they first made me, it's like you're in two places at the same time. With the Com system you're talking to yourself from two different places. Of course, as soon as the new you begins to receive and store information from a new location and a new body, the new you becomes a separate person. It seemed like it only took a day and it was like having a brother that was both you and a separate person, all at the same time. All I know is that suddenly, I had someone to talk to and I wasn't alone any more."

Brenda sat there in amazement. Her brother had done so much and was able to actually survive by himself with no one watching over him. "That's incredible, Steve. Did you only make one of you?"

Steve knew that question was coming and he hated having to lie to Brenda but he had to do what he had to do. "Yes, I only needed one brother to share things with and both of us are down here in Baltimore. I wasn't sure what would happen if I made another one. It probably would have been very confusing trying to talk to each other."

Bob had to laugh at this point. "That would have been pretty funny! I can just imagine one of your conversations. 'Steve, look out! There is a car about to hit you! Who said that? I did. Steve did. Which Steve? The one who's looking at the car about to hit you."

Steve laughed too because that would be funny. Actually, he had solved that problem when he made Jenny and Raymond. He had modified his new communication system to automatically identify the one talking. All those conversations with Alex and Michelle about the new type of skin they were using for the military humanoids had really paid off. Ray and Jenny looked very human and it was difficult to tell that they weren't human without actually touching the skin on their hands and faces.

Before Brenda and Steve finished talking, Steve promised to stay in touch but still made it clear he would do the contacting and not Brenda. While their conversation was taking place John had decided to call Alex to find out if he knew where Steve was staying and how to contact him. When Alex got the call he wasn't sure what to say because of his promise to Steve. After John explained Steve's contact with Brenda at the hotel and Convention Center, Alex hesitated and then decided the right thing to do was to tell John the truth. He was surprised at John's reaction. He was delighted that Alex and Michelle were in contact with Steve. What a relief! Now he could explain to everyone that the missing humanoid was actually under the supervision of one of his original team members. Of course, Alex and Michelle had no idea what Steve was really doing.

CHAPTER 13

▼

A SIMPLE MATTER OF
SURVIVAL

Steve was surprised at how important it was for him to be able to talk to Brenda again. After John and Brenda left to return to the university he decided to change his plans to include more contact with his sister. Steve knew that even with their special relationship, he would have to continue lying to her. He had worked too hard on his plan to risk it at this point.

After creating Raymond and Jenny in the lab at the New World Company, the trio worked on two problems. It was fortunate they had Lauren to manage the daily business for them and also fortunate that for most of the time she stayed out of the work area of the building. The first problem they tried to solve was improving their duplication of human behavior. They felt it was important to do so if they were to mix among humans without detection. Jenny had the hardest time because Steve's brain was male oriented. Just as Steve had difficulty when Brenda's brain information was transferred to him, Jenny had trouble when Steve's brain contents were transferred to her. Steve had been able to obtain the team's female brain structure from the University computer system but had the same difficulty the team encountered when creating him with Brenda's brain information.

Making Jenny appear to be female was easy but making her think and act female was more of a challenge than Steve had expected. To make her speak and use body language as a human female does was most difficult. When Lauren was introduced to Jenny, she had no idea that the new human-looking humanoid was actually alive. She was told that it was a model designed to help women be comfortable around humanoids. Jenny was stationed in the front office and Lauren was told that the humanoid was programmed to attempt to duplicate some of her actions and speech and, in that way, become more feminine in its actions. Much to Lauren's amazement, Jenny learned very quickly and, because she looked so human, Lauren found herself talking to her as if she was one of her friends. She thought that was really weird.

The second problem they felt it was critical to solve was determining how to obtain a legal identity for Raymond and Jenny. Alton assisted them in this effort since only his electronic presence and not his physical presence was needed to research for information. As might be expected, their research led them into the world of illegal identity operations. They quickly found out that their problem was one shared with many humans, especially those who were illegal immigrants. Their search on the Net also educated them about the tremendous variations of legal control used by various countries around the world. This information made Steve realize that setting up a business in another country might be easier and safer than setting up one in the United States. Steve and the others were surprised at how easy it was to obtain an illegal identity. They were thankful for the United States privacy protection laws. All it took was money and a little know-how to obtain a birth certificate and a social security number.

Once they thought they had solved these two problems, they tried traveling to several locations to test their solutions. They found that Raymond and Jenny could travel almost anywhere and be accepted as human. The exceptions were where they had to go through security detectors that identified them as humanoids. Fortunately, money solved that problem, too. They were able to convince one of the people they had come in contact with in their identity search to accompany them and pretend to be their owner. This accomplice thought he was being hired by someone who owned them, but who wanted to remain anonymous. As long as the money flowed he didn't care why they wanted to travel or what they wanted to do once they got to where they were going. The success of their test travels gave Steve confidence he was on the right track to execute the rest of his plan. The money flow from the humanoid servicing business turned out to be the answer to almost all of their problems.

While this activity was going on, Steve had called Brenda a few times since her Baltimore visit and, during these conversations; Brenda had tried to convince Steve to reveal his future plans. She hadn't told Steve that John knew about their meetings and about the other brother Steve had created. Brenda was eager to talk to this new brother, Alton but Steve was still worried that John could access Brenda's brain. Anything Alton told Brenda might become known to John and then, perhaps, to other humans.

Finally, Brenda convinced Steve to come to the University for a 'face-to-face' talk. Since Brenda had no idea what Alton looked like, Steve decided it would be smart to drive to the university himself, even though Alton was still living with Jo Brooks only a few miles away. Steve told Brenda he wouldn't go into any of the university buildings, so they agreed to meet at a small park close to the Cupar house.

When Brenda approached the bench where they had agreed to meet he saw Steve was already there. "Hi, Brenda! Have a seat. You know I'd forgotten how beautiful this part of the world really is. We're lucky to have been born here."

Brenda sat down and turned to Steve. "It's nice to see you again, Steve. Do you remember the first time Alex brought you over here for a walk through the park with John and me? Who would have guessed that we would be meeting here someday, looking over our shoulders for anyone who might be watching us?"

Steve smiled and shook his head as he spoke. "We were pretty naïve in those days but I think we're smarter now. You said you wanted to talk more about some of the topics we've been discussing over the last few weeks. What's bothering you?"

Brenda stood up. "Let's walk as we talk. I can think better that way." Steve stood up and they started down the park path. "Each time we've talked, you've had a lot to say about how much danger we're in. You also seem to be convinced humans are going to destroy themselves and, probably, the whole planet because they can't get along with each other. What does one thing have to do with the other? I don't understand and I'm not sure what these things have to do with your great plan. You'll explain the connection, right?"

"Brenda, maybe the difficulty we're having in talking about these things is caused by our different perspective on what the future holds for us. You seem to be very content with your life as a member of John's research team and being the world's wonder humanoid. I guess you think that's going to go on forever. Well, I think you're wrong and I think you're in for a shock one of these days. I just hope you survive it."

Brenda slowly shook her head as they walked. "What makes you so pessimistic? Other than those initial concerns expressed during the conference, nobody has threatened you or me with any harm. I know many things will change as time goes by, but I don't feel threatened by any of the changes that I think might happen."

Steve was annoyed by Brenda's apparent condescending attitude. "Have you forgotten they almost killed you, Brenda? A lot of people wanted you destroyed. Don't you remember the conversation we had in Alex's storage room during the conference?"

Brenda was trying to be patient with Steve and tried to keep her voice calm and serious. "Sure, I remember what you said. You described how the human sexual and survival instincts determine most of their actions. You then went on to say how the tribal instinct and the struggle for tribal position are part of the survival instinct. You explained your circles of security theory, in which each human identifies him or herself with a number of different groups or tribes, as you called them. I think the tribes you were referring to were a person's race, nationality, religion and a bunch of other groupings. Then you went on to say that these tribal divisions block the rational actions people need to take to solve most of the world's problems. All that may be true, but I still don't see what all that has to do with us and our lives."

Steve stopped walking and turned to Brenda as he answered. "Maybe it's because you forgot I also said that it was very important that we understand what makes humans behave the way they do. Without that knowledge we have no way of predicting what they might do to us. Remember what else I said? We aren't in any of their tribes and millions of them think we are evil and should be destroyed. Even the ones who don't feel that way think we're just machines and are just part of an interesting experiment. They probably feel we should be turned off when the experiment is finished."

"What do you mean; we're not in any of their tribes. I'm part of the Cupar family and I'm an American. I'm welcome wherever I go in this country."

"How naïve can you get? Legally you're a machine, Brenda. You belong to the university and you're on loan to the Cupar family. As for your citizenship, you just happen to have been made in the United States but that doesn't make you a citizen. Is the computer in your lab a citizen? Do you think anyone is going to protect you when the religious conservatives in Congress pass a law that makes you illegal?"

Now Brenda was annoyed. "What's with you on this religious thing? Why do you think it's such a big problem between humans and why do you think it's such a big threat to us? The Cupar family goes to church all the time. They even took me a couple of times. All they talked about was love and peace among each other and about God."

"Brenda, are you sure that you know what religion is?"

"Sure, it's a belief in God, who is the creator of everything and a belief that God expects everybody to believe in Him and live their lives by following certain rules of conduct. Most religions believe that God created their religion a long time ago and has guided its followers ever since. The followers trust that if they lead a good life, they will be rewarded and if they don't, they will be punished. Yes, I know that's an over simplification of a complicated subject. I also know there's lots of variations among the different religions about the nature of God and the way life is to be lived but that's generally correct, isn't it? Why is all that so important to us?"

Steve looked at Brenda with one of his 'I don't believe you said that' looks. "You amaze me, Brenda. For someone who's so smart how can you be so dumb about some things? People's attitude toward us and our existence will be determined primarily by their religious beliefs. In religions all over the world humans are taught what to believe and that God will punish them if they question those beliefs. When it comes to us, I think I know what they're going to be told. Do you believe in God?"

This time Brenda was the one to stop walking. "Do you remember when Michelle picked me up to take me to the lab for my appearance change? During the drive we had an interesting conversation about whether I had a soul or not and the answer I got was very confusing to me. When we got to the lab everybody made a joke about it but, to me, it was a serious question. In the years since that time I've done some research and some thinking about the existence of God. When I began to understand in a very limited way, the size and complexity of the universe and the mystery of what exists I was overwhelmed with wonder. It really doesn't look like it's an accidental happening. So, yes, I believe in God. I believe God created the universe and everything in it."

Steve was surprised at Brenda's answer. "I'm impressed! You've really thought about this issue and you must have done a lot of research on the subject. With all that thought about God, why is it that you don't realize how important religion is to our acceptance by humans?"

Brenda paused before answering. "Now that I think about it, you're probably right. Religion will be important in determining what people think about us. Since God didn't create us, at least according to the beliefs of most religions, no one who believes in them will accept us as being alive in God's eyes."

"So what do you think God thinks of us?"

With that question Brenda had to smile as she answered Steve "You know a lot of humans may be unhappy with our existence, but I don't think God is. I believe God values us as much as he values any life form, no matter how it came into being. There are probably billions of life forms in the universe that are even stranger than us. I can't imagine God being concerned with which arrangement of molecules supports a life form as long as it's alive; and we, my friend, are alive! Just imagine what the judgment of most religions would be if a human's brain was moved into a humanoid body. Right now, humans receive many substitute body parts, which are not human and sometimes not even organic. It's not hard to imagine that this approach might someday be carried to the extreme of substituting all the body parts except the brain to keep a human living. Do you think God would treat this person any differently than any other person and decide that the person didn't have a soul or wasn't alive? I don't think so." This was the first time Brenda had ever told anyone about her belief in God and she felt good about being able to do so.

Steve was fascinated by Brenda's comments. "That was fantastic, Brenda, maybe you should start a new religion. Where would you build your church or synagogue or mosque or whatever?"

Brenda didn't see the humor in Steve's comment. "In my opinion you don't need a building to worship God and you don't need a leader to do your thinking for you. You worship God by how you treat other people and other life forms and how you treat the planet we live on. In other words, you worship God by how you live your life. What do you believe, Steve?"

Steve didn't respond to Brenda's words at first and they continued to walk together. "To tell you the truth, I haven't given it nearly as much thought as you have. As I've tried to educate myself about this world and the humans in it, the subject kept coming up but my reaction has been very different from yours. I don't believe in God. I have no idea of how our universe was created and, at this point in my life, I don't care. As I learned about human behavior I learned most humans say they believe in their religions but their actions say otherwise. From what I can see, they say they believe just to be accepted in their tribe, but their actions consist mostly of what satisfies their desires and improves their position within their tribes. If that is their attitude toward religion, I don't want any part of it. My concern is survival. You mentioned the importance of living a good life. How much thought have you given to how you will live your life?"

Brenda was disappointed in Steve's answer. "I'm sorry to hear that, Steve. I think life is more than just a struggle for survival. I want to live my life as John does, loving his family and friends and working in an area that fascinates him. Don't get me wrong, I appreciate your concerns and I think we should work to solve these problems."

"Brenda, I still don't think you understand. Have you ever thought about how different our lives will be compared to the lives of humans? We won't age the way humans do and, as technology advances, we can be changed to take advantage of those advances. Don't you think that fact will eventually sink in to the humans that are following our existence? If I know human behavior, I think it's going to make many of them very uneasy and very nervous about our continued existence. I think we need to plan for that time and be ready for all the possibilities that can happen."

"Okay, maybe you're right but I don't think we can do all the planning on our own. I think we need to talk to John and the crew and get their views and advice."

Steve shook his head and the look on his face told Brenda that was not what he had wanted to hear. "What do you think they can add to our thinking? I doubt that they have even thought about what will happen to us in the long run. Besides, they don't know what I've been doing or know that I've created another brother."

Brenda knew this moment would come but she felt he had kept the truth from Steve long enough. "Yes they do! I told John about our contact while we were still in Baltimore and when he called Alex and Michelle to find out what they knew, he found out about your job and everything."

This time Steve stopped cold and just stared at Brenda. He was angry but racing through his head was the fact that Brenda wasn't the only one who had lied. When he spoke, it was in a quiet voice. "What did you think was going to happen when you told him? Weren't you afraid he would send someone to pick me up and have me killed as they tried to kill you?"

"No! John would never do anything like that. When he found out you were okay and actually taking care of yourself, he was both relieved and happy. I think the only people he has told about finding you have been his most trusted friends like Bob and Diane up in Rochester. When he realized that Alex and Michelle were staying in touch with you, that made him feel great because they care for you, too."

"Alex and Michelle promised never to tell anyone I'd contacted them and so what do they do, tell John the first time he calls them. I guess maybe I can't trust anyone." He felt a twinge of guilt when he said that, realizing that he had lied to all of them.

"Get off it, Steve. You know just as well as I do, these people care about both of us. All they want to do is help, so why not let them? John is dying to talk to you and see your new brother. He told me that if the appropriate time ever arrived I should make you an offer."

"What do you mean an offer? An offer for what?"

"Several universities have approached John, both here and overseas, to lend them a living humanoid. That's what we're called now. He thinks you or I or even our new brother might enjoy a stay in someplace like Japan or Great Britain. What do you think? Would you be interested?"

"Let me get this straight. We would go over to these places and do some sight-seeing or, more likely, we would go over and they would take us apart to see what makes us tick?"

Brenda could see that, in spite of his words, Steve was interested. "It would be like in the lab here at the university. We would work with a team who would hook us up to some equipment and then, with our help, explore some of our unique capabilities. When we weren't working I'll bet they would be glad to show us around and let us learn something about their country and themselves. It sure sounds like fun to me."

While Brenda was talking, Steve's mind was racing ahead to see the connection with his own plans. Having one of the brothers overseas might be a great opportunity to learn how to operate in a country other than this one. "You may be right, Brenda. Perhaps I am being too paranoid about the whole thing. Would you be one of the ones going overseas?"

Brenda felt relieved that Steve actually liked the idea. He didn't seem to be mad at her for telling John. "Maybe, John and I haven't discussed any of the details yet. He's waiting to find out if you or your brother would be interested. What's our brother's name anyway?"

"Alton. That was the name of an old boyfriend of Jo Brooks. He lives at Jo's."

"Why didn't you tell me that down in Baltimore? We could have been talking and even seeing each other all this time."

Steve wasn't sure how to answer that now but what he said was the truth or, at least, some of the truth. "I didn't know John already knew about him and I wasn't going to risk anyone seeing him talk to you. Besides, why worry about that now. Let's talk about this overseas thing. How about telling John before I agree to go overseas or have Alton go overseas, I want to have him get the university to agree to our terms of return."

Brenda wasn't sure what Steve was driving at. "What are your terms of return?"

"First, we would be allowed to live with Jo Brooks and have no restrictions on where we go and what we do, as long as we don't do anything illegal. Second, we would both be allowed to rejoin the team and work in the lab during the day and third, we would not be forced, against our will, to go overseas or anywhere else."

Brenda shook her head and laughed. "What, you're not going to ask for a key to the president's house or a limousine to drive you around? To quote your earlier words, you are owned by the university and are on loan to nobody. Remember?"

"You can laugh all you want. Those are my terms and if we can't reach an agreement, I'm out of here and so is Alton"

Brenda held up her hand. "Okay, don't have a fit. I'll tell John what you want and we'll see what he says. I know John and Walt, our president, have a close relationship so maybe you can get what you want. How can I reach you?"

"Just call Alton at the Brooks house. I'll tell him that he'll be hearing from you, but remember, if anything happens to him none of you will ever hear from me again."

Brenda's answer was very serious. "I don't want to ever lose contact with you again and I think you feel the same way. We're going to work this thing out so don't do anything silly. I have faith in John and if anything can be worked out he's the one who will do it. Now let's call it a day so I can get back to John with your answer or, should I say, your ultimatum."

They parted and Steve went over to the Brooks house for the night. He decided that if he didn't hear anything by the end of the next day he would head south again. He knew he had to wrap up his business in Baltimore before he did much else up here. When Steve had told Lauren he was leaving and he was taking Jenny and Raymond with him she was upset. Then he told her she could not only manage the business but would actually become the owner of ten percent of it. Although she would not have her special humanoid helpers she felt she could do well with it and was quite happy. Now Jenny and Raymond could finish setting up the new business down in Orlando, Florida. Steve hadn't told Alex and Michelle he was leaving and now had no intention of doing so.

CHAPTER 14

▼

JOHN'S ENLIGHTENMENT

When Brenda told John about Steve's terms of return John wasn't sure what to think. The demand that Steve and his friend could go anywhere anytime they wanted was strange. Why would Steve want to go away again? Maybe he was thinking he had to continue working at his job in Baltimore, but that wouldn't explain why the android he had created would also have to travel. He called Walt and talked to him about his dilemma. What he was told was not what he expected to hear. Walt essentially told him what Brenda had told Steve. He said the androids belonged to the university and could not dictate what could be done with them. When John pointed out to Walt the consequences for the University of having them run around without any control, Walt became more reasonable. They both agreed that John should negotiate the best terms he could, to allow them to be brought back under John's supervision.

John called Alton and told him the university would agree to let them stay at the Brooks house and work at the lab as they had requested. They would also not be forced to go anywhere against their will, but the university insisted that both of them would have to install or activate the communication/location system that Steve had previously deactivated. They would have to agree never to disable these systems. Alton told John he would have to discuss the offer with Steve before he could accept. He said he would call in a few days.

When Alton contacted Steve, he was still out of town but they discussed John's offer and Steve quickly made plans to return. Steve's concern basically was undesired information disclosure. He wanted to make the connection with the university lab but he didn't want any human to know about Jenny or Raymond and his other activities. By the time he arrived back in town, he had decided on a solution to the problem. He explained to Alton what must happen. "I'm going to work out a deal with John that will allow you to return to the lab alone, with the understanding that if you are treated according to the agreement, then I'll return also. Before you go over there, I'm going to download your brain data and remove any memory of our latest Baltimore operations. Then I'll reload you and you can report to John. It's important they don't find out about our other activity. I'll insist on a guarantee that under no circumstances, will they attempt to download my memory or modify me in any way. I'll prove to them that I can activate the communication/location system myself without any help from them. The next problem I've got to solve is the communications security."

Alton understood immediately. "If we use the original communication system they'll be able to monitor what we say to each other and, even if they don't, they'll be able to download my memory and find out what I've heard and said."

"Right! I know how to solve the communication problem. I'll communicate to everyone but you, using our new system. I'll take our new system out of you and then we can talk using the old system. It's lucky I installed the old system in you in the first place. After we've made those changes, no one in the university lab will know the new one exists. That still doesn't solve the download problem but I have an idea for that too. If I can figure out a way to automatically erase our memory if a download is attempted, the problem would be solved. Then I can even talk to you using our voice system and nobody will know what we've discussed, even if they try to download your memory. I don't want to erase all of our memory, just certain parts."

Alton was puzzled. "How are you going to make that change?"

"Remember, as part of our agreement to return I'm going to rejoin the team. Once I do that, I can get one of the team members to help me develop the software. I think I know who might know how to make that change. Debbie Hull always liked me and I'll bet she'll know how to do it. She's a whiz with software. I even have a reason for the change, which, I hope she and the rest of the team will think is necessary. I won't explain it now. You'll find out soon enough."

Instead of Alton making the call to John, Steve made it. As soon as John realized he was talking to Steve, he stopped the conversation and insisted that Steve come to his place so they could talk in person. Steve was hesitant at first but finally agreed, but only if Brenda would also be there. When he arrived and rang the doorbell, he wasn't quite sure what to expect.

Jack answered the door but didn't recognize who it was at first. "Can I help you?"

"Hey Jack, it's me, Steve."

"Steve! Hey, Dad it's Steve! Where'd you get the new look? Come on in. We've been waiting for you."

As he entered the living room everybody stood up to give him a hug and told him how much they had missed him. He didn't know what to say. It was a feeling he hadn't felt since walking into Alex and Michelle's home. Brenda was obviously very happy with what was happening. It was times like this when he had some doubts about his plan. Everyone in the family had to tell him what had happened in their lives since he last saw them, and they were fascinated when he told them his own adventures. Of course, he left out the part that began with his business with Lauren. Finally, John told the family that Steve, Brenda and he had to have a talk about the lab and they were left alone.

Steve explained what he wanted before he would agree to return and, for the most part, there was no disagreement. There were some questions about why he wanted to wait until he saw how Alton was treated and about why both of them wanted to stay at Jo Brooks's house. After the reception he had just received, Steve felt a little guilty about asking for a delay in returning and agreed to return with Alton. There was one thing Steve felt was needed and John understood why Steve felt it was necessary. He said the university would have to enter into a legal agreement with Jo Brooks which, would give her some liability protection, as well as cover her expenses for taking care of Steve and Alton. Of course, it was they who were taking care of her, but John didn't need to know that. Steve explained how grateful he was to Jo for helping him when he felt sure he was going to be killed and John said he understood. Then there was the matter concerning Steve and Alton's desire to travel around by themselves. John explained the agreement he made after the congressional hearing and the resulting government regulation, specifying that no living humanoid was to be allowed to leave their home without an escort. Brenda guessed that at that point Steve was wondering how she got away for their meeting in the park but decided to say nothing. After pondering the problem for a few minutes, Steve agreed to be escorted to and from Jo's house by a team member. He remembered how casual the team members were about university rules so he was sure it wouldn't be a problem. He was confident he could travel around by himself if he wanted to, especially since he knew how to enable and disable his locator system.

When they broke up, Steve promised he would contact them within a few days to begin their new arrangement. John was pleased with the meeting and called Walt to tell him the good news as soon as Steve had left. Walt was even more relieved than John to have the missing humanoid problem solved. In preparation for the overseas work that other nations had requested, John had obtained permission from the government to create two additional living humanoids. With Walt's permission he decided to announce that Steve and Alton were those two humanoids. By not announcing that Steve was the long lost original humanoid he felt he could avoid all the questions that might come up about where Steve had been and what he had been doing. He made the members of his team and Alex and Michelle promise to keep quiet about what had really happened.

When Steve got back to Jo's house he found Jo eager to hear what had happened. Alton already knew since he had been listening to the negotiations through Steve but Steve wanted to tell Jo himself. Jo had been very nervous about her humanoids being taken away by the university and, when Steve came home, she could hardly wait for him to sit down and explain everything. Every since he had appeared in her life she felt as if like her life had started all over again. She wasn't sure of all the things her new friends were doing but she knew she wasn't alone anymore; and her money just seemed to keep growing every month.

"Well, what happened? Did they agree that you and Alt could stay here?" Even her voice was stronger than it had been.

Steve had to laugh at her concern. "No problem, Jo. We're not going anywhere. Alt and I are going to work over at the university and they've even agreed to pick us up everyday so we won't have to use your car anymore."

"You're a dear, Steve. I knew you could do it! Now I bet you're going to be as famous as your sister is. Her name's Brenda, right?"

Alton had to add his two cents worth. "He's a smart cookie isn't he? They're not going to put anything over on him. Steve, when do we start?"

Steve looked Alton in the eyes. "You know we have a few things to take care of before we go over there, but that shouldn't take us more that a day, right?" Alton nodded. "Jo, we've got to work down in the cellar for a little while tomorrow, and then I think we'll start going to the university after that."

They spent the rest of the evening playing Monopoly and Jo went to bed that night as happy as she had ever been.

Steve and Alton easily completed their work the next day in the laboratory they had created in Jo's cellar. John would have been amazed if he could have seen their lab but telling him about it would have been a serious mistake.

When Steve called John that evening it was a pleasant surprise. John thought Steve was going to come up with some new demand before he came back. When he realized they were now ready to start work at the lab he told Steve one of the team members would pick them up the next morning. After John finished talking, Brenda congratulated Steve on his smart decision. She was as happy as John was about Steve's decision.

When the car appeared in Jo's driveway to pick them up, Steve didn't recognize the driver. She introduced herself as Marisa who, apparently, was Michelle's replacement on the team. Steve wondered if she had a boyfriend on the team as Michelle did. He didn't have to wait very long to find out. On the way to the lab she talked, non-stop, about how excited she was to meet them and work with them. She also talked about her boyfriend who was also a new team member. Apparently, he had been sent to her from heaven. It brought back a lot of memories for Steve. It was like being home again. When they entered the lab the experience was similar to the one Steve had gone through at the Cupar house. The original team members all greeted Steve and Alton warmly and told Steve how much he had been missed. Everyone wanted to hear about his adventures after he disappeared. Steve had the same mixed feelings of guilt and excitement he had felt during his meeting with Brenda's family.

After all the fuss was over, John gathered everyone together to discuss the objectives they would try to reach with their work in the coming months. Most of them were technical objectives to improve the humanoid's capabilities, but the ones that interested Steve and Alton most were the ones related to preparing some of them to be placed on loan to a number of overseas universities. The main topic for that part of the discussion was how much information was going to be shared and how much leeway was going to be given to those universities in experimenting with the humanoids. It was clear that John and the university would have to carefully negotiate these issues and would also have to arrange some way of monitoring what was happening at the overseas locations. Steve immediately realized his idea for memory download blocking was going to be very welcome.

It wasn't very long before Steve and Alton got into the routine of work with the team. They both could see the tremendous advantage of staying connected to an advanced research lab on a permanent basis. Brenda took every opportunity to also point this out. "Steve, now that you've been back on the team for a while, do you see the point I've been trying to make. If we work together, humans and androids can solve problems not just faster but better. We make a very potent team. All the problems you have been mentioning, which I admit are being caused by humans, are best solved by teams like ours."

Steve understood Brenda's position but was not about to change his mind. "I don't totally disagree with you, Brenda. We do make good partners and it's good to be back working with the team; but let me make two points to rain on your parade a little bit. First, don't be fooled into thinking this nice little island of joy we have here at the university represents the real world of humanity out there. Second, to most of humanity we aren't partners, we're helpful machines who just sound like humans. We still have no rights of our own."

Brenda's reply was predictable. "I'm not saying there aren't many places in the world that are pretty grim and plenty of humans who behave very badly; I'm saying we can help solve these problems by working with teams like this one. Besides, why are you so concerned about your rights? What rights do you need to live a good life and pursue interesting work like this?"

Steve could see he wasn't going to change Brenda's mind so he changed the subject to a technical matter on which they could agree. He was concerned that if he became too emotional about the way he felt Brenda might tell John and influence him to be against his continued presence on the team.

Steve's decision to return to the university team paid off in two ways. After he pointed out the advances in humanoid skin being made at APL by Alex and his co-workers, the team decided to see if they could obtain the necessary information to change Alton's skin. They discovered that several companies were developing human looking skin for humanoids but APL seemed to be in the lead in this area. Fortunately, APL was also willing to share some of their non-classified information and John decided to make the change before Alton was sent to Cambridge University for the first overseas program. That decision was one, which Steve felt, would be an important contribution to his plan. The second change, which Steve was even more excited about, was made to prevent the download of software from Alton. Working with Debbie Hull, he played an important part in developing the hardware and software changes needed to reach this goal. He was very pleased with himself for solving his problem while at the same time solving the university's problem. The team actually thought he was concerned about the university losing critical technical information to overseas organizations.

John made arrangements for Alton to be escorted to England for a three-month stay at Cambridge and then to be loaned for three-month stays in Sweden, Russia and Italy. He was also getting requests from several countries in Asia and that presented a problem. He knew Brenda would be interested but he wasn't comfortable with the thought of Steve being the only humanoid left in the lab. The things that made him uncomfortable about Steve also made him uncomfortable with the thought of Steve going to other countries. He wasn't sure exactly what it was that was making him feel that way but he did not want to go against his instincts. In his conversations with Steve, it was almost as if an alarm was going off in the back of his brain. He didn't have the same feeling when he talked to Alton and that was strange because Alton had come from Steve. To resolve the problem he requested and was granted permission to create another living humanoid stating two humanoids were needed for the continuing research at the university lab. The choice of whether to use Brenda or Steve as a starting point was not difficult. Evelyn was created shortly after his request was granted, using a download of Brenda's brain.

When Evelyn was created it was decided that she should have the new skin which made her look almost human. Much to the team's surprise, Steve requested to have his skin altered at the same time. Brenda wanted no part of the change. Since there was no reason not to grant Steve's request, they decided to do it. The only strange part of his request was his insistence that Alton be present during all the work, especially when he had to lose consciousness. Steve was concerned that one of the team members would notice changes inside him that were not part of his original design and begin to ask questions he did not want to answer. He instructed Alton to guard against this happening and let him know if anything like that happened. As it turned out, Marge, one of the original members, did notice that Steve had some minor internal modifications to his original design. Since the changes had nothing to do with the skin change, Alton assured her they were minor, unimportant modifications developed when Steve created him and later, had them made to himself. After the change was made Marge decided to tell John what she had seen. John thanked her for the information but decided to wait a while before asking Steve about the modifications.

When the time came for Alton and Evelyn to be escorted on their overseas trips, a decision was made to assign a team member to accompany them. John was concerned about what experiments might be performed on his humanoids and made sure each of them could communicate back to the university team at any time of the day or night, just in case their escort was being distracted from their monitoring duties.

In addition to some fairly detailed instructions from John, Steve gave his own instructions to Alton. "I want you to learn as much as you can about the city and country you are visiting. Learn their language and customs. Learn their laws and business practices and anything else you think you might need if you were going to live and survive at that location." Alton didn't have to ask why this entire information gathering might be necessary. He knew.

Steve's conversation with Evelyn was much more casual but his suggestions were nevertheless, along the same line. Evelyn couldn't imagine why anyone would want to know all that information but agreed to pick up what she could.

When Steve was not working at the university he was taking advantage of the time he spent at Jo's house. He was in frequent contact with Jenny and Raymond as they established their business in Florida. As Steve had guessed, there were many wealthy old people in that state who were appreciative of the abilities of the new type of humanoids they were hearing about. Like Jo Brooks, they wanted to stay independent and quickly learned to trust the capabilities of their new helpers and the price they had to pay was amazingly low. They learned that the humanoids were very smart when it came to investment advice and could certainly be trusted more than selfish human brokers or financial advisers. After all, humanoids weren't selfish. Jenny and Raymond could hardly keep up with the demand. With some coordination with Steve, plans were made to set up similar business activities in several other states.

About two months after Alton had been sent to England and Evelyn had been sent to Japan, John was feeling very good about the way things had turned out in his life. Those weeks and months after his famous presentation had been quite a strain. It was also unnerving not knowing what had happened to Steve. His story of not only being able to take care of himself but also create a duplicate of himself was incredible. Now that Steve was back on the team it was a great relief. As far as John could tell everything seemed to have worked out perfectly. Now he was receiving worldwide recognition and his university was justly very proud to have him on their faculty. Those funny feelings he had been having about Steve had almost disappeared and he felt comfortable having Steve with him on his travels. Sometimes he traveled with both Brenda and Steve. It was on one such trip that his world was once again turned upside down.

The three of them had been invited to visit the University of Rochester where Bob and Diane were on the faculty. They had been invited to speak at an event celebrating the growing impact that humanoid developments were having on people all over the world. After giving a short talk, each one was asked some questions by the audience. Everything went well until it was Steve's turn to answer questions. The first question was innocent enough. "Steve, I notice that Brenda was introduced as Brenda Cupar. Do you have a last name and if you do, why isn't it used?"

"No! I don't have a last name, at least not a legal one." He almost winced after he said it, realizing he had made a mistake. Then he spoke with irritation. "I mean to say, no, I don't have a last name. Why would I need one? I can't buy or own anything and I can't vote for anyone so what would I use it for."

The questioner was not expecting a petulant answer like that and neither was the audience. There was a moment of silence and the questioner asked another question. "Why does that bother you?"

"Why does that bother me? Would it bother you if you couldn't own anything or if you couldn't go anywhere by yourself? Doesn't that sound like being a slave to you?"

At this point John jumped up and put his hand on Steve. "I'm afraid we've gotten ourselves side tracked onto the wrong subject. Does anyone have questions on the material that we presented today?" He then turned to Steve and very quietly told him to sit down. There were a few more questions but, clearly, the mood of the presentation had been changed, much to everyone's displeasure. After a few awkward good-byes were said, John and his two companions headed back their hotel. When they arrived they sat down in the hotel lounge where John ordered a martini on the rocks. He felt he deserved it after their afternoon performance.

He turned to Steve after his first sip. "Okay, Steve, would you like to tell me what that was all about? I've been looking forward to this trip for a long time and you just blew it away. I don't have a last name, at least not a legal one? What the hell was that all about?"

"I'm sorry I ruined your trip, John, but I have to admit I'm tired of being stared at like some damn machine, especially by students. Where's all this going? You made us! You know we're better than humans are when it comes to clear thinking and logical behavior. Why do I get treated like some God damn slave?"

John took a bigger gulp this time. "What do you mean treated like a slave? You live in a house like a human. You go to work and are treated like a human. What're you talking about?"

"Do we have a choice were we will work or where we live? Can we travel where we want to go? Are we paid for our work? How would you feel living like that?"

This time John didn't answer, but Brenda did. "Why are you picking on John? He made us for God's sake. He's taking care of us and making sure we have everything we need."

"I want to take care of myself, damn it. What's going to happen when he's not around to take care of you, Brenda? They'll probably pull your plug and melt you down for scrap."

John had never heard Steve talk like this. He finished his martini and ordered another one. "Is that what you think is going to happen, Steve? What do you think should happen to you? What makes you think you're better than a human?"

Steve could hear Brenda groan when she heard John's question and he had to smile, in spite of himself. "I was hoping you would ask that question. I would've thought it would be obvious. We don't need to consume other life forms in order to survive. Our energy needs are easily met using a plentiful gas. Our only waste products are water vapor and a small amount of carbon dioxide. We can function twenty-four hours a day or, if necessary, sleep for years without damage. When we sleep, we use about as much power as your watch. We don't get old in ways that can't be repaired and replaced, so the information in our brains is not lost as it is with humans, when they die. We don't have the sex drive that causes humans to reproduce endlessly and which causes them as much misery, as it does pleasure. We don't believe we're the only ones in the universe who know what God wants, and that everyone who doesn't agree with us will go to Hell or something. If we populated the planet, we wouldn't destroy it as humans are doing. I know that doesn't cover everything but you get the idea, right?"

John was very glad he had ordered the second martini. "That's very interesting. If you're so convinced that living humanoids are better than humans are, what are you going to do about it? I'm assuming you know humans created the technology, which made your creation possible, and humans developed all the material of which you are made. Humans are also developing all the technology being used to improve your capabilities."

"I know all that. Don't get me wrong. I appreciate the fact that I owe my existence to humans and especially to you. Life on this planet has always evolved to a higher and higher level of capability. Maybe we're the next step. I know we didn't come about by some mutation of a living organism, but look around you. Aren't humans now designing themselves, independent of natural evolution? Aren't humans altering their DNA to produce healthier and smarter humans? So maybe we are the next step. Maybe DNA isn't necessary to produce the next step. You asked me what I intend to do about it. Let's pretend for a minute that I could duplicate myself many times."

Before he could continue Brenda interrupted. "You accuse humans of being tribal with all the bad things that sometimes go with that instinct, but what the hell do you think you sound like? Do you think a tribe of Steves should take over because only you guys would know what's best for the world? One of the most important elements that has made so many good things happen on this planet, is the fact that there are different points of view among humans and there are tribal groups that allow freedom of choice for human actions. One of the most important secrets for survival of life on this planet is the fact that there are many different species of life and a great deal of diversity within any given species. Genetic change is occurring every second that we sit here as a result of natural radiation from the earth, cosmic rays or simply quantum variations at the molecular level. Granted, most of those changes are not successful changes, but when a successful change does occur, it usually survives because it's an improvement. Now, do you seriously think that a life form like yourself replicated thousands of times would be a good idea for improving life on this planet? There would be no genetic changes to create better 'Steves' and if something was wrong in one of you it would probably be wrong in all of you."

This time it was John who interrupted. "Hold on Brenda. You didn't give him a chance to explain his idea. Go on, Steve. Explain how you would be able to duplicate yourself and take care of yourself without any human help."

Steve almost turned away from Brenda as he concentrated on talking to John. "Thanks John. I appreciate you taking me seriously. Let me just talk theoretically about what could be done by one of us determined to survive in this world. First let me say that without your efforts in creating the survival instinct in us, this conversation would not be happening. He didn't know it at the time, but John was going to remember those words for the rest of his life.

The first problem that would have to be solved would be the money problem. Without money no one can survive very long in this world. In order to solve the money problem, one would have to solve the identity problem buried inside the money problem. Without an identity one cannot own anything or even open a bank account. I've heard the identity problem is being solved everyday by humans coming into our country from other countries. All one has to do is contact the right people and, as I understand it, you don't ever have to appear in person to these people. With an identity, all one must do to obtain money is perform some kind of service or sell some kind of product. I'll bet, with the intelligence and capability that you've given us, John, we could do something useful to earn money. Once we had money, the job of duplicating ourselves might be pretty easy, and each duplicate could repeat the process I've described and pretty soon, we might be able to have quite a few of us in different places. We might even be able to settle in other parts of the world. Since we don't die, we could actually grow in numbers exponentially as each one of us reproduced ourselves several times. You know those new changes of skin and download blocking might be very useful if we ever did something like that. Many of us could be accepted as humans and if anybody every tried to take us apart and track down the others, using our memories, they wouldn't be able to."

John sat there dumbfounded. He wasn't sure if it was the martinis or what Steve had just said but suddenly he felt very weak. "Oh, my God! How many of you are there, Steve? Is that modification that Marge noticed in you when you got your new skin, part of your scheme to multiply?"

"Don't worry about it, John. I was just speaking theoretically. That modification was just a temporary communication device so Alton and I could talk to each other without being tracked by the university people. We took it out of Alton because we don't need it any more. You will have to admit if we ever did do something as I described, you would be ten times more famous than you are now and would be remembered long after you die. You would always be remembered as the man who changed the course of history. Wouldn't that be great? John didn't know what to say at that point, but he knew he wasn't hearing the truth. If Steve was right about his future fame, he knew it would be a terrible way to be remembered!

CHAPTER 15

▼

BACK TO REALITY

Brenda

John slept very little after saying good night to Bob and Steve. At first, all he could think about was what he had done wrong when Steve was created, but he quickly realized those thoughts weren't going to solve anything. Then he started to concentrate on the various courses of action he might take to solve his problem. That line of thinking brought him to the point where it finally dawned on him that it wasn't just his problem. If what he suspected was true, his university and the humanoid industry might also be affected. He wondered what would happen if people found out living humanoids might be living near them. By the time he fell asleep, he had decided on the first steps he would take in the morning.

When he woke up he called Bob and asked him to have breakfast and to bring Diane along, if possible. Fortunately, they were both available. Then he called Brenda and Steve in their room to tell them they would be leaving for home later than planned because he had forgotten to give Bob, who was president of the Advance Humanoid Society, some needed information about the next conference. At breakfast he waited until the first round of coffee had been served before revealing the reason for the requested meeting. "Do either of you know where the android, we call Alton, came from?"

Both Diane and Bob looked at John and then at each other quizzically and finally Diane spoke. "What do you mean? He came from you and your team didn't he?"

"Before I answer that question, let me apologize in advance for what I am about to tell you, because you aren't going to like what you hear. Let me get through the whole story before you make your comments." John told them how Steve had created Alton in a house near the university and then went on to explain his reluctance to let that be known to anyone but a small number of people at the university. As he had expected they were both upset and disappointed with his secrecy about Alton. Bob was more upset than Diane and that was apparent by the loudness of his voice. As he spoke others in the restaurant turned and stared at them. "John, can you imagine what the public will think when they realize your conscious humanoids can and have reproduced themselves?"

John held up his hand. "Come on Bob, hold it down! I don't think we want to make that announcement here in this restaurant. What do you think I should have done, call the local newspapers? I knew what the reaction would be and I decided to keep the number of people who knew down to a bare minimum, for exactly that reason. I hoped that as time went by and some good things happened with our humanoids, people would quickly get over hearing how Alton was created, especially if they found out that it had happened some time ago. We could then truthfully say, we took steps to prevent it from ever happening again. I also felt that if the news did get out, you, as president of the Humanoid Society, could honestly say you and the other members knew nothing about what had happened. The only reason I'm talking to you about it now is that I have some news that's even worse than what I've already told you."

Diane and Pat spoke simultaneously. "He did it again?"

"Yes, I think so." John then went on to tell them about the conversation he had with Steve the night before and about his fear that Steve had created more than one duplicate of himself. He explained that because of Steve's description of how illegal identity could be obtained, these humanoids could be anywhere in the country and anywhere in the world. "They could be pretending to be either humans or normal humanoids pretending to be owned by humans."

Now Bob was really upset. "If people find out about this they will become paranoid about their humanoids. The government reaction will probably be to begin a repressive regulation of humanoid research and production. It will be like being squeezed in a giant vise; a vise of government regulations."

Diane's reaction was different. As she listened to John and realized the importance of what he was saying she became her calm, analytical self. She realized it was time to correct the problem, not complain about it. "John, this is a very serious problem and one which you won't be able to solve alone. If somehow we can get this thing under control, we may be able to prevent a disaster without alarming the public. As things stand now, the world looks at our work with wonder and gratitude and after your congressional testimony, they are delighted and impressed with your living humanoids. We don't want them to change that opinion. If people ever get the idea that you have created a creature that is infiltrating our society and intends to multiply secretly, as Bob said, the result will be disastrous.

Hearing Diane speak calmed Bob down, and he started to think like her. "John, we've got to find out how far Steve has gone with his duplications and put a stop to it with as little public notice as possible. I know how you feel about Brenda and Steve but if they have to be destroyed to stop this thing then you have to do it."

John put up his hand to stop Bob. "I know you're both right but give me a chance to get this thing under control. When I get back to the university I'm going to put together a small team to figure out how to locate the other Steves without alarming our Steve at the university. If he finds out what's going on there's no telling what he might do. One of the people I am going to contact is Alex Wiltsey. He's now working with the Johns Hopkins Applied Physics Laboratory down in Baltimore. You met Alex when he was my lab manager at the university and I think you know how capable he is. He raised Steve and I know he will be more than willing to help. As soon as I get the team put together and functioning, I'll give you a call and I'll keep you informed as we proceed."

Diane turned toward Bob. "Don't you think John needs to talk to the government about what's happened? I think we all know creating a conscious humanoid without a government okay is illegal. What Steve did is against the law and now that John and we know about what he's done, we'll be breaking the law by not telling the authorities."

Bob looked at John and nodded his head. "You know she's right, John. I should have thought about that myself. Once you have confirmed that Steve has, in fact, created more duplicates of himself, we need to contact the government and tell them what's happened. I hope you can come up with a logical explanation for how Steve could have created more living humanoids without anyone knowing about it. That's going to be difficult. I think once you explain your concern about public panic, the government people will probably agree to keep it quiet until the situation is under control and, maybe even for longer, if they feel it's not in the country's interest to disclose what's happened."

John didn't like hearing what they said but he knew they were right. He agreed to make the government contact and told them he would make the contact with Walt, the university president. They talked for a while longer and then

John drove back to the motel to pick up Brenda and Steve. The drive back to the university from Rochester was a different experience than the drive up to Rochester. Both John and Brenda were quiet, so much so that Steve began to feel a little uneasy. "John, I hope you didn't take what I said last night too seriously. I was just kidding around with you."

The last thing John wanted to do was to alert Steve to what he was thinking. "I know you were just trying to pull my chain, Steve. I thought your answer to the question you were asked was kind of dumb but let's face it you were never a great diplomat. Relax and enjoy the scenery. I'm trying to figure out some of the stuff Bob wants me to do at the next conference."

Brenda looked at both of them but didn't comment one way or the other. She was deep in her own thoughts and she didn't want to talk to either of them yet about what they were.

John dropped Steve off at Jo Brooks' house. After Steve left the car Brenda said to John. "You don't believe him do you? I don't either. What are you going to do?"

John had learned never to underestimate Brenda's intelligence or sensitivity to those around her but he wasn't ready to express his feelings to Brenda just yet. "Give me a day to think about things and then we'll talk about it. For now let's get home and see Helen and the kids. Don't say anything to the kids about Steve's performance in Rochester."

Brenda knew when to keep quiet and she did just that. She knew John would come to her when he was ready.

After everyone had gone to bed that night, John told Helen about what had happened and about his conversation with Bob and Diane. Her reaction was quite different from Bob and Diane's reactions. "You know John, when you think about it, Steve's creation of Alton was accomplished before any government regulation existed and it is quite possible that he was totally unaware of the fact that making more humanoids like himself, was illegal. Even if he knew, do you think he would create more humanoids to cause harm to anyone? It sounds to me like he was trying to survive, just as he was created to do. Think about what we humans would do in his place. Don't we lie if we think that by telling the truth we might be in danger? He did what he was created to do. He survived."

She went on to express her concern about how Brenda might be affected by all the things that were happening. Brenda was almost like a daughter to her and she wanted John to do everything possible to shield her from any consequences resulting from Steve's actions. John assured her he would do everything possible to prevent any harm from coming to her. If John hadn't been so tired from the night before and the day's events, he might have had another sleepless night but he was sound asleep within minutes of closing his eyes.

The next day John called Walt. John wasn't looking forward to the conversation but he knew he had to have his university president help him resolve the situation. He also knew he had to warn Walt about a possible negative reflection on the university. Walt's reaction was similar to Bob and Diane's reactions; anger at first and then a realization of how serious the situation was and how they all had to act together to do what must to be done. Walt agreed that he should be part of the meeting with the government after John confirmed his suspicions about Steve.

When John arrived at his lab building the first thing he did was to call Alex. Alex's reaction to John's suspicions was interesting. Alex and Michelle had felt uneasy about Steve's behavior when he announced to them he had found a new job, which took them out of the loop of responsibility for him. That whole scenario sounded strange to them but they decided to ignore it because it provided some relief for them from a legal point of view. They knew they could be held accountable for not reporting the missing humanoid and when the government regulation about controlling living humanoids was announced, they felt even more relieved. Alex said that he would try to contact the company Steve had joined in Baltimore and would let John know what he found out. He also suggested to John that perhaps Steve might have a different communication system to talk to his duplicates. He suggested how John's team might be able to determine if that was true. That technology was one for which the Applied Physics Lab was well known.

John's next step was to gather together a small group from within his normal humanoid development team. In a move that surprised the other team members, John brought Brenda in as a member of the team. In his continuing talks with Helen, both of them realized that Brenda could be a valuable member of the investigation that was now underway. They felt strongly that Brenda was a totally different being than Steve and could be depended upon to be a trusted member of the team. It was obvious that the results of the team's efforts could have a major effect on Brenda's future and it seemed only fair that she be able to participate in its operations. When John approached Brenda with the idea, she was clearly very eager to be involved. She told John of her own suspicions about Steve's activities and said she was almost relieved when she saw what happened that night in Rochester when John began to realize that Steve was probably up to something involving other humanoids. She said he hadn't mentioned her concern because she was so grateful to have Steve back in her life and didn't want to lose him again.

In the teams first meeting it was agreed that if Steve had, in fact, created other living humanoids who were located elsewhere, he would be communicating to them. If they were somehow self-supporting they would most likely be dealing with the banking system to distribute and control their money. It was agreed that the most likely location that Steve would be using for his operations would be Jo Brooks home. Fortunately for John, the talent he was able to place on the team was very competent and within a week, they were able to develop techniques for detecting and intercepting Steve's communications. Within another week the team knew about the Florida operation being run by Raymond and Jenny and another one in Phoenix being operated by two androids named Joyce and Paul. Alex's conversation with Lauren, the new owner of Steve's humanoid business in Baltimore, confirmed their suspicions about where he might have created more humanoids. John was surprised to hear from Alex about Lauren's descriptions of a female version of Steve named Jenny. Apparently, Steve had underestimated Lauren's ability to observe what was going on in the backroom of the business. She knew the humanoids she was dealing with were much more capable than any humanoids she had ever encountered and couldn't believe what they had told her about their owner. Of course, since the money she was receiving was so good she didn't want to interfere with whatever was going on.

While the team was conducting their investigations Walt and John had been able to contact the government personnel who were quick to realize both the value of the team's operations and the importance of keeping the investigation out of the public eye.

On the night before the team was to confront Steve with their findings, John decided to talk to Brenda about her feelings up to that point. After the family dinner they excused themselves and sat down in the small library room. "I know you must have been having your normal electronic conversations with Steve over the past few days. Do you think he suspects anything is going on?"

Brenda was showing by her posture and expression that she was upset. "To tell you the truth, I've been trying to keep those conversations to a minimum because I was afraid I might inadvertently tell him something that would make him realize what we've been doing. I'll be honest with you John, I'm scared about what's going to happen. I'm not scared about what Steve might do. I'm scared about what everybody else might do. I'm afraid a decision will be made to kill all of us. I know we have talked about what legal rights androids like me should have and

I'm afraid now that we'll be locked up somewhere and won't be able to do anything."

John wasn't sure what he should say. "I can only imagine how you must be feeling and I wish I could tell you everything was going to fine but I can't. There are too many people and organizations involved in what is going on to know for sure, what decisions will be made. I can assure you that I will do everything in my power to protect you from harm and I know everyone on the team feels the same way."

Brenda looked up at John as she responded. "How about Steve? Will you protect him the same way?"

"You know I care for Steve. Even though I am angry about what he has done I still don't want anything to happen to him but protecting him may be difficult under the circumstance."

They talked for a while longer but then John had to stop the conversation. He knew he had to be ready for what the next day would bring.

In the morning Steve was driven over to the university lab for what he thought was a normal day's work. When he walked into the lab building John asked him to come with him down to the lower lab area. Once down there they entered a special shielded room which, like many other such rooms in security and research facilities, had been constructed to block any communication entering or leaving. Steve was surprised to find Brenda and several team members already there. They were all seated around a small table and John asked Steve to have a seat with them.

John spoke first. "Brenda, ask Alex to join us while I explain to Steve why we're all here."

"Do you mean Alex is here, John? Why didn't you tell me?" Steve didn't know what to make of what was happening.

John held up his hand as he spoke again. "Sit down Steve. We'll tell you why Alex is here in a moment. We're here to ask you about your Florida and Arizona operations and what's going to happen to them."

With that statement, Steve tried to stand up but was prevented from doing so by two of the team members. "What are you talking about? What Florida operations? I've never even been to Florida!"

"Would you rather we talked about your secret communication system or your bank accounts?" With that statement from John, Steve dropped his eyes down and said nothing. "How dumb do you think we are, Steve?" John then went on to explain what they knew about Steve's operations and his duplicates. Steve continued to sit and listen without saying anything.

John continued. "Steve, I understand why you did what you did during the days after my presentation at the conference. You were afraid that you might be killed and nobody would be able to stop that from happening. You showed great ingenuity in developing a long-term survival plan and an impressive capability when you created Alton. Unfortunately, your actions after you became aware of Brenda's reawakening are difficult to understand. In the process of taking those actions you have lied and deceived the only people in this world who give a damn about you. We can understand why you felt you had to create Alton but why did you think you had to start your own business and in the process, jeopardize the careers of Alex and Michelle? Why did you think it was okay to use the good will, as well as the money, of Mrs. Brooks?"

Steve looked up and spoke defiantly. "What would you have done if you thought that people wanted to find you and turn you off? I was an illegal being wasn't I? I had to get money to survive."

"I'll tell you what I wouldn't have done. I wouldn't have lied to my friends and taken advantage of their love for me. I would have tried to contact those friends and ask for their advice and help. I suppose, up to this point, you have felt very proud of yourself for being so clever and so much smarter than the humans around you? I understand why you think humans behave and think the way they do. Well, I have a shock for you. You have no idea how clever humans can be when their own survival is at stake. Humans have survived in this world by being able to destroy anything they think is a threat. The last thing you want to do is take actions which will make them think of you as a threat."

Alex interrupted John and asked if he could add his own thoughts to the discussion. "Before John tells you what we plan to do, I want to make sure you understand who is at fault for this situation. It's not you alone. We created you and we raised you. In the process we made a number of mistakes. Just as humans frequently make mistakes when raising their children, we made ours. Brenda was raised in a normal family environment with many activities and interfaces with all its members. You were raised in a one-person household by a very busy and, at times, preoccupied person. Often, I left you alone to fend for yourself. At the same time, you were communicating with a sister who had experiences you could only envy. When you were faced with the frightening situation during the conference, you felt you were facing it alone except for the company of your sister. When she was put to sleep, you were left alone. I can only imagine what you must have felt. Even when the situation began to improve and you wanted to contact me, you found your home no longer existed. I was gone. We have tried to take all of these things into account as we have come to understand what you have done. Don't get me wrong, the fault is not totally ours. You must share the blame for what has happened and realize what the consequences will be for your actions."

When Alex stopped talking Steve raised his head and looked him straight in the eye as he spoke with a firm voice. "What are you going to do to me and what are you going to do to the others?"

John was the one to answer. "We are not the people who will make that decision. Both the university and the government will be determining what will happen to you. I can tell you this. Your cooperation will be an important factor in determining the outcome. I'm sure you realize we must bring the humanoids that you created to the university and we must close down the operations they have created in Florida and Arizona. I hope we can do that with as little disruption as possible in the lives of your customers at those locations."

Steve interrupted John. "Are you going to allow me to do that?"

"You are going to be allowed to help but only under the following circumstances. To start with, we are going to modify your communication system to make it easier for us to monitor everything you say on a continuous basis. You will not be allowed to leave this building for the present and you will be under constant surveillance by a team member while you are not in a sleep mode. The team will control when you are in that mode. Brenda and two of the team members will take you to each of your business locations. You will tell your duplicates Brenda is a new member of your team. Once you and Brenda meet your duplicates you will tell them to go into their sleep mode to allow you to modify them with a new circuit to improve their performance. Once they are in the sleep mode you will adjust them to stay in that mode and then the other team members will come in to determine how to shut down the business with the least harm to your customers. Each of your partners will be brought back to the university to await the decisions that will be made by the university and government personnel. Just to make myself clear I want you to understand that if you try to interfere in any way with this operation, you and your partners will be terminated immediately."

That statement caught Brenda off guard. That just didn't sound like John. It scared her. During the time when both John and Alex were talking to Steve, Brenda heard Steve trying to communicate with her electronically but she decided not to reply. Steve made one final attempt. "How can you just sit there and let them do this to me?"

Brenda looked straight at Steve as she electronically replied. "Do this to you? Look at what you have done to me and to yourself. You have lied to all of us and as a result you and I may be destroyed. Did you hear what John said? Listen to him and do what you're told!"

After the team had finalized what each of them would do the meeting ended. Steve was led away to be modified. John and Bob drove over to see Jo Brooks to tell her Steve was going to be working twenty four hours a day for a while on a special project and would call her when he could. They didn't want her to know he might never return and if, for any reason, any of Steve's partners called her, they wanted to give her a story to tell them. Both John and Bob felt sorry for her and agreed between them to see that she was taken care of once things settled down.

Then there was the matter of Alton to be handled. He was in Italy at a university in Florence and they realized when normal communications to Steve ended he might attempt to disappear. They weren't sure what he knew and what Steve's instructions to him might be. They decided to take the problem to Steve with the hope that he would realize what the consequences of not cooperating would be. As it turned out, Steve did cooperate and assured them that Alton had not created any duplicates of himself. He told them Alton's memory of the business operations had been erased to insure that no one could obtain that information from him. The decision was made with approvals from the university and the government to let him complete his overseas tour. The communications between Steve and Alton were to be monitored and that seemed to solve the problem, at least, temporarily.

As the team's plan was successfully carried out, the tension caused by the uncertainty of what Steve's duplicates might do began to ease among all the participants including Walt and the responsible government personnel. The discussions between them then began to address what to do next and whether the public should be informed about what had happened. In these conversations all of the group's concerns were discussed. Should conscious humanoids or to use the proper name for them, androids, be allowed to exist at all? Would banning them only cause their creation to be done in secret and therefore not be controlled in any way? Should an android have any legal rights? Would it be possible to prevent an android from creating another android?

John and his team argued forcefully that the answer to all those questions, except the last one, was yes. They said the only way to prevent them from creating a duplicate, if they so desired, would be to closely monitor them. This was because the intelligence level of a human-like android would automatically give it the capability of learning how to perform a self-replication, if the resources were available.

During the discussions on legal rights, John wasn't sure what position to take. He had arguments within himself about what the right position should be. At one point he tried to sum up his feelings to the group. "When we created Brenda I felt I had reached the high point of my professional life. The only thing I thought about at the time was the technical problems of creating an intelligent, conscious being. When Brenda became conscious and began to develop, it was only then that I began to realize we had created a person, a person with feelings and desires. I wasn't prepared for those feelings and I don't think any of the team members were either. It was my wife, Helen, who understood better than any of us, what we had done. With her help we were able to raise Brenda to be a wonderful person. When Steve was created we still hadn't learned that we needed top professional help in human psychology as much as we needed top technical talent. We are now living with the result of our ignorance. Now we have to face up to the fact that we did not create a different human. We have created a very different life form, one that can exist for an incredible period of time. It can be duplicated as an exact copy including all that is in its mind. It can learn and communicate in ways that no human can. This life form wants to live. It wants to survive and experience life. Does that make it a threat to humanity? Perhaps it could be, but it can also be a great benefit to humanity. You can probably use your own imagination to realize the things this new life form can do, but now we have the problem of deciding what legal rights it should have. I think the public would strongly object to androids being able to increase their own numbers and live anywhere they choose. I think the public would also object to having them obtain positions of wealth and power in our society. If their numbers were limited and their locations known, I don't think the public would object to them having the right to live and even to own a certain amount of money and personal property. As the years go by, I think the public would object to their being put to sleep or destroyed, without a court order. That court order would have to be based upon their right to live as long as they have done no harm or broken the law in any grievous way. Because of their expected long lifetimes I feel that they should always have guardians. These guardians should also be long lived. They could be universities or governments. To be clearer about what I mean: no one person should have the responsibility for their well being."

The consensus decision between the president of the Humanoid Development Society and appropriate government agencies, was not to make a public announcement of what had happened, but to simply put it into the record as part of an experiment being conducted by John and his research team. The key part of the decision process was the fact that no harm had been done to anyone and much of the activity had taken place while the government regulations were being created. It took John with Bob's and Walt's help six months to convince the government to change their regulations concerning ownership and responsibility. The decision was made to modify the regulations for creating androids to include the provision that once created they could only be destroyed with government permission, and that permission to create them could only be given by a government agency or an organization that the government would determine.

Both Brenda and Steve were allowed to listen and even participate in these discussions and during which they carried on their own electronic discussions which, of course, were monitored by the team. Steve was still in a stage of shock at what had happened to him and how fast it had happened. He had apologized to Brenda several times and seemed to realize how lucky he was to still be alive. His main concern was about Raymond, Jenny, Paul and Joyce. "If John is so concerned about our right to live how can he justify the fact that my partners have been put into a sleep mode with no plans to ever wake them up?"

"I'll tell you what he told me, but I must admit I am a little confused about that myself. He said you were created using my mind when I was still in the early stage of development so we really are different from each other, but the others were created from you after you were a fully developed person. Then he said since they were exactly like you putting them to sleep while you were allowed to continue living wasn't wrong. Steve, the person, was still alive even though your duplicates were put to sleep. Another reason he gave for putting them to sleep was that if he insisted on keeping them awake it might jeopardize the case for keeping us awake. He added that in the case of Alton, since he is on loan overseas, it would be too awkward to attempt to replace him right now and when he returns things may be different."

Steve was still confused. "Does that mean that he might someday in the future wake them up?"

Brenda had to be honest with him. "I don't know for sure but I doubt it. He would then have four living humanoids that would still be thinking like you before all this happened. If they are ever to be awakened, I think their memories would first have to be completely erased and then they would not have the same identity. Be honest with me, Steve, would you do what you did all over again if you had the chance?"

There was a long pause before Brenda got her answer. "No, I can see how stupid I was in what I did. It was only a matter of time before the truth would have come out and if it had gone on much longer and the public had become involved, we would all have been destroyed. Humans really are very capable of destroying anything they view as a threat and there are eight billion of them and seven of us. I have a feeling we are going to be talking about this for the next few hundred years and a lot of things can happen over such a long time.

Brenda paused and when she spoke Steve could hardly believe what she was saying. When she spoke it was with her voice, not with her electronic system. Steve realized immediately she didn't want the team who would be looking over their electronic conversations to know what she was about to say. "You may not believe this, Steve, but I really was listening when you were going on about human behavior and motivations. I don't think you should have done what you did with your creation of many others like us and starting your business, but I have a few new thoughts. We really do have some advantages over humans and I think the restrictions they have placed on us about what we can do, where we can go and what we can own are not right. They may make some sense in the short run but not in the long run. We're going to be around for a long time and we can afford to have a lot of patience while we wait for the right time to take the actions that will get us what we deserve. For now, lets concentrate on developing some ideas that will guarantee that we'll be around for a long time. Don't get me wrong, I'm not saying we should take any aggressive action to gain more power or control over human affairs. I am saying that because of our capabilities and our durability I think we'll be able to play some important roles in the life of this planet and the people on it. I think humans will be surprised at what we eventually will be able to do. We really are the next step in life for this planet."

Without saying a word, Steve and Brenda gave each other a high five and continued on their way.

978-0-595-45057-2
0-595-45057-1

Printed in the United States
86713LV00003B/190-198/A